The House of Miranda Alba

PART I

L.A. Sosa

Editorial San Miguel S.A.

Every believer runs the risk of becoming blind to what they do not want to see.

Herodota

The fact that a believer can be happier than a sceptic is as true as saying that the drunkard is happier than the sober man.

George Bernard Shaw

Contents

1

Leonora
Brussels, 1965-1975

There are very few photos left from that period of time; the time when my family fell disastrously apart.

We lived in the tranquil city of Brussels, at number 30, *Rue de la Science*; a beautiful building from the nineteenth century. On the huge front door was the official seal of the United States: a stern eagle holding in his talons both olive branches and arrows: symbols of war and peace. I was afraid of that eagle.

In one photo I'm with my two sisters at the entrance to the Consulate. We had been carefully placed there by the photographer, forming a triangle by the side of the door, each of us with our musical instrument: Rosa with her viola, Nikita with her child-sized violin, and me with a small flute. This photo was destined to form part of the group of family photos in my father's office, proof to the public of his daughters and their talents.

We looked like three spoiled girls, with our velvet party dresses, our Mary Janes of black patent leather and our little white socks folded precisely at the ankle. The tumultuous decade of the sixties was already in progress, but we looked like creatures from a previous era; from a time of peace and conformity. While in the big cities of the world, protestors marched against war and injustice; while the adults worried about communism and hippies, and the young people became obsessed with rock music and the idea of free love; in Brussels, in the home of the U.S. Consul General, the three of us lived, set apart in our innocence. We attended the *Lycée Français Jean Monnet*; we had private classes in music and languages, and we were photographed in the entryway of a beautiful nineteenth century building.

In that time, I was famous in the family for being very dramatic, for being able to make others laugh or cry with my acting and improvising. I imitated people I saw in the street, on television, in my father's office. I invented little scenes, with the characters excessively comic or overly tragic. Melodrama was my forté. At home they called me the "little Charlie Chaplin". I don't know where this talent came from; surely not from my mother who was of a serious nature. Possibly I got it from my father. In the coming years we would have ample expressions of his falsity. And later on, I would have a dire need for the acting arts; the future of all of us depended on them.

In another photo, we are all together. There is my father: tall, thin, with a new moustache in order to appear more "modern"; there I am, chubby and with a smile that stretched from one side of my face to the other; there is Nikita, taller than I was, and already giving signs of growing into a beautiful woman. And there is our mother, who, unknown to all of us, was carrying within her the beginnings of our youngest sister, Adriana.

On the back of the photo I can see the names and ages; Rosa, sixteen, me, six years old, and Nikita, four. But the letters of my name are hardly visible; the ink has faded and you can hardly make out the word. No matter. Names can be deceptive.

In the third photo the three of us, Nikita, Rosa and me, stand not at the front door but instead at the small back door, the one we used every day to go into the garden, or out into the street. This photo was for us to look

2

at, to have in the house, not in my father's office. In that photo we looked the same as we were in that moment, and capable and fortunate family.

And who was the most capable of all of us? Rosa, clearly.

As a child, Rosa had all her clothing organized by type and color. She stored her many toys according to size and use. She had a special place for all her Barbies and another for her Ken dolls. All her things were hanging or stowed where they were supposed to be: her books, her notebooks, her pens and pencils, everything. Like me and my sisters, Rosa grew up speaking English, French and Spanish, but she also spoke German pretty well. With little effort she got good grades in school and won prizes. She played the viola, which is not an easy instrument to play, and she painted artistically and well.

And she loved me. Rosa wasn't the typical older sister who gets annoyed by her younger siblings and doesn't let them touch her toys. On the contrary, she played all the time with me. She treated me as if we were the same age. And I loved her just the same.

In adolescence, she started getting interested in politics and would find opportunities to speak about it with whomever she found in the consulate. She followed avidly all the news about the student demonstrations in the U.S., in Paris, in Berlin. When she finished her studies at the *Lycée,* she said she wanted to do university in Chile, which precipitated a crisis in the family. My mother was in favor of the idea; my father was violently opposed. He said that his colleagues in Washington would look askance at the idea of her studying in a communist country, because by then, Chile was heading in that direction. My mother defended her, saying that Rosa had the right to live her life as she saw fit.

When Rosa left Brussels without even saying goodbye to my father, he stopped talking about her completely, almost as if she had died. This was the first of many doors that closed in my family.

At first my mother received news from Rosa regularly. She was studying art. She met a fellow student, a law student named René, and they quickly fell in love. Soon after, they got married in Chile. Nobody from our family in Brussels went to the wedding, and we hardly spoke of it. Then, via my aunt and uncle in Santiago, we learned that Rosa and René had gotten involved in the student movement there, and my mother became very worried. Later, we discovered that they were active in worse things, clandestine things. My father knew what it was about; he was cognizant of the political climate in Chile; I was not. I remember that I often asked about Rosa, but my mother would never answer with anything concrete. I had the impression that she couldn't answer honestly, and what she **did** say, were memorized phrases, pre-approved by my father.

Rosa became pregnant very soon and the next year their daughter was born. Despite the obstacles posed by the politics of my father's job, my mother was able to go to Chile to see her. During her absence my father was in a foul mood. Adriana, the youngest of us four girls, had begun to show evidence of a serious defect in her speech. And when she couldn't make herself understood, she became infuriated. Then it began to seem as if she couldn't hear very well either. She was only able to understand speech if she stood directly in front of the speaker and could see their face. My father didn't have the patience to deal with her, and in the absence of my mother, the situation worsened.

Upon her return to Brussels my mother told us that Rosa seemed happy and that her daughter was named Miranda. But she didn't say a word about the political activities that were happening there. It felt like a prohibited topic, so we in turn did not ask.

On top of all this, my father's job put enormous barriers to any free communication between Rosa and us. We always had to be aware of the strictures and rules of his position in the government, even without knowing very well what those strictures were. Also, my mother, wanting to protect her daughters from the rough world outside our home, never spoke to us about the things that really mattered. In this way, a wall was built between our different lives. We couldn't know what, exactly, was going on with her, nor she with us.

One day we got the news that Rosa was no longer in Chile, but instead had gone to Mexico. My mother fell into a panic; it was clear she knew what this meant. I remember that seeing her, with her reddened cheeks, her reddened, watery eyes, put me in a panic as well. She breathed with difficulty. It was very frightening.

We found out that René, Rosa's husband had been detained by the security forces in Santiago, and had been sent to Asuncion, Paraguay. There, they questioned him. Paraguay was where they sent all the inconvenient young people who were causing problems in Chile, and it was known that many of them never returned home. My father, despite his diplomatic power, was unable to do anything and René disappeared. My father was informed by Washington that René died of a cerebral hemorrhage in Paraguay, and that it was too dangerous for Rosa to return to Chile.

From Mexico, Rosa communicated with my mother, asking her to go urgently to Santiago and get Miranda, and to bring her to Mexico. Miranda was just six years old. My mother did this, but just the same as the last time, she returned melancholy and bitter to Brussels.

Very soon Rosa became involved with another man; a Mexican painter. In that time, I was the typical teenager, focused entirely on myself and knowing little and caring less, about the lives of others. How I regret that! I wish with all my heart that I had paid better attention to the situation with Rosa. But I didn't. And I never will forgive myself that that.

Then… something happened that should never have happened. Our mother died. She died after finding out that my father was having an affair. And not just with one woman, but with various. It came out in all the media; a complete disaster. After a public apology organized by his chief in Washington, my father resigned his ambassadorship. My mother was undone, and she started spending a lot of time away from home, away from us.

We thought at the beginning that she had committed suicide, but the autopsy results were equivocal. The amount of drug in her system was not enough to have killed her. Outside the family, it was thought to be an intentional overdose, but I refused to believe it. I imagined that she had simply wanted to give my father an idea of how desolated she was. But there was no way to know with any certainty what my mother was thinking at that time. So, with the death of my mother and the disgrace of my father, my sisters and I were left with nothing; bereft of the protection of an intact family.

With regard to my father, I gave little importance to an idea that floated on the edges of my consciousness: the possibility that my father was innocent and that the information about the adulterous affairs was a type of sabotage; a calumny organized by his political enemies. In that era, it was not possible to be a diplomat without having enemies. The ambience of fear and paranoia of the cold war caused many questionable acts and dubious scandals, even in a place as tranquil as Brussels. But I wasn't conscious of any of that then. The possible innocence of my father simply did not fit into the schema I was constructing about his character.

I had, in fact, seen that my mother was acting very strange in the days before her death. I asked myself if it were something more than the disillusion in my father. But of one thing I am certain: she did not have to die. She wasn't the one who committed the mistake. She wasn't the one who caused the destruction of the family. But she died anyway, and neither the doctors nor my father could explain to us what happened.

Rosa came for the funeral but she didn't bring Miranda. She said that she was too little and that the change in routine would be too upsetting for her. She told us that Miranda was well cared for by Diego, the painter; that his abilities for care-giving were that of any natural father. With our father, Rosa spoke very little. In the chaos and tumult of the events, there was no opportunity to explain anything, nor to ask any important questions. Rosa returned to Mexico with all her mysteries intact.

And now? What would Nikita do? What should we do with Adriana? Adriana was twelve years old, and she had problems. As for me, I didn't know exactly what I should do, but I knew that I wanted nothing more to do with my father. I was furious with him, disgusted by him, blaming him not just for the death of my mother, but condemning his behavior afterwards. He acted like nothing had happened; he was more worried about his own future than the present time of his daughters. He shut himself up in his office for hours on end, talking on the phone. Finally, he told us that by the following month, we would have to leave the embassy.

Nikita didn't want to continue living with him either, and less still when he said he was going to New York. She opted to continue her studies in Paris. And Adriana? Poor Adriana, who hardly understood that we weren't going to continue living in the beautiful nineteenth century building, with its ivy-covered walls and its charming garden in the back, that she was not going to be able to ride her little bicycle anymore through the paths of the park across the street; that everything was going to change for the worse.

"I have to be very frank with you", my father said after the funeral. "I'm going to have to travel a lot in the coming year and I can't take Adriana with me".

"But, what can we do? Where will we live?"

"You both should stay in Brussels, stay where she feels comfortable".

"Are you saying that I should take care of her?", I asked him incredulously.

"It's what your mother would have wanted", he replied.

I found myself, therefore, in the peculiar position of being the guardian for my little sister, with no mother to support me, without the confidence that a child would normally have in her father to support her, with no job or career, and very little money. Very suddenly the real world presented itself at my door.

I did the necessary things. With the help of one of the consulate secretaries, I found an apartment and work as a private English teacher. My father was in a hurry to leave Brussels, but he left me with some funds. Rosa also sent money, although she refused to return. She said it was impossible for her to do so, and she asked that I not inquire further because it was a very delicate situation.

For me, this was an extremely difficult period. The family that I once had, no longer existed. We were isolated one from the other, each of us wrapped up in a private mourning. I blamed my father for his acts, my mother for letting herself get taken over by sadness, my sister Nikita for going off to Paris, and Rosa for not being in Brussels to help us.

With the little money I earned, plus the assistance of Rosa and my father, we managed to live more or less well. Adriana continued studying at the *Lycée*, where, thank God, the teachers tolerated her, remembering perhaps the importance of the family in times past. But Adriana grew up without a mother and effectively without a father as well, since her own never cared much about her. During the years that we were alone, Adriana and me, I only received two letters from the ex-consul, and even though I answered them as soon as they arrived, they were both returned to me with "address unknown" written on the envelope.

It was then that the *coup de grâce* happened. In December Nikita came from Paris to celebrate Christmas with us. We went to the *Gran Place*, in the center of the city. This was an old custom of my mother's; to take us to one of the pastry shops there to eat *gaufres*, which are the cookies that one eats in Brussels, and to drink hot chocolate, in the afternoons in winter after school.

Upon our return from the *Gran Place* I saw an envelope on the table in the foyer of the apartment building. It was crinkled and worn, as if it had travelled for a long time in the corridors of the postal service, and indeed, it had the date of the previous month in the postmark. The letter said that Rosa had had an accident in his painting workshop, in his house; that her death had been investigated but that there were no definitive results; that there was not going to be a funeral or anything because Rosa had left instructions that she did not want that; that we should rely on him, on Diego, to take good care of Miranda and that he had someone there to help him and that she would have the best of care.

Suddenly I couldn't handle the shock and vomited everything I had consumed in the pastry shop. A torrent of chocolate came out of my mouth, demonstrating how much I wanted to be done with Brussels, how much I wanted to leave it and all the terrible things that had happened there. The city of my childhood, with its beautiful, well-cared-for old buildings, its polite traffic and tranquil nature, its' pretty flower pots and parks and gardens: all that I threw up and away.

By then my family was so fractured, that the death of Rosa almost did me in completely. But I had to gather myself together, for me and for Adriana. There was no one else that could take care of her. I had to keep going. I fled from the sadness by focusing on my work, on taking care of my sister, on maintaining contact with Nikita. With the few weapons I had, I fought to remain afloat. I remember that I gave up on knowing the truth about my mother's death. I lost all hope to discover what really happened. But the death of Rosa had to be uncovered, had to be explained, had to become known. I felt the responsibility to bring it out of the shadows, so that the memory of my sister did not vanish, so that the truth about her life and about her death would be revealed.

2

Rosa
Santiago de Chile, 1968

The trip had been going on for hours and the plane's motors droned on and on. Everyone was asleep. Except me. I hadn't slept in two days.

I take out my passport and look at it: navy blue, with a smooth and comforting cover, its beautiful eagle alert with its wings extended and its claws full of arrows and olive branches. I feel proud to carry it, but I also feel repugnance. Pride, because it is the passport of my father's country. The USA; the most important and most powerful country in the world; huge in territory and resources, frightening in its military power; its people the most optimistic and ingenious of all; the country with the most freedom and liberty in the world. My father's words come back to me: "Rosa, never forget that you are very lucky to live under a system that gives equal opportunity to all of its citizens and rewards them equally for their efforts". My father had his capitalist ideology well formulated, and an arsenal of vocabulary to defend it.

But I feel repugnance too. The government of this powerful country has committed horrors in the name of promoting its ideology. Businessmen, backed by the government, have become rich on the labor of the poorest, in the poorest of countries. It is shameful the number of places where the

U.S. has interfered: Dominican Republic, Cuba, Iran, Guatemala, Vietnam, Tibet; places where they have placed puppets or dictators who continue to support this robbery... so many abuses in the name of free enterprise and democracy. In the country of my father, the words of the government sound very noble, but their actions reveal a horrible schizophrenia.

My mother and I often discussed this phenomenon, but then she would scold me, saying that I should not condemn what also sustained me. My father's position provided us with a life of luxury and it was very disloyal of me to criticize it. Besides, there were many good things in the capitalist ideology.

With my sisters it was impossible to discuss this. On top of being very young, they didn't have the head for such logic. Leonora liked to play act and make people laugh, play her flute, play with her toys. Nikita only liked dolls. They were not interested in politics even when the politics of the entire world seemed to be entering in crisis.

I put away my passport and look out the window. I'm worried about the details of my immediate future. I'm going to live with my aunt and uncle, but I don't know them. How will they perceive me? A show-off? Silly? Me, Rosa C. Burleigh, daughter of Robert C. Burleigh, U.S. Ambassador in Brussels, and daughter also of María Luisa Fernández, born in Santiago de Chile; my mother.

Surely my aunt and uncle will ask me about my mother. They must still wonder over the path she has chosen: she, a young journalist, ardent supporter of social justice in her country; falling in love with an American man whose passions were distinctly different. No, it didn't make sense. And then, for my mother to have abandoned Chile in order to follow him first to Bloemfontein, South Africa and then to Brussels where he would carry out his diplomatic mission and where my sisters and I came to grow up. To live so many years so far away from her home, so far away from the rest of her family? My aunt and uncle considered it very sad.

The plane lands. My new life starts.

3

Rosa
Dreams

Saying goodbye to my family almost broke me in two. "Rosa, don't cry, don't cry", I told myself and I didn't. Excessive crying was something that Leonora did, not me. To cry in a moment like that was *de trop, exagerado,* too much, *übertrieben.* I had to maintain my composure because I am a serious, dedicated young woman.

But later, in the plane, I did cry. I cried and cried and I couldn't stop. Each time I thought I had it under control, the tears would begin to slide down my cheeks again. When the stewardess came around with the coffee, I grabbed it, desperate for something to calm myself. But then the fragrance of the coffee reminded me of going to the *Gran Place* with my mother and of the day that she allowed me to exchange the hot chocolate, which was the drink of my little sisters, for coffee, saying that I was old enough for it. Oh, how I esteemed my mother! How I loved her. She was so special and no one else seemed to recognize it. No one remembered, or knew perhaps, that she had been influential as a journalist in Chile, that she had moved many people with the force and sincerity of her newspaper articles. I cried then, for the loss of so many things, especially the loss of my father's love.

I'm not wrong when I say I was his favorite. After I was born, the doctors told my parents that they couldn't have any more children, and for ten years this was true. But then when Leonora, Nikita and Adriana were born in rapid succession, my father was unable to show to them the same affection he showed for me. Maybe it was because they didn't resemble him; neither in appearance nor in character. My father and I are resolute people; we are concerned with how the world is best managed, how human systems are best governed, how best to live with one another in a global sense. I love my sisters dearly, but they are frivolous; they aren't interested in those topics. That is why, starting now, I am writing everything down; so that when they are grown and able to judge for themselves, they will have a record. It's impossible to put everything down, I know that. But at least they will have a partial history of the family, and can understand things for themselves.

As a child, my father and I conversed a lot. In his few free moments, he would listen to me, answer my questions. As a teenager, we spoke about what we were most interested in: politics. And the most important question we asked: was the involvement of U.S. military justified in Vietnam? I reminded him that the war there was a civil one: Vietnamese against other Vietnamese, and not between that country and any other. He would answer emphatically that we could not just stand by and let the country turn Communist. "Communism is…..

"What's wrong with Communism?", asked naively my sister Lea.

"Would you like to choose for yourself where to go to school, what to study, where to live or where to work?", asked my father agitatedly. "Or would you rather have the government decide these things for you?"

Talking about Communism always put my father in a foul mood, as if he had to defend himself from attack. I didn't like to see him like that: consumed by the certainty of his opinions. Nevertheless, I enjoyed talking with him, even when the debates became heated.

But when I told him that I wanted to go to university in Chile, that all changed. I explained to him my reasons, I tried to convince him to the best of my ability, but he remained intransigent. After an enormous number of conversations, he simply told me "no". He said I could study in Paris or in Berlin, or in any other place, but not in Chile.

I felt like the bonds between us had broken. My father always lauded the great freedoms and liberty of the U.S., but it seemed that those freedoms didn't really pertain to me.

In the first letter I wrote to my mother from Santiago, I told her about my aunt and uncle, about my classes, about everything except my father and what happened between us. But she answered me with a scathing letter. She asked how I could be so ungrateful, so hateful, to have left without even saying goodbye. She was completely disillusioned with me, broken over my behavior. Her letter felt like an arrow in my heart. She reminded me that despite my disagreements with my father, I was still his daughter and owed him my loyalty. My hand trembled as I wrote her back. My God. I couldn't avoid having lied to her and to him, in order to leave. Lying to my mother; I never thought I would get to that point.

But there was no other way. In those days, my parents were not getting along. They argued a lot when they were alone and when we were all together they treated each other with a frightening coldness. So, in order to get ahold of my passport, I had to ask my mother for it, knowing that she was unaware of the prohibitions my father had put on my plans. I had to do the unthinkable from pure necessity, because I knew that my mother, as a good and dutiful wife, would prohibit me just the same, if she were aware. I know that my mother loves me, that she was on my side in this situation, but she would always be more loyal to my father than to me. I don't know whether to condemn her or admire her for this, but that's how it was.

In any case, my mother didn't know me as well as she thought when she told me that my disagreements with my father weren't sufficient reason to leave Brussels. She didn't know about the existence of René. And with René, everything changed.

4

Rosa
René

Now I must speak about René, the young man I met only six months ago; the man to whom I was rushing now with all the forces of my being.

We met in the *Gran Place,* in the most banal way possible. I was running, late to my piano lesson, fearful of arriving tardy because every time I did, *Monsieur Lebeque* would tell my parents and I would be scolded. René was coming from the other direction and we didn't see one another. We crashed and René fell to the ground. I remained standing and I quickly helped him up, saw that he was laughing and so began to laugh as well. We started to speak in French but I quickly noticed his Chilean accent. That there was another Chilean family in Brussels, that my mother didn't know this, seemed incredible. My mother took her diplomatic and social duties very seriously, and as the wife of the ambassador it was unusual for her to have missed this.

We stayed for two hours in the café in the *Gran Place*; the piano lesson completely forgotten. We talked about everything. René was just as passionate about politics as I was, except that he admitted to being a socialist, clearly and plainly. His idol was Allende, Salvador Allende, the same leader that was the enemy of my father. My father spoke often about the instability in all of South America caused by this man and by his politics, saying that Allende represented the worst tendencies of that ideology. Allende was proposing to break down the capitalist system -the freest and fairest system of all, the system that keeps the whole world afloat economically- and replace it with Communism. That must never happen. Allende was the worst nightmare for the world, and René represented the same thing in my little family world.

So, I had to keep my relationship with him a secret. I couldn't tell my father about him, of course. But neither could I reveal anything to my sisters or to my mother. Not even to Lea, who was my soulmate in everything. Lea, Lea, how I miss you! Leonora always had a way of getting me out of a bad mood, or making me laugh, of helping me see that things were not as serious as I thought. Lea was like a mirror to me; reflecting back my own better self. And I think I was the same for her. We even looked very much alike, despite the difference in ages. We had the same voice, the same strange accent: a mixture of South African, American and Chilean. Together, we were something much bigger than two people; we were a force for understanding, for tolerance, for humanity. There was no one else who could do for me what she did.

That's why it hurt so much to leave Brussels without explaining anything to her; without explaining that I had fallen in love with someone who was returning to his home, and my desire to go to Chile was much deeper than a simple desire to study there. I couldn't say anything at all to her, because I knew that even though she was adept at her little theatricals, the truth eventually would escape from her lips.

During those six months, Rene and I fell profoundly in love. I was nineteen, he was twenty, but our love was not merely a love between young people; it was based as well on a shared ideology, a strong sense of justice, a sentiment and a feeling that we could change the world; to make it a more fair and just place, that we could alleviate the suffering of the poor and the oppressed. René had come to Brussels on a scholarship, but he was not going to remain there with his arms crossed, doing nothing, while the possibility of working for real change existed elsewhere.

When René told me he was going back to Chile, I had to go to the end of my courage. I had to find the will to put everything at risk: my existence as a good student, as a good daughter, as an obedient woman. I had to abandon everything I knew in order to follow my heart and my conscience.

5

Rosa
A New Look

"You don't believe.... we're on the eve.... of destruction?", the Turtles song asked. The record was a gift from René from just before he left. With her voice a mixture of a lion's roars and a murderous growl, Lea used to sing this song over and over, making us laugh each time. Luckily, our bedrooms on the fifth floor of the consulate building were out of earshot from the rest of the house. In those bedrooms, lots of things went on that would have been met with great disapproval from our parents, but were things that interested us very much. *The eve of destruction...* the destruction of what, the world? Of us? To my sisters it didn't mean much, but to René and I, it was portentous. The marches for peace, the demonstrations, the strikes in the universities... all this portended great changes in the world, and we both wanted to be part of it.

Lea loved the song, as well as Nikita, and even Adriana managed to sing it fairly well. Poor Adriana. She has a pretty face, delicate hands, long, strong legs; everything about her made it seem she would turn into a beautiful woman. But her mind was fractured. She spoke in a language of her own making and only our mother could really understand her with any consistency. At times Lea could communicate with her, but neither my father nor Nikita had the patience, and all of them would routinely get frustrated in the attempt.

The song was resonating in my head when I arrived in Santiago. Warning. Prohibition. Risk. Questions. New beginnings. Happiness, yes, happiness even. The destruction could refer to the ending of old injustices, old habits, and this was a good thing.

René went into a delirium when he saw me. He said he couldn't believe that I would leave my family, my whole previous life, in order to be with him.

"I couldn't do anything else", I told him.

He brought me to his house, or rather, his apartment. He didn't live with his parents anymore, a fact which surely caused a great scandal in his family. And there, in his flat, we made love for the first time. Our bodies came together so naturally that it felt like we had been lovers for years and years. I had never felt such pleasure, as much physical as emotional. I had never felt such love.

Then we went to a meeting of law students. They were going to discuss things with the leader of the student union of the law school. René didn't tell me until the meeting was underway, that he himself was the leader. This made me very happy. The students spoke of Allende, of the possibility of having him speak in a forum of students, for the following Saturday. After the meeting ended, René kissed me and said that it had been the best day of his life. I felt illuminated inside, as if there were a candle burning, burning with passion and ideas.

I confess that there were other things, less serious things, that pleased me in my first days in Santiago. The clothes I had brought from Brussels, I threw in the trash. Modest dresses, boring skirts, sensible shoes. I bought a pair of bellbottoms that fit me just right, accented with a wide belt at the hips, as well as a leather jacket with fringe at the hem that swung like the mane of a horse as I walked. I felt completely new, more open, ready for anything.

My art classes were enchanting. I have always loved to draw and paint, and in Santiago I felt very inspired. The teachers were very good. The Chilean students were completely different from the students at the *Lycée*. There, everyone obeyed the teacher without questioning anything; here, they ask before doing any obeying at all. The men had long hair, the girls wore earrings made of feathers and walked around braless without any shame. They exhibited a kind of freedom I had never seen before, a kind that had been denied to me in my family's house and which I now tasted hungrily. René and I forged ties of freedom stronger than any my father had tried to use on me.

But I also confess that I had many moments of great sadness, of weakness. I missed my family, the happy times we spent together. I missed the talks I used to have with my father and I felt a huge hole in my heart, knowing that he thinks badly of me now, that he doesn't love me as he used to, that perhaps he will never love me very much again.

My mother, on the other hand, supported me completely. After her first letter to me, in which she described how disappointed she was in me, she returned to her usual loving self. She always answered my letters the same day she received them, but even so, the mail service sometimes took a month or more for us to exchange news. She told me about my sisters: that Nikita had not gotten the good grades she had hoped for, that Lea had done very well in a play at school, and that Adriana had managed to say two complete sentences without error, and that a whole week had passed without her becoming infuriated. My mother never wrote to me about my father, nor about their relationship, but I knew they were not getting along well. And I knew the reason. My father had a lover. It's natural, I suppose that men in positions of power tend to feel omnipotent. Everyone does what they are asked to do, they are lauded for their decisions and never questioned.... everything is justified. Whatever scheme, whatever behavior, for as illogical or harmful as it might be, is worth it if it achieves the required objective. I wondered if perhaps this woman served some purpose in the political machinery in Brussels; it was possible that the love affair was a cover for something worse, something covert, something illegal, maybe. But the means justify the ends, as my father used to say, as an explanation of the interference of the U.S. in other countries' internal affairs. If what he did worked against the spread of Communism, it was permissible.

Oh, but if my father could have heard the discourse of Allende! The first time I heard him speak, I felt my heart explode. Allende spoke about the enormous injustices in his country; for example, that the large landowners had so much money that they could leave fields fallow, while the farm workers had such little land that they could not feed their families. Allende explained that the International Monetary Fund and the World Bank are controlled by the U.S., and are forced to lend money to Chile at interest rates so steep that it was never going to be possible for the country to progress. All this and more Allende explained, in such a lucid manner that nobody who heard him, could doubt the legitimacy of his words.

What I most liked about Allende was that he frequently spoke about the role of students in the coming time. We, the students, had the ability to change the system. In us was the energy and the creativity necessary to organize a new system based not on the needs of the dominant class, but on the needs of all the people. Every time we went to a Socialist meeting, on returning to the apartment, René and I would spend hours evaluating his ideas, ending up expressing ourselves in the ardent union of our two bodies, in love.

It was during those days that René introduced me to his friend Isaac. I liked him immediately. Isaac and René were childhood friends and treated one another like brothers; soon I was included in that friendship. Isaac worked in a union called *Triunfo Campesino*, working to better the lives of the farm workers, and he would often come to see us with news of improvements in their salaries or other such things. We always felt so optimistic whenever Isaac visited.

Isaac wanted René to leave law school and join him at *Triunfo Campesino*, but René wanted to finish his studies, and I must modestly admit, I advised him that being a lawyer would be more useful to Socialist party than not having the degree. Besides, René's parents would have been furious if he had changed his academic plans.

René's father. I have to talk now about René's father. He was the son of a military man; grandson of a military man; married to the daughter of a military family; proud of his military service; one of the most patriotic people I had ever met. But the military in Chile did not enjoy much prestige in society, and I think he suffered from an inferiority complex that he was not always successful in hiding. He was also very much a believer in the traditional culture of his country, a culture in which the stratification of the economic classes remained unchanged. The rich remain rich while the poor remain always poor. This is what Allende wants to change, but this change scares and discomfits people like René's father.

Nevertheless, he is not a bad person, not at all. The year before I arrived, René's father had been sent to Pisagua to participate in military maneuvers, and when, as the chief of security, he discovered Socialist pamphlets in the bread basket of a woman worker, he believed he did nothing wrong in imprisoning her. He told me, in our many discussions, that the Leftists were not simply another political party but a group focused on fomenting the hatred between the poor and the middle class, leaving the Chilean people without faith or hope in anything. For René's father, the world was black and white, clearly divided between good and bad, and he was unable to discern any nuances there.

When the massacre of My Lai occurred, in which 500 Vietnamese villagers were killed by U.S. troops, René's father remarked that it was "lamentable"; a term that the upper echelon of the military used to describe the horrendous act as more of a bit of bad press than anything else, and his use of the term rankled heavily on us, and served to further separate René and his father.

That is why René had to leave his father's house and live apart. His mother cried, his father got depressed, but for me, I was happy because this meant that we could be together. In other circumstances we would not have been able to do this. And my aunt and uncle? What did they think about all this? Surely they kept my parents well informed of all these events. When my mother heard that René and I were living together, she urged us to get married. My father didn't say anything.

So, we married. And one day later, I discovered that I was pregnant.

6

Rosa
The Birth of Miranda, 1970

I was nine months pregnant when the art faculty honored me with an exposition of my paintings. They were simple things, made of geometric forms and vivid colors, and I didn't think them very sophisticated, but they appealed to the judges. There was a little party on the opening night, with wine and guests. There was much to celebrate: the paintings, the hope that Allende gave us, and for René and me, the anticipation of being parents.

The first labor pains began in the evening and by two o'clock in the morning we went to the hospital. At three o'clock, with a cry more of confusion than of pain, our daughter was born. It was the same day that Allende won the election.

They say that newborns don't see very well, but I can attest to the fact that this isn't always true. From the first moment, Miranda gazed at me with luminous, brilliant eyes, of a dark brown like her father's. Her eyes were more unusual still because most babies are born with blue eyes and they acquire their natural color over the course of the next few months, but Miranda's eyes were already completed. Nor did she cry like other babies;

she just looked at me with her intense stare that seemed to comprehend me completely.

To feed her it always happened like this: I felt a little tickle in my breasts in the exact moment that she stirred and gave a little sound to indicate her hunger. I don't know if this happens to other women, but the result was that Miranda never had to struggle or suffer in any way. I was already unbuttoning my blouse before she had to cry. We were two; following the same rhythm, in the same physical state.

My mother arrived as soon as she could, but even still it was a month before she could get to Santiago. She said that my father did not facilitate her trip at all. I could understand my father's anger for me, but what blame did Miranda have? Not even the birth of his first grandchild could mitigate his disdain for me. I guess that my leaving home was so terrible that he could never pardon me, nor celebrate anything good either. I realized then that neither Miranda nor I would come out unscathed from his fanaticisms.

With regard to public life, we were all very happy. All our friends, our fellow students, were ecstatic with the idea that Allende had won the election. We could hardly believe it. It was like a dream that you think could never come true, but then does: a dream made into reality. Very soon, the reality of his winning would come to affect me and René very personally.

Because of his work as the leader of the union of law students, René had attracted the attention of some important people in Allende's government. They asked him to accept the position of leader of all the student unions in the country; a huge honor. René could not refuse. Suddenly, he began spending many days away from home, missing many meals, leaving me alone with our new baby. I missed him. And I found it very difficult to continue my studies, because I had no one with whom to leave Miranda.

My aunt, when she discovered the situation, sent me her maid, named curiously enough, Rosa.

During the first days of Allende's presidency, things went very well. There were jobs, many more jobs available; and the inflation rate which had been a problem for some time, abated. But none of this lasted. Very soon there were shortages of foodstuffs, like sugar. Rosa spent hours and hours in line at the store, and once it opened, they would only sell a half kilo. There were shortages of coffee; of toilet paper; even toothpaste. And René spent more and more time away from home.

I could have withstood this, but one day I found out about something that truly filled me with fear. Isaac, René's friend, came to talk to us about his work in the MIR: the Revolutionary Leftist Movement. I know about that group. They were not satisfied with the rate of Allende's progress. They wanted more changes, more quickly, more in the style of the Marxists. Isaac wanted René to join the MIR. I begged him not to, but I felt impotent to change his mind. René had become very frustrated with his work in the unions; Allende himself had proved an impediment to strikes, because of ideological conflicts in his party. He was having trouble pleasing the groups with different interpretations of progress, and he made some strikes illegal. The MIR did not abstain from violence if they thought it necessary, and René knew this, but out of his frustration he felt drawn, as if to a romance, by the concrete action they advocated. Their methods began to feel right to him, more passionate, more romantic in a way. René was a student of the law, but he began to lose faith in the law to solve the country's problems.

It was then that my milk dried up. I no longer felt the tickling feeling in my breasts and the baby cried desperately, sucking with all her might, but it was useless. The anguish of not being able to feed her drove me crazy with grief. Rosa suggested that we give her sugar water in a bottle, but there was no sugar. Nor was there cow's milk, neither fresh nor in powder. When René arrived home that night, I screamed at him like a crazy woman. I screamed out the desperation of a broken mother, a mother driven mad by anguish.

René went immediately to his parents' house but they had no milk either. They knew where to find some, however. When the baby had had her fill and had fallen asleep, worn out by the crying and the hunger, we sat down to talk.

"So you see what happens when the big farms get invaded by leftists?", remarked by father-in-law. "There are shortages of milk because they don't produce what they used to".

"Let's not discuss this now, responded René.

One day later we found out that the MIR group had put explosives in an electric tower in the south and a young technician had been killed in the explosion. Isaac was in the south, and if it hadn't been for the crisis of the milk, René would have been there too. To think that my husband was so close to being involved in the death of an innocent person filled me with fear.

But not everything was so black. When Fidel Castro visited Chile, René was invited to Santa Elena to speak at the meeting, together with a group of union leaders. This was a tremendous honor and it made me very proud to see that René had gained the confidence of such important people. This period, then, was a mixture of happiness and fear; of advances and retreats; of improvements and setbacks.

Until the fatal day arrived.

7

Rosa
The *coup d'état*

The upper class in Chile had always been opposed to Allende and his leftist ideology. With the expropriation of private property, they felt even more threatened. The middle class watched disappear its privileges and felt alienated from the process as well. If you had asked him, my father would have said that the middle class is the basis of society, and to separate it from its sources of wealth, is a grave error. But my father could never see the benefits of changing this: instead of a small middle and upper class and a large working class, we would have an equitable distribution of income that would include everyone.

But like every radical change, it was necessary to undergo a period of instability while the new norms were solidified. What Allende didn't perceive was that this period of instability was going to be his downfall. The sense of imminent loss felt by the upper and middle class extended to all reaches of society. The church was opposed to Allende's proposals because of the Marxist education system that interfered with its dominion over catholic schools; the doctors, lawyers, and nearly everyone else, could not get a job without being a member of Allende's political party; even the copper miners, long a stalwart group in favor of socialism, tried to strike but were prevented by the new regime, and returned to the mines with only minimal salary improvements. No one was happy; no one was in favor of the new system, even the most fervent followers.

René and I, along with our school friends, spent hours and hours debating the pros and the cons of Allende's program. There were some of us who began to doubt its wisdom. Others believed that more radical changes were necessary. The friendship between us began to fray. And between René and me, began a period of misunderstandings, of doubts and anguish. I sensed that my husband wanted to become more involved with the radicals, but I could not then, and never would, be in favor. I felt like I couldn't stop him, however.

At the same time, René's parents never wasted an opportunity to express their disdain for the socialist system. They believed that the soul of the Chilean people was in danger of disappearing. They complained, saying that for the previous one hundred and fifty years, Chile had had a democratic government; we responded that socialism provided for an even more democratic environment; one in which the decisions were made jointly by many people, but my in-laws could not see it that way. René got so disillusioned with them that he stopped all contact and I had to serve as intermediary between them and us. I didn't want what happened in Brussels between my father and me to happen again in René's family, but it was hopeless. The only thing I achieved was making the distance between my husband and myself bigger.

In the streets, there began to be talk of a *coup d'état*, an overthrow of the government by the military. There were rumors everywhere. You couldn't believe the news; some said that the fears of a coup were being flamed by anti-progressive forces; others said it was the CIA. There was no way to be sure of anything.

In June, the *tancazo* happened. A regiment of soldiers with tanks attacked the Ministry of Defense, killing several bystanders, which provoked

Allende into proclaiming by radio that the country was under attack and begging for people to defend it. Obeying the order, the MIR group expropriated more than half of the factories in the country, arousing even more hysteria and confusion. The inflation rate rose to incredible heights: what today cost ten escudos tomorrow cost one hundred. The commander of the army resigned his post and was replaced by Augusto Pinochet. I had not heard of him; later on he would become our worst nightmare. In sum, what began with such high hopes started to fall apart. Some would say that Allende himself caused the disintegration, others that it was the machinations of the CIA; others that it was simple nature of fickle human beings.

I cried daily in that time, for the frustration of everything. Art was the only thing that alleviated my anguish. I painted as if my life depended on it. And in a certain sense, it did. I think that if I had not had painting as a way to express myself, I would have gone crazy.

When in September the Hawker Hunter fighter planes discharged their rockets at La Moneda – the building where Allende and his aides had taken refuge – destroying the windows and setting alight the curtains, many people cheered. Finally, this period of fear, of instability and anger, was going to end, and Chile would return to its civil ways and its democracy before socialism came into view. But this was not to be. Allende died, and Chile did not return to democracy for a long time.

8

Rosa
René arrested

Communism in Chile had been destroyed. And to make sure that it would not return, it was necessary to put our trust in the military. That's what my in-laws professed, along with many others. Besides, the military would only be in control for a limited time, a few months, only until things returned to normal.

But things did not return to normal. One day after the coup, the military declared a state of siege, which gave them immense powers. Nearly all the normal activities of daily life: going to work, getting together with friends, studying, came under their auspices. All the news was censured; all political parties dissolved; all the unions were prohibited. The congress was dismissed.

The upper class behaved like ostriches; putting their head in the sand to avoid knowing anything or participating in anything. They had been so afraid during the previous three years that they were ready to submit to anything in order to survive. Then, we learned that in the days immediately after the coup, several thousand people had been detained; most tortured; many killed. Some people refused to believe it, but I was certain of it. Our friends kept us well informed of things like this. René's father characterized it like this: "nobody likes it, but if your house is full of pests, you have to exterminate them". It made me angry to hear him describe our leftist friends, noble people, like Allende, and like their own son, as "pests".

But Chile was not the same now. The democratic country in which political differences could be discussed politely, disappeared. Before, it was said that there were no political arguments that couldn't be resolved by sharing a bottle of red wine between adversaries. No longer. Parents and children disagreed, fought, and became estranged; brothers became enemies over political questions that before didn't have the power to divide. A type of craziness took over, or a blindness; and it kept its power over the country for a long while.

And between René and me? Well, the actions of the military made worse what was already a bad situation. We had passed through many months of antagonisms. A disaster of this type is something that either separates you from the people you love, or brings you closer together. It's not like we didn't try to remain close; every day we held each other like you hold on to a lifejacket in stormy seas; every night we made love like we were the last remaining people on earth, but our differences continued. I was never going to be in favor of violence to solve problems, and I sensed that René might be.

He tried to continue his studies and I did as well, but we suffered from a great depression; the failure of a utopia. Because it was really going to be a utopia. We were constructing a new country, a new society. We were going to include the working class in the government; giving them the dignity they deserved. We were going to make Chile a thousand times better than it had been before. But the word *revolution* sounded too much like *destruction* to the people, and our dream failed.

We kept on the best we could but it wasn't easy. The day that a friend came to tell us that Isaac had been detained, was extremely difficult. René put aside his frustration with his parents and pleaded with them to help, but they achieved nothing. They had been tainted by association with their son, and all their old contacts in the military dried up.

Then we learned that Isaac died; during a supposed attempt to escape the cell in which he and others were being held. Our friend told us that the military had tortured him, to make him reveal the identity of others in the MIR. Together with Isaac, they tortured a fifteen- year-old girl, the daughter of a steel worker in Quiriquina. She survived and told us what happened. She said that Isaac never lost his courage or his dignity, nor did he reveal a single name.

We were in the depths of the most unbearable agony, when my father came to visit.

It had been eight years since I had seen him. He looked older, but he had not lost any of his fine manners from his years as a diplomat. He told me he had been invited by Pinochet to assist with some economic issues. I can hardly describe how this unexpected visit felt. On the one hand, it gave me great pleasure to see him again. I loved him for the simple fact of being my father. But on the other hand, I still felt dubious about his activities in Brussels; his possible involvement in something that might harm our family. Therefore, a huge emptiness existed between us; a huge darkness of secrets and unknowns, and to see him so unexpectedly caused me to cry for the lost times of the past, those times when we used to converse freely without the doubts that now circled round us.

René was worried about the reason for my father's visit, but he wouldn't elaborate. René at that time was going through a depression; his school friends had all fallen into a demoralized state that he could not penetrate. It was a passivity, a sadness. Nobody wanted to risk their job, their academic career, or anything at all because the powers of the military were omnipotent. They controlled all the ways to get jobs, to be able to study. They eliminated classes; removing books from the library; firing professors, erasing entire faculties. For the military, the universities were symbols of the worst of Allende; they were where the most damaging ideas started, and for that reason the schools were where the hand of the military came down hardest.

I think that it was because of this that René entered more thoroughly into the resistance. He took on the task of uniting students against the military junta, but he found it difficult. Everyone had doubts about everyone else; no one trusted anyone. One day, René started to cry, remembering the day that Allende won the election. That day, Allende had come to speak to the students. He was up on a balcony and down below, the students were delirious with joy. When he finished his speech, they began dancing and playing music, and continued throughout the whole night. Now everything was so different.

The only thing that helped me stay calm was my little daughter. Caring for her helped me remember that the world still had beautiful things in it; that there was still a way to live without being judged, condemned, and sent into nothing. Watching her made me think also of my sisters, above all of Lea, because Lea was the same way: playful, active, light-hearted. I could see the links among the women of my family, like a thread that comes unwoven and rewinds itself regardless of the distance and time.

So, we barely held it together. But then one day, the unthinkable happened. They arrested René.

9

Rosa
An exchange of favors

Chile was in chaos; it had been changed into a country of enemies. And my worst nightmare had come true: René had been arrested.

The first thing I did was go to his parents' house. But they couldn't do anything. They no longer associated with any of their old friends; another casualty of the political situation. They seemed isolated and depressed.

I didn't want to ask my father for help but I had no other option. I had to speak with him.

"I know about René.", he said as I came into his office.

"How?!"

"I can't tell you how."

A long moment passed.

"You're not here in Chile only as economic advisor, are you?", I asked him, already knowing the truth.

"No", he admitted.

This was not the moment to investigate the professional life of my father; I had other, more urgent matters to attend to. I needed him to help me locate René.

"I know where he is being held", he said, "but I don't know if I can get him out."

He gave me the address of the place. It was a common house in the outskirts of the city. By then it was night, but I didn't care. It wasn't permitted to be outside of your neighborhood at night and I ran the risk of being detained as well, but it didn't matter.

I asked the officials there about René and they told me to wait. I waited until one o'clock in the morning. I asked again and they told me to wait until eight a.m., when they would publish the updated list of prisoners. By seven a.m. there had gathered a group of family members, all with the hope of at least knowing that their loved one was inside. Together we waited until two o'clock in the afternoon, with no news. I had not eaten, nor slept, nor used the bathroom.

At five o'clock a soldier came out and read the names of the detainees. René's name was not on the list.

When I returned to my father's office, he wasn't there. Desperate, I returned to my flat where Rosa and Miranda were waiting for me. Rosa had saved my life many times before during that difficult period; I was completely sure that she was taking good care of my daughter. Miranda was napping, and I too tried to sleep a bit.

I woke up from an anguished dream hearing the voice of Rosa telling me that my father had arrived. I hurriedly got dressed.

"Rosa. My Rosa", said my father.

"What has happened?", I asked in a panic.

"They've taken René to another location. It's not good news."

"Do something, Papa! You have to do something!"

I thought about all the questionable matters in which my father had been involved during our years in Brussels, all the dubious problems that he had helped solve, all the midnight phone calls in order to help a colleague, a friend, a friend of a friend. Surely my father still maintained some of his diplomatic ties. Surely he could help me get my husband back.

"I have something to propose to you", he said. "It's a plan that my chief in Washington has formulated. It's an exchange of favors."

I felt sick inside.

"What kind of favors?", I asked, imaging the worst.

"Can you listen for a moment without judging me?", he asked. I nodded. Anything for René.

"There are people in our government who are trying to fix the economic mess that Allende left. These people need our help. And there are Chileans who are committed to solving these issues as well. They need our help."

"Yes, I can imagine that", I responded, my insides a churning mess of conflict. My father could not avoid noticing my state of mind. And I could not help noticing that he referred to the U.S. government as "our" government. I did not consider myself part of that government at all.

"Rosa, I know you don't agree with the junta, but you have to see that the country is in dire straits."

I was growing impatient with this talk of political issues; my only concern was René.

"Please don't lecture me, Papa. This isn't the moment. What is the exchange of favors?", I said, putting a black tone over the last words.

He sighed, knowing I was right.

"All right. Pay good attention. In Mexico there is a subversive that the junta wishes to silence. This man is fomenting socialist behavior in all of Latin America. He is the leader of a group of leftists that represents a threat to the whole continent. My chiefs in Washington are working with Pinochet and his security forces to discredit this man because they too want to see him gone."

"What does this have to do with me?"

"Let me explain. I know this man. He was in Brussels for a while. And I know he has one weak point. He is an artist and in the past he was accused of fraud. Some people, people high up in the art world, thought that he had taken ownership of a painting that he did not paint. Now, his biggest fear is that something like this happens again."

I didn't want to hear any more. What did the fate of this unknown Mexican painter matter to me? Less still, since it was about harming a leftist? Could my father perhaps have forgotten about my sympathies for socialism?

"The subversive is named Diego Alba."

My father waited for me to make some reaction, but I did nothing. The name meant nothing to me.

"It will be easy. You will travel to Mexico. You'll contact certain people who will help you prove that he has committed fraud, and you confront him, offering silence in exchange for him discontinuing activity with his group."

"But…"

"Let's not talk about it anymore. Here."

He handed me a folder.

"Read this. You'll see that it's very easy. You won't be any more than ten days in Mexico. Then, when you return, René will be home."

I felt nauseous. I felt like I was falling into a deep hole. But I had no other option but to accept.

10

Rosa
In Mexico

The plan was not that easy, despite what my father told me. It concerned the movement of some paintings, some calls to places where the person would not identify themselves, a countless number of lies and deceits. If Diego Alba was not a fraud, what my father was proposing was a calumny of the highest level.

The following day my father came with the airline ticket and a passport with my photo, but a different name. Rosa helped me pack. We discussed what she needed to do for Miranda, and she assured me that all would be well. I made her promise to call my aunt and uncle and my in-laws if I were not back in ten days. Hurriedly I wrote a letter to my mother, informing her of everything that was happening. I was afraid. I didn't know what influence my father actually had with the junta. If he failed me, neither my aunt and uncle nor my in-laws could help me. No. I was flying solo.

In the folder, I read about Diego Alba; his past, his present activities. My role was to pretend to be a representative from an art gallery in Santiago, interested in acquiring some of his paintings. I read about how I, as an art student, would find it easy to gain his confidence. I read about how I was going to destroy him.

The first thing I had to do was get in contact with a woman named Esmé Moreau. She was French; the owner of the gallery in Mexico City where Diego showed his work. I was to propose a lucrative deal between our galleries; pure business, like the good capitalists that we were. This poor woman had no idea of the intrigues in which her painter was to become involved. After arriving in Mexico and settling in to the Hotel Geneve, I went to her gallery.

I didn't have to pretend to admire the paintings of Diego Alba. They appealed to me enormously, even in my worried and anxious state of mind. But I had to focus on the task before me, even though it seemed to me, in equal measures, to be both absurd and absolutely necessary. Esmé and I were deep in conversation when Diego entered the gallery. At that moment, everything changed.

Diego affected me like an X-ray; penetrating my deepest secrets. I got the distinct impression that he didn't believe my story of the gallery in Santiago; that in fact, he was enjoying the game. But then I thought he did in fact, believe me, and was quite enthusiastic with the idea of his work being shown there. It was impossible to be sure.

He invited me to his house to see more paintings. This wasn't part of the plan written in the folder, but I wanted to go. I noticed that his invitation to me annoyed Esmé, although she tried to hide it.

The entrance to his house was bordered on both sides by huge, tall trees, whose trunks and branches were an unexpected white color. We passed through his front door: a massive wooden entrance carved in a Moorish style, and into a large interior patio. I felt my worries begin to diminish a little. Diego served me a white wine that didn't taste of alcohol but rather of honey, and he spoke to me about his art, about the history of the house, about his past. He asked very little about me. Diego was somewhat older than I, and he had lived a lot. He started painting at a young age and his work became well-known when he was only eighteen. His conversation, his voice and his manner contributed to my sense of ease, a sense of relaxation that I had not felt in many days.

Then, perhaps because of the wine or perhaps the warm sunlight that bathed the patio, I felt very sleepy. I could hardly stay awake during the meal and afterwards, Diego offered me a place to lie down. He took me to a beautiful, high-ceilinged room, full of books, with lace curtains that moved in the breeze. On a large leather sofa, with my head on a velvet pillow, I sunk down gratefully.

When I woke, I felt a delicious warmth in my whole body, and a delicious sense of freedom. I stayed immobile for a few minutes, loathe to lose the feeling. It had gotten late. Diego returned me to the city, to the Hotel Geneve, a trip of two hours. We conversed; intimate things. I felt like I had met the most interesting and sympathetic of friends. I talked to him about some paintings I had made, and he was enchanted with the idea that I was an artist as well. Inventing as I went along, I spoke about the new economic opportunities in Chile now that the Marxists were gone. I wanted to see how he replied, as a kind of experiment.

But Diego didn't take the bait. He gracefully avoided talking about politics at all, and soon we were at the hotel. It felt to me that the deal between the French woman gallery-owner, the Chilean representative, and the Mexican painter was going to work perfectly.

11

Rosa
The Death of René

In the following days I dedicated myself to the task of ruining the reputation of Diego Alba. There was the purchase of the paintings, which put me in contact with Esmé Moreau once again, and the arrangement of them to an anonymous buyer. I fought with myself to banish the bad feeling that was growing within me; Diego didn't deserve this. But I felt trapped, a prisoner of forces much bigger than me, and over which I had little control.

I had nearly finished with everything I had to do in Mexico when two men, dressed in coat and tie came to see me at the Hotel Geneve. Suddenly I felt a tremendous fear. What had happened? I thought quickly to go the front desk and call my father, but they stopped me. They were speaking English; they were from the U.S. embassy. They showed me a telegram from Chile and I took it, but I couldn't read it. I felt a fear that took the breath from my lungs, the sight from my eyes. I felt like something terrible was going to happen.

The men took me to a sofa in the lobby and we sat down. They explained that their colleagues in the embassy in Chile had informed them that René had died. They said it was a cerebral hemorrhage. While he was in custody. That I could not return to Chile at this time because I would be in great danger, that…. that…

The information came to be in pieces. Fragments of phrases without meaning. Then an American woman came over. She was to stay with me for the time being. We went to my room, but I was in a daze. I couldn't stay there, like a caged beast. We went out into the street. I began walking at full speed, leaving the poor woman to come after as if she were in the wake of a crazed ocean liner. We walked I don't know how many miles, paying no attention to the traffic, to the stoplights, to anything.

When we finally returned to the hotel I went to the bar and ordered a whiskey. Then another. I felt then that I could return to my room and read the telegram. There were two; one was from my father, saying more or less what the men had told me. But in one thing he made special emphasis: that under no circumstances was I to return to Chile. He said that the DINA was looking for me; the Chilean National Intelligence Agency. I knew about the DINA; I knew what they were capable of. Some months before the coup, they had put a bomb in the car of Carlos Prats, a commander of the military under Allende. Prats had been against the junta. He and his wife died in Argentina, where they had taken refuge from Pinochet and his aides.

I sent an emergency telegram to my father, asking him to call me by phone. But instead of a phone call, I received another telegram, saying that he couldn't call me because he did not trust the telephone line; he suspected that the DINA might have bugged it. He explained that now more than ever it was important that I complete the plan; that we achieve the desired results. I was horrified at his words. He said that his own security in Chile depended on it. All this felt like the most grotesque blackmail imaginable.

Meanwhile, I could not stop thinking about Miranda. It was if I had to postpone my anguish over the death of René, in order to put some order to things. I didn't have the luxury of mourning my husband right then. I had to save my daughter.

I called Brussels. I tried to talk to my mother but the call couldn't be completed and I went to wait in the lobby for the operator to try again. I took advantage of these moments to write an urgent letter to her, asking her to go to Santiago and take charge of Miranda. No other plan occurred to me other than bringing them both to Mexico. To be together. To protect ourselves from the insanity that surrounded us.

I was in the Hotel Geneve for four more days. They were the worst four days of my life. The only thing that saved me going under completely were Diego's visits. He came each day to take me out for a meal. I wouldn't have eaten otherwise. He walked with me when the fury and the anguish threatened to overwhelm me. He listened to me. He listened to me when I told him that my husband in Chile had deceived me with another woman; that he had waited until I was out of the house to tell me this; that the woman in question was the owner of the gallery that I supposedly represented; and that now he was asking me for a divorce. Diego understood me completely when I explained that I was now without a husband or a job. I don't know where so many lies came from; I don't know how I was capable of doing this.

Finally, my daughter and my mother arrived in Mexico. The relief was intense. We spent a long time then discussing the future. How was I supposed to carry on, now that my life in Chile had disappeared? We discussed the possibility that Miranda and I would return to Brussels, and I had nearly decided to do that, when Diego came back into the picture.

We were in the restaurant of the hotel when he came up to us. My mother stopped short; it seemed that she might know him or recognize him in some way. But the moment passed and I thought I must have imagined it. Diego didn't react upon seeing her, nor did he comment in any way about my plan to return to Brussels.

But later, when my mother had taken Miranda out for a walk and we were alone, he began to speak.

"You are an artist. You're a mother. And now...."

THE HOUSE OF MIRANDA ALBA

"Now I'm alone."

"No, you're not alone. You have your mother."

"She can't stay here. She has her whole life in Brussels."

"So, you plan to return to Europe?"

"I don't see any other option."

But to tell the truth, I did not want to go back to Brussels. Since leaving there, I had constructed a new life; an independent life; a life of passion, of work; of ideals; a life I was not going to be able to re-create there. I was used to living outside of those limits, outside of the stifling conformity of that European city. Brussels had rules that I couldn't follow anymore.

"Stay here," said Diego. "Esmé could give you a job in the gallery. Mexico City is a beautiful place to live."

I didn't say anything.

"Rosa, you need time to consider your options. I was thinking…., would you like to spend some time at my house while you decide what to do? It's large; you and Miranda would have your own suite of rooms. I have a woman who helps out there; she could take care of your daughter when you need her to. She has a son who is five years old; he would be good company for her."

Later, when Diego had left, I spoke with my mother.

"I don't advise you to accept his offer, Rosa. You hardly know this man. Just a few days ago you were trying to ruin him and now you plan on being his guest? It makes no sense."

"I was never in favor of my father's plan", I responded. "You know that very well. If it hadn't been for René, I would never have accepted being his accomplice. All this has been horrible, Mother. Horrible."

"Your father did what he thought was right, what he thought was the best way to proceed. He didn't have anything to do with René's death."

"You can't tell me you believe that René died of a cerebral hemorrhage?!", I asked incredulously. "It was the DINA. They probably tortured him, and my father did nothing."

At this point I could no longer contain the tears that had been building up inside me during these last days. I cried and cried, soaking the pillows, the sheets of the bed. There was no way I could stop the tears from coming. My mother could do nothing but sit by the side of the bed, watching. My poor little daughter got frightened, and still the torrent of tears continued.

By the next morning, I had decided. I would stay in Mexico. My mother was still in league with my father, still united with him in some inexplicable way. I wanted to talk to her about the rumors about my father and his relationships outside of marriage, but I couldn't find the words. Moreover, in my position as daughter I felt uncomfortable judging or meddling in her personal affairs. You can never really know your parents completely.

So, I made the decision. To return to Brussels would signify a defeat for me, an inglorious return to the past, and I didn't want to return to the past; I wanted to go into the future.

Before leaving, my mother gave me one of my old Barbie dolls. It was my favorite; one of the many that my sisters and I played with as children. I remembered that it was also the favorite of Lea; she always wanted me to gift it to her, but I never did. It was one of the few things I ever denied her. To think about Lea now, about Nikita and Adriana, gave me a longing for those days; those simple days when we all lived together as a family. I wanted to see them again, but they were still young. They still had their whole lives ahead of them; lives that I hoped to God were not tainted by the same mistakes I had made.

12

Rosa
Mrs. Poncia

René was dead. My father had betrayed me. My life in Chile no longer existed. I was now in another life altogether, and I found myself once more passing through the line of tall white trees that led to the house of Diego Alba.

But this time I carried with me a sense of sadness that covered me like a shroud. All the fury that possessed me in the days after Rene's death had gone, leaving behind a crushing depression. The movements of my body cost me heavily. Instead of internal organs I had inside me a blackness that choked. I went to bed and I couldn't get up.

But Miranda needed me. She wanted to investigate the house, which was large and very complicated, and she insisted that I accompany her. Together we spent hours going from room to room, down corridors, up and down stairs, through patios and archways. It seemed to have no end. One day we walked up the hill to a little house that had a view of the pyramids in the archaeological zone nearby. There was a small pond there with water lilies and pollywogs. And in the immense solitude of Diego's property, I began to heal.

Diego gave me the materials for painting, but I still did not have the energy. What I most liked to do was wander alone in the hills and the woods that surrounded his house. There I could think. I left Miranda in the care of Mrs. Poncia, who at the beginning gained my trust. Her son Cecilio was five and played well with Miranda. There was a piano in the main living room and Miranda liked to play her little songs there.

Mrs. Poncia had an unusual appearance. You could say her eyes were blue, but they were of such a light blue that they seemed almost transparent. Her skin was extremely white, so white that you could see the veins in her forehead. Her hair was long and coarse, with streaks of grey, while her eyebrows, which formed a single line above her eyes, were bushy and dark. All this gave her the appearance of something from another world, a ghost or a spirit, and her voice, which was rough and deep, just emphasized this. I understood that she was from the countryside, but from what kind of countryside I couldn't imagine.

But leaving aside her appearance, she was an excellent cook. The food she prepared was excellent and when my apatite came back, I loved to eat her meals. I tasted for the first time, mixtures of tastes that were new to me: spicy and sweet, bitter and earthy; fruits I didn't know, meats I had never tried.

Cecilio took after Diego, not so much in his physical appearance but in his manner. His speaking voice was a carbon copy of Diego's. It occurred to me that Cecilio might be his son, an unacknowledged son, but as a guest in his house I didn't feel right asking.

Diego took very good care of Cecilio, nevertheless, the same way he cared for Miranda. He was the most marvelous substitute father. He played with them, gave them everything they needed to express themselves creatively, like crayons, paints and clay; everything they needed to mold their childish fantasies. He built two small easels for them to paint *en plein air,* as they say in French, and it gave me great pleasure to seem them in the garden with their canvases and their paintbrushes.

In this way, three months passed. It had now come the time to move ahead with my life. Miranda needed to go to school, I needed to find a job. I asked Diego to take me into the city to meet with Esmé Moreau, and he said he would do so the following day. But the following day we discovered that Diego had left on a trip. And Mrs. Poncia began to show her true character.

When I asked her about the bus to take me into the city, she said that the bus stop was very difficult to find and offered to take me out to the highway to show it to me. We went there and I saw a small wooden stake, not at all official looking, with the number 123 painted on the side. Mrs. Poncia said that this was the bus stop, and she then returned to the house with the children. Something in all this didn't seem right, but I chalked it up to the pain and upset that still resonated in me. I tried to repress my fears. Miranda was a smart, alert little girl and I had to rely on her powers to take care of herself.

I waited an eternity for the bus to come, but it never came. So I decided to walk to town and try to catch it there. Once I got there, I asked about the bus stop at kilometer 123, but they told me there was no such bus stop. It occurred to me that Poncia had deliberately misled me, and from that I sensed that my presence at the house was not agreeable to her, that she possibly was jealous of me, even.

When I got to the city I tried to focus on finding Esmé's art gallery. It wasn't hard. Speaking with her was a delight; her light French accent reminded me of my friends in Brussels. She was dressed in a style *tres chic,* which made me look at my own clothes with consternation. I would have to buy new ones if I was going to work with her in the gallery. After our talk, she took me to see some apartments; one of which was perfect for me and Miranda. The elementary school was nearby. All the aspects of my future seemed to be resolving themselves, except for money. Before returning to Diego's house, I passed by the telegraph office to send a message to my father. He owed me.

13

Rosa
Miranda and Diego

In the three months we spent at his house, Diego behaved in the most gentlemanly way possible. I was very grateful and perhaps because of that, I did not have my defenses up as well as I should have. When he returned from his trip he began to treat me differently: with great tenderness and affection. This affected me greatly. Diego is a very persuasive man.

He told me about his trip: he had been in Cuba. He came back with a suntan and smelling of cigars. What was happening in Cuba was exciting; the arts were flourishing under Castro. Our conversations reminded me of the ones I had with René when we first met. When Diego asked me to consider the possibility of staying longer, I told him I had to think about it, but I really didn't. The money that my father sent me was not even half of what I needed.

"Is there a school for Miranda in the town?", I asked him.

"There is, but it isn't of the highest quality. But perhaps that doesn't matter for a short time. Mrs. Poncia can take both the children and pick them up.

With the mention of Poncia I felt the little hairs on the back of my neck stand up.

"And me? How will I go into the city for work? It's almost two hours by bus."

With this, Diego appeared to grow larger; his ability to solve problems even greater, to straighten out the road even more, to offer me what I most needed.

"You don't have a great need to work right now, Rosa. Besides, you are in a fragile state. You've suffered a trauma. Let the house give you what you need right now: peace and time. You need to feed your body and your soul. Let me help you."

I felt the tears on my cheeks. It had been a long time since anyone had offered to help me in this way. With René, I was always the strong one, the independent one. He always valued me for my ability to take care of myself, but now….

"Thank you. We will stay. You don't know what this means to me, and to Miranda."

I wanted to keep talking but Diego stopped me.

"It's you who should get the thanks. You've provided what was most lacking here."

He closed his eyes, as if delighting in the anticipation of what he was going to say.

"I was very alone here. I have my work, my trips…. but I felt very alone. Now, I hear music, laughter, conversation. The house has come back to life. It has been so good for me to have you both here. And you….."

He couldn't finish, overwhelmed with emotion.

"I've never known a woman quite like you before", he said.

From that point on, things changed between Diego and me. I saw that he was falling in love. And me? Was I falling in love with him? I couldn't admit it. It felt like disloyalty to René, to his memory, to our past together, to everything that Chile represented to me in my life. No. I couldn't put all that aside.

What I did in the face of all that was dedicate myself to my child. I took her to the primary school in the town, but Diego was right. It was very bad. So I decided to educate her on my own. She was seven years old. She could read in Spanish, so I began to teach her to read in French as well. After all, most of the world's knowledge is in books anyway. And Miranda had a huge desire to read. We went frequently into the city, to the bookstores and soon the bookshelves at the house became full of children's books, as well as books and newspapers for me too. I needed to know what was going on in the world.

I also painted. Painting calmed me down wonderfully; helped me forget about the peculiarities of my situation.

One of these peculiarities was Mrs. Poncia. I hadn't mentioned anything to her about the bus stop that didn't exist, and she probably thought she had me daunted or afraid. She always pretended to be the lady of the house; in some way, she exercised a control over it and everything that happened there. She was in charge of the shopping, the cooking, the cleaning, the washing of clothes. She had been with Diego for a very long time, since he was a child. Poncia was fifteen when she was contracted by Diego's mother, as a nanny for the precocious boy. I imagine that at some point, she must have married and had Cecilio. But no one ever talked about Cecilio's father, so I continued with my doubts as to his parentage.

With regard to Miranda; she had fallen in love with Diego. He spoke to her as if she were an adult; he made her feel important and respected. He listened to her little stories in a solemn silence; he laughed at her childish jokes. He also told her stories, stories the like of which she had never heard before. He told her about the Indians who had lived here before; and he was an excellent story teller: emotional, dramatic. In the world of Diego and Miranda, there still existed these tribes from the past, with their ceremonies and their sacrifices. They still wandered about, were still dangerous.

Miranda was enchanted by these stories. They fed her imagination.

Cecilio, on the other hand, was jealous of Miranda and of Diego's treatment of her. He was only five. It's normal. He had been very doted upon by his mother, very spoiled. Poncia could not see a single defect in Cecilio, and he had many very serious ones. He liked to trap the baby chicks that lived in the back patio and cut their feet to see the blood. He did the same to the kittens. It made me sad to see how Miranda tried to pet the kittens, but they wouldn't come anywhere near her from their bad experiences with Cecilio.

And Mrs. Poncia never let the opportunity pass to look down on me, always when Diego was not around. I remember, as if imprinted on my memory, my new dress that later disappeared from the laundry. I had bought it to wear when Diego was returning from a trip, but the dress was not in the basket of dry clothes, nor was it hanging on the line. And when I asked her about it, she said it had never been in the basket, that she had never even seen it, and she even got angry, saying that I was accusing her unjustly.

Then, she would speak poorly about me to Diego. This never had any results, except for once. One night, very late, Diego arrived home very tired. Mrs. Poncia, who never stayed the night at the house, had remained. She waited until Diego came in to tell him that she had seen me enter his studio and come out with some of his drawings. Diego went immediately to his studio and the drawings were not there. The following day he asked me about them, and I found myself in the ridiculous position of having to defend myself like a common thief. What would I want with those drawings? Poncia had told him that those same designs appeared in some of my own work. There is nothing worse for an artist to be accused of plagiarism. But when Diego asked to see my paintings, there somehow was a resemblance to the sketches. I don't know how she did it, but she managed to put me in a very awkward position.

What she had that was good, was her culinary expertise. She used many spices and plants that were native to the area, like cilantro and epazote, plants I had never tasted. I ate for the first time tunas, which are the fruit of the cactus, and mole, a chicken dish with chocolate. I had never tasted such wonderful food. And since there was always wine in abundance at dinner, our meals at Diego's house were lively.

It was about this time when I began to feel nauseous after eating. I believed it was nerves, my nervousness. So many things had happened to me recently; deaths, lies, losses. It was logical to think that all that was taking its toll on my physical health.

But there were too many coincidences. I would feel fine all day and then, just after eating something she had prepared, I would feel sick. I had nausea, dizziness. I vomited regularly. I felt like my legs weren't working properly, and I had to fight off the desire to return to bed and lie there all day. I didn't feel like doing anything, talking to anyone. My appetite disappeared, and my clothes felt loose on me. I didn't know what was going on.

14

Rosa
Mrs. Poncia in Town

A long time passed without any trips for Diego and I felt much better. The memory of the sickness nearly vanished.

Even though physically I felt better, my sixth sense started to tell me that something terribly wrong was occurring in the house. Diego had told us that the house stood on the grounds of a much older dwelling, that had been in continuous use since the distant past, since even before the archeological ruins ever were first built. That is, the house had a thick coat of history upon it, a great heap of dust, of spirits, covering everything, flying into the most remote corners, inserting themselves into every space. I know it sounds absurd, but I felt a bad energy there, especially in certain areas. In some rooms, the furniture changed position without reason, as if to trap or trip up the person inside; from underneath the doors would sometimes flow a current of hot air, or cold; objects would become lost to later reappear in other place; the curtains moved even when the windows were closed, or, would not move despite the breeze outside; sometimes it would get dark inside the house as if the sun had passed behind a cloud, only to find when you went outside that it was a sunny, cloudless day.

I never dared to say any of this to Diego; it sounded implausible and ridiculous. The house he had constructed was beautiful, and the gardens were divine. But beneath all that beauty existed some contrary force. In my entire life I hadn't felt anything similar; in fact, my most salient characteristics are seriousness, pragmatism, concentration and logic. It was difficult for me to believe in something so clearly antiscientific, but I couldn't help it. According to Mrs. Poncia, the house breathed, it saw things, it heard what was being said. Whenever she talked like this, Miranda would look at me with big eyes, Diego would laugh, while Mrs. Poncia would smirk with a secret understanding.

One thing I **did** mention to Diego. I asked him to build a door in the wall that surrounded the grounds. Because of the same suffocation that I felt in the house, I often needed to go outdoors, and I wanted to be able to go into the town. But walking along the highway was dangerous, as I well knew from Mrs. Poncia's trick on me. When I explained this to him, he didn't hesitate to build a small gate. It was well concealed and in this way I was able to escape from time to time without anyone noticing. I liked this, but I'm not sure why.

One day I was wandering the streets of the town when I saw Mrs. Poncia come out of her house. It was Sunday, the only day she didn't work at Diego's house. The bells of the church were ringing and she was dressed to go to mass. From inside the house I heard a male voice shouting at her to return inside. Poncia paid no attention. She got to the next block when the man slammed open the door and caught up to her. He grabbed her by the arms but Poncia resisted. She is short but strong and knew how to defend herself. But soon she was overcome and they both returned to the house.

When I got back, I found Diego and Miranda reading together. It was such a quiet domestic scene that I did not want to sully it by mentioning such a disagreeable matter. Later, I didn't see the necessity of telling Diego. Things like that are always known in towns like Comala anyway.

If the circumstances of Mrs. Poncia were infelicitous, her character was even more so. And when she began to mistreat Miranda, things got worse. It was never anything overt; always just the most subtle insinuations, disrespectful gazes. I didn't say anything to Diego about it because I had no solid evidence. And even Miranda seemed, for the most part, oblivious to her behavior. I didn't want the situation to degenerate into one of her word against mine; Poncia and Diego had a long history together and I was hesitant to interfere, especially since everything was so intangible.

But that changed the day that I discovered Poncia telling a horror story to my daughter. It was about one of the tribes of yesteryear, a warrior group that was fighting with the Aztecs to dominate them. Poncia spoke as if the tribe still were present, still existed. She described with a wealth of grisly details, how the warriors attacked the Aztec village, how the arrows flew and the blood flowed.

"But, why did they attack them?", asked Miranda.

"To take away their women. And the children."

"And what did they do with them?"

"Into the women they put something that would make them pregnant. And they trained the children so that they would become part of their tribe."

Miranda was perplexed. After a pause, she said:

"I don't think that the children would like that. I would want to be with my own father always."

I felt a cry of anguish deep inside me. René was no longer here to be with his daughter.

"But now the children are part of the winning tribe", explained Poncia. "The stronger ones. Isn't that better?"

"I don't know", she answered in an uncertain voice.

"And when they grow up, they become warriors too. Being a warrior is the best thing that can happen to a person."

Some moments of silence passed. I thought to interrupt at that point, but suddenly Poncia began speaking again.

"Cecilio is training to be a warrior. Mr. Alba is making him an obsidian knife like the ones they use in that tribe. You should see the tip. It is sharper than you can imagine."

"Cecilio is going to kill people?"

"Only his enemies", she responded.

At this point I had to stop the story. I could see that Miranda was becoming upset. Besides, now I had sufficient evidence to accuse her to Diego.

But when I told him about it, he didn't take it seriously. He said that all children love horror stories.

"Besides", he continued, "Mrs. Poncia is just a harmless witch. Leave her in peace."

"But, what about Cecilio? That he's training to be a warrior? That you're making a sharp knife for him?"

"Don't pay attention to that. That is just Poncia talking."

When I wanted to reaffirm my distaste for all this, Diego didn't let me. He told me to wait and left the room. When he returned he showed me something very beautiful.

"I am making something of obsidian, but it isn't a weapon." He opened a polished wooden box and inside, on a velvet pillow were three paintbrushes of different sizes. They were exquisite. The handles glowed with the blackish green tone of shining obsidian.

"These are for you. So that you have something beautiful in your hands."

He took my hands in his. " Because these hands deserve …."

I didn't let him finish. I embraced him and he returned my embrace with tenderness. He kissed me. We kissed one another. The world became full of this kiss, it was taken up by his face, his breath, his trembling body. Everything else faded away.

"I have to tell you something important", I said.

Diego stepped away.

"I don't like this seriousness. What is it?"

So I told him. I told him all about my true life in Chile, about René, about the exchange of favors that my father had compelled me to do, about the plan to cause the painter to fall into disrepute. I couldn't squash all the lies any longer. In that moment, I felt that I loved Diego Alba very much, and that there should be no lies between us. Nevertheless, some intuition told me to save other details for later. I told him nothing about my sisters, about our life in Bloemfontein, or in Brussels, very little about my parents.

Something happened then, that I did not expect. Diego became infuriated. I thought he would hear my story with sympathy, with forgiveness, but he did not. His face darkened, his mouth formed into a disdainful grimace, and he turned away.

"And when we met in the gallery, when I brought you here, when I offered you everything I have, put it at your disposal, when I tried to help you the best way I could... how is this possible?"

I didn't say anything.

"And now, at this late date, after spending six months with me, **now** you decide is the moment to liberate yourself from these lies?"

"Forgive me. I haven't been well since my husband died", I responded, nearly drowning in remorse.

A long silence passed. Finally Diego turned back to me and showed me a measured smile.

"Come."

He enveloped me in his arms like a bear, like a silk blanket, like a tree that hid me in its topmost branches.

"We are like the obsidian paintbrushes", he said. "And now we should begin to paint with them, don't you think?"

15

Rosa
Black and White Clouds

I felt much better being in Diego's house without the weight of those lies on me, but I still had moments of pure anguish. They came without warning, like an attack. I felt like I couldn't breathe; that the air wouldn't go into my lungs; I got dizzy; I felt like I was going to die. The image of René being tortured by the DINA, even though I didn't see it, flashed vividly before my eyes. In those moments I could do nothing except fall to the floor face down, trying desperately to get a breath of air. Luckily Miranda was never present to see me in this state.

Then sometimes I would get depressed, a state that did not allow me to arise from the bed. I didn't have the energy. I had to ask Mrs. Poncia to take care of Miranda, which always gave her a perverse pleasure. I don't know what other stories she told her, I don't know what other ugly things were communicated, I don't know in what way she might have hurt her that wouldn't become visible until later. I didn't know. But I was paralyzed by doubt, paralyzed by anguish and fear. Those were horrifying moments.

But despite all that, I managed to improve. The attacks and depressions came less frequently. I could eat, speak, teach the school lessons to my daughter, paint. The long walks I took through the countryside helped as well. I often went into the town of Comala.

Comala was a strange place. The people did not greet one another on the street; the stores obeyed no normal rules for opening or closing; the hour of the siesta was so quiet that the town appeared abandoned. I had lived in Bloemfontein, in Brussels and in Santiago de Chile, and I never felt anything like that in those places. In any case, I liked to wander around there, perhaps propelled by the same uneasiness that haunted me in Diego's house.

But then something happened that gave me a solid reason to continue struggling. Diego asked to paint my picture.

He sat me down in many different poses; he put in different positions; he manipulated me like a mannequin. And the feel of his hands on my face, on my body, functioned like a kind of medicine for my soul. His intense gaze while he painted filled me with tranquility; it filled that terrible vacuum in my mind. The little songs he hummed while he worked relaxed me, and when he finished, it was as if a black cloud had finally lifted.

The painting was beautiful. Diego had captured some essence of me that wasn't visible in my face, but rather existed only in my spirit: courage, pragmatism, resistance. I was enchanted with it.

It was clear that Diego had fallen in love with me. And I with him? I still could not let myself feel it fully. Instead, I expressed myself in music, in art. I occupied myself with reading, with taking care of Miranda. In this way a year passed.

I was feeling much better when something happened that, curiously enough, was not altogether unexpected. In some way, I knew that my mother wasn't well. It was nothing she mentioned in her letters, but somehow I still knew. When I received word of her death, it hardly surprised me. I didn't feel the pain or the upset that one normally feels in these occasions.

They said she died of an overdose. It almost didn't matter what the reason was; her death passed over me like the temperate rains that used to pass over Brussels; insistent and moist, but without strength. What I felt most was an anguish for my sisters. Lea was eighteen, Nikita, sixteen. They could take care of Adriana, who was twelve. But without a mother it would be difficult. And our father had proved himself to be useless, morally empty.

I went to Brussels. It was immensely pleasant to be with my sisters once again. Lea was delirious to see me and I felt the same. Together with Nikita, we spent long hours sitting on the sofa without saying much, but holding each other's hands. Adriana scribbled in her notebook at our feet. My father had returned to Brussels from Chile, but I spoke very little with him. Nobody noticed. We were so wrapped up in sadness that the everyday things of life -eating, dressing, conversing – happened automatically and were of little consequence. I returned to Mexico with a huge weight in my heart and a huge worry for the three Burleigh children: so young and so alone.

When I got back to Mexico Diego told me he had something important to tell me. Should I accept his proposal of marriage? After a moment to think, I told him yes. It was a kind of surrender. Life had put so many obstacles in my way that now my only desire was to rest, to recuperate. And in Diego's house, I could do that. Did I love him? I couldn't tell. I don't know if it was love that caused me to marry. But in any case, things were going to be solved.

16

Rosa
Comala

The dinner that Poncia prepared for us the night I returned from Brussels was the most exquisite I had ever had: duck breast with a sweet and spicy glaze; rice with mushrooms, and a creamy flan with cinnamon for dessert. I couldn't imagine how a woman from the countryside could know how to cook to expertly, but I never wanted to ask her because it would only serve to elevate her over me. There was always this rivalry between Poncia and me to be the cleverer one, and even though it was repugnant to me, I couldn't avoid it.

Some hours after dinner I felt a slight illness in my stomach. I thought it was nerves; the marriage proposal had understandably been an upsetting event, albeit a pleasant upset. Or perhaps it was the champagne; I had drunk a lot. But the discomfort soon passed. That night, Diego and I made love for the first time. These were moments of tenderness, of sweet passion. But I could not erase the image of René from my mind. I probably would never be able to make it so that he was not present in some form, in my memory. René was my first love. He would always be that.

The next day Miranda guessed that something had changed in the house. When I told her that soon Diego would be her like a new father for her, she said that he already was, and had been for a long time. She asked when she would have a new brother or sister. How did Miranda know about that? I had never explained any of that to her.

"Mrs. Poncia told me all about it", she said. I felt a hatred for that woman.

"She says that I am going to marry Cecilio".

This was over the top. I could not permit that she express herself this way with my daughter. I went to talk to Diego, and he promised to put an end to her attitude. I had to accept his promise, which really did not promise anything, because Poncia was in no way going to leave the house, and some admonishment from Diego would change nothing.

I was upset, and abruptly left the house. I got to the gate in the wall, slamming it as I went out.

There were very few people in the town. I walked down a solitary street, and in the silence I could hear the furious tapping of my footsteps. Suddenly I sensed that someone was walking behind me. I turned to see the man who had shouted at Poncia that previous day. I felt a wave of fear, and began walking more quickly. He followed me at an increased speed. I looked around for someone to help me but there was no one. Not one soul. All the doors to the houses were shut. I tried to control my panic and not run. But I felt his steps coming closer. I started to run.

More quickly that I could imagine, the man had me trapped. He pushed me backwards until I was pressed against the wall. With one hand he held my two hands, and with the other he covered my mouth.

"If you scream, I'll cut you, understand?"

I nodded. He remained like this for a long moment, as if to make me understand that it was impossible to escape. Slowly he took his hand from my mouth. He looked me up and down, his head tilted to the side, like someone evaluating a possible purchase. He tried to kiss me, but it was not a kiss but an attack. The stubble of his beard scratched my face; his breath smelled of alcohol; his lips were horribly hard. He tried to put his tongue in my mouth, while at the same time putting his hand under my skirt. He pulled my underwear down and put his hand where just recently Diego had put his. In that moment, I screamed.

The man let me go and took off running. I pulled up my underthings as best I could with trembling hands, and I looked around for help. There was no one. No one had seen, no one had heard anything. "Don't cry, Rosa", I told myself. "Don't cry."

When I told Diego what had happened, he became enraged. There are no words to describe the depth of his anger. He hardly waited until I had finished before running out to his car and taking off, with a spray of gravel from under the wheels.

I thought he would go to the police, but he did not. Later, he explained to me that he knew exactly where to find that man. He made him pay dearly for his misdeeds to me.

"He doesn't have any unbroken fingers left", he told me.

I felt like I was living in the old west, where violence was repaid by violence, where there were no police, no courts of law, nor judges. Mexico felt to me for the first time, like a third-world country, and it made me miss Brussels where something like this would never have happened.

But neither were there people like Diego in Brussels: men capable of doing what he did. Vengeance is a primitive emotion, but one feels it notwithstanding the level of culture. And I, in that moment, I felt the love that Diego had for me like a force more powerful than any police, any judge, any court of law could offer. That night he covered me with kisses over my entire body, completely erasing the stain that that man had left on me.

17

Rosa
The Plaid Notebook

The nausea and dizziness returned. I thought I might be pregnant, but I was not.

The house continued with its spells and obfuscations. I kept getting lost in it. I bumped up against the furniture, the walls.

Diego had to leave for a business trip, and he would not heed my implorations that he not go. With this, I felt even worse.

When he returned, he took me to a doctor in the city, but all that the doctor found was a slightly lowered blood pressure. I managed to write a letter to my father, but the pen seemed to have a mind of its own and the sentences wavered across the page.

Miranda disappeared for long stretches of time but I didn't have the energy to find her. Then, she would come to my room to play with her Barbie. She said she had named her Minx. I didn't understand very well what she was saying

Mrs. Poncia brought my meals on a tray because I couldn't remain upright while I was seated at the table. With great difficulty I went to Diego's studio to ask him to help me. He was concentrating on his work and hardly paid me any mind. I felt like I was dying. I was very thirsty and saw that there was a pitcher of water flavored with melon on the table. I had some and felt a bit better, though still very weak. I told Diego I was going back to my bedroom to lie down.

When I woke up, I felt very bad once more. Very bad. I found my diary and tried to put down what was happening. My diary, a gift from my mother, comforted me, with its cover of scotch plaid. Thinking about my mother also gave me some strength. Suddenly, though, all the sadness that I should have felt when she died came crashing down; all the feelings that I should have felt but had not because of the complications in my life, complications with Diego, with his house. I missed my mother with my whole heart. I missed my family, missed being with them free of the problems that surrounded me now. How had all this happened? I felt bad, very low.

18

Leonora
Trees and Walls

The address was somewhat mysterious: Kilometer 123, Mexico-Comala Highway. And worse still, because it was stained by the chocolate that I had vomited over it. The address was unlike any I knew in Brussels, and the number could have been 123 or 163; it was impossible to discern.

"Oh, Comala. That's on the way to the ruins", the woman in the hostel told me.

She was kind to us, showing a kind of maternal worry, surely because she had a daughter the same age as Adriana, and because we must have looked like the orphans that we were, wandering about in Mexico City.

We left Brussels without much sadness. What kept us there? Nothing. Just a broken family and a shattered past. And there was something, some spiritual or material force, something that had long disappeared in Brussels, that called to me from the new world.

"You must go first by bus to the town, and from there in a *combi*. Ask the driver of the *combi* for the address. He will be able to orient you", she said with doubt in her voice.

The bus station was packed full of people and it was hard to find the right bus. We got on with a big crowd, and had to stand for a long time until some people got off. In the bus were travelling different types of people, but as we got further and further out of the city, the more prosperous got off leaving us surrounded by only the very poor.

I felt extremely alert, and very happy. The two weeks that we had spent in Mexico had been like an extended emotional voyage. I hardly ate. I hardly slept. When we walked in the streets, the men followed us with their eyes, said things to us. Even grown men in suits and ties made comments. There was a vitality in the air that had long since evaporated in Brussels.

The city enchanted and repulsed me in equal measure. There was poverty, there were beggars. There were some streets in the downtown that were modern and logical and that reminded me of Brussels, but there were others that were rough, acrid. We walked those streets untiringly, absorbing the smells of the spicy food, listening to the people shouting, the music blaring from the shops, the feeling of a society that was still in the process of being tamed.

Looking out the bus window I observed that the streets were wide, with many lanes, but had little traffic. At the intersections, often there would be only one stoplight, hanging loosely from above. The buildings did not seem old, but many of them looked permanently shut. It was hard to tell if they were abandoned or if they never had even opened.

We passed neighborhoods of little houses all alike; this, after going through long stretches of nothing. A woman started talking with me. As we passed one of these isolated communities, she remarked that there had recently been a scandal there. Many children had gotten sick from the water. The houses all looked very pretty, but every time there was a heavy rain the water infiltrated the sewers, which had been poorly constructed, and contaminated the drinking water.

"How often do heavy rains happen?", I asked,

"You aren't from here, are you? Well, in the rainy season they happen every day."

"And they never came to fix the sewers?"

"No. That's how things are. The people responsible got paid and left, leaving their mess behind.

I thought again of Brussels, a city precisely cared-for, a city of parks and gardens, a dry, stifled place of bureaucrats and business people.

Finally, the bus arrived in Comala. Nobody got off but us. It was afternoon, siesta time, and everything was closed. It was a bit chilly and Adriana very soon began to whimper. She said she was thirsty, hungry, but all said in her peculiar manner that only I could understand. I lent her my sweater when I saw that she was trembling. I looked around for the *combies,* but I didn't not see a single one.

At the other edge of the plaza there was a long street stretching into the distance; further out was the countryside; and beyond that was a line of hills. There was a profound silence smothering all sound, even the moans of Adriana. We sat down to wait.

When the shops finally reopened, and people returned to the street, they looked at us like we were from another planet. Maybe it was our clothing, or maybe it was the look of uncertainty that marked our faces.

"Kilometer 123? That must be over there", answered the first woman I asked. She pointed with her hand to indicate the road leading out of the plaza.

After walking for twenty minutes, I realized that we were going nowhere, so we returned. I asked a gentleman the same question and he pointed in the opposite direction.

"Go two blocks, and you'll see the cemetery. Turn to the left and you'll see a road heading downhill. That will take you to the highway.

"And the *combies?*, I asked.

"Miss, there are no *combies* here", he answered.

We followed his directions but we never got to the highway. Once again we returned to the plaza. I decided to ask several different people to see if any of their suggestions coincided, but none did. And as I went asking it appeared that each person became more annoyed than the last, more suspicious. It got colder.

I remembered something from Diego's letter; something about an irrigation ditch that ran alongside his property. We had seen such ditch earlier; now we returned to it and began to follow it out of town.

The further we got from the town, the worse everything looked. Dirty, unkempt. At the bottom of the ditch was a slow-moving current of filthy water. We had to be careful walking; the streets were poorly paved with a variety of materials; brick, concrete, stone badly placed, or simply not paved at all. There were no trees, no flowers. The air smelled of garbage and dog feces. Nevertheless, I felt very happy. Very alive.

When we came across a young boy, I asked him about the highway.

"This is the highway", he answered.

"This?"

"Yes, Miss."

So, we were going on the highway, but it was uncertain if we were going in the right direction. The only thing I knew to do was to keep going.

We walked for two hours. Little by little we left behind the dirtiness of the town and we entered into the countryside. Little by little I felt better, more confident. The countryside, which at first was mostly treeless and dry, gave way to green. I smelled the fragrance of bushes I didn't recognize. Now, instead of rocks and barren hills, we started to see grass, and the trees were tall and graceful. In the distance I thought I saw a wall that extended to the horizon. We went towards it.

The wall was very long; and even though it wasn't tall, we still could not see over it. We followed it for a long time until we reached a small opening. There was a wooden gate there; it was rustic but well-made. Adriana was afraid and wouldn't come close. I tried the gate but it wouldn't open. In the shadows next to it I saw a small sign made of tin which had the numbers "123" stamped on it.

I went back to where Adriana was waiting.

"It's here!", I said. She looked at me with a blank face, erased of hope or enthusiasm. Suddenly I felt all optimism vanish. Yes, we were there, but now what? I had wanted to find Diego's house, in order to do what? I had abandoned the only home we knew to come here, and discover what? I had uprooted poor Adriana, brought her all this way, with what objective? Until that moment I hadn't doubted myself, even though I didn't clearly see my goal, but now, now I felt all my plans come crashing down. I had wanted to investigate Diego, penetrate into his life, with what idea? Vengeance? A desire to rid myself of all the injustices that plagued me? It was if the dishonor of my father, the death of my mother and the death of my older sister had come together in one single expression of fury. And that fury was pointed directly at Diego Alba.

Standing at the gate I felt impotent. I squeezed my nails into my fist not even feeling the pain, I breathed agitatedly, ground my teeth. I was in the throes of the most annihilating frustration.

But I didn't see that inside me, an idea was forming. I was hardly conscious of it; it was coming from somewhere far away, and only in pieces. They say that God is in the details, and if that's so, then I have to be thankful to him. Little by little, the details of a plan were coalescing in my brain.

19

Leonora
The Plan I

The complete solution came to me in a dream.

In that peculiar way of dreams, I saw myself from behind, seated at a desk, typing at a typewriter. I heard the tac tac of the keys. Suddenly I could see what I was typing: a letter.

Dear Sir:

This letter is to inform you of the coming investigation into the life insurance policy of the recently deceased Rosa C. Burleigh. It is customary in cases of accidental death to conduct an inquiry before disbursing the funds to the beneficiary.

Please indicate your availability for April 15, 1979, by return letter to us at our offices. If convenient, our representative, Margarita Lopez, will visit your home at three o'clock in the afternoon to take charge of the investigation. She will need to speak with all persons who were present in the home during the period of November 3 through 6, 1978.

We hope this will be agreeable to you, and we look forward to your prompt reply.

Yours truly,

When I awoke from the dream I was trembling over the audacity of my plan. Enter the house of Diego Alba? Pretend to be a professional from an insurance office? Interview the people, pretend to be writing a report? As a child I was applauded for my little plays, my invented scenes; this would have to be the best of them all.

During the next days I worked hard on the details of the plan. I needed to get ahold of paper with the logo of an insurance company on it, and a typewriter with which to write the letter. And above all, a way to disguise myself. When we were young, Rosa and I looked alike and even though the years had changed our appearances somewhat, there were still familial similarities. I needed to look older, much older. Surely Diego would know that Rosa was the oldest; if I looked even older it would make the connection less obvious.

As for the stationery, after a lot of deliberation I decided on the simplest thing of all: place an order at a stationery shop for a quantity of paper with a logo of my own design; use the address of the hostel as the invented address of the company; and finally, buy a typewriter. Maybe a used one wouldn't be too expensive.

In all these deliberations I felt the presence of Rosa. I felt she was inspiring me, that she was lending me her cleverness, the intelligence I needed.

One by one I gathered the necessary materials. When I finally posted the letter, it was with an emotional release. That night I slept well for the first time since arriving in Mexico.

More quickly than I imagined, Diego responded. The day was convenient. But there was more. He said that since his house was difficult to find, we should meet in the town of Comala, and he would pick me up there and take me to his home. He also said that if I needed more than one day for the investigation I was welcome to stay for the days necessary. Everything seemed even better than I thought.

The only worrisome thing was what to do with Adriana. But this too, was solved. The woman who was in charge of the hostel offered to watch over her; she had taken a liking to the poor girl who hardly spoke.

The day was coming near. I practiced the walk, the attitude of a professional woman. Thanks to a very confused hair stylist, I had my hair dyed grey. I practiced with the makeup; with my new name; with the information that I presumably would know about the insurance business. In a certain sense, what I was proposing to do was not too far from a lie: interview the people who were near to Rosa when she died. Except that I was doing it for myself, and not in any official capacity. I liked the idea of playing at being a detective. Very soon I would be meeting this man, this famous painter. Very soon I would be under his roof, under the same roof where my sister lived, touching the things she touched, seeing the things she saw, sitting perhaps, in the chair she sat in. Very soon I would meet my niece, Miranda, the daughter of my beloved sister Rosa.

20

Leonora
The Plan II

The car was big and black, with tinted windows. It reminded me of the cars that my father used in his official travels around Brussels when he was the ambassador: a car full of secrets and tension.

I looked quickly at my reflection in the shop window: yes, I looked very much like a woman of fifty, with my grey hair, my dark, shapeless skirt, a white blouse, thick pantyhose and sensible shoes. I carried the typewriter in its case and a briefcase full of the stationery I had ordered, with the emblem of the insurance company at the top.

In the days leading up to this one, I had thought obsessively about the painter, oscillating between various emotions. On the one hand, I felt for Diego Alba a deep suspicion. The letter he sent me about Rosa's death did not explain anything. He said she had not wanted a funeral. How did he know that? The letter explained nothing about the accident itself. How did it happen? He didn't explain anything about her frame of mind in those days. Was she happy? Depressed? Was she working? In Brussels, after I got his letter, I immediately wrote a response with all these questions and more, but he never answered. I wrote another and he didn't respond to that one either. Nikita said that the mail in

Mexico wasn't reliable, but all the same it wasn't very believable that two letters had gone astray. My mother probably knew more about what was happening with Rosa, but those answers died when she did.

On the other hand, I tried to be logical about Diego, as I knew that Rosa would be under the same circumstances. I actually did not have any solid evidence against him. In fact, I knew very little about him at all apart from the fact that he was supposed to be quite rich, and that for a time, he had loved Rosa and been loved by her. Or at least, one supposes that. The absence of information does not necessarily signify guilt or bad intentions.

The town of Comala was sleeping its siesta once again. The shops, all closed, the streets empty of people. From the car parked across the street stepped a man: tall, muscular, with powerful hands and a sturdy gait. His voice, when he addressed me was deep but pleasant.

"Mrs. Lopez? I am Diego Alba. It's nice to meet you."

Diego offered his hand to shake, and looked directly at me, his eyes connecting strongly with my own. I didn't know what to say. I felt naked, helpless. Face to face with Diego Alba the husband of my sister, my words evaporated from my mouth.

"I hope the journey hasn't been too difficult. Comala is quite far from the city."

"Yes, it is. A little", I stammered. "But it must be nice to live so close to the pyramids…."

I hardly had begun to talk when Diego became startled. He looked even more fixedly at me, and instantly I realized the problem: my voice. I had forgotten that Rosa and I had the same voice. Surely Diego would hear the resemblance. I panicked, thinking that the trick was over, that I would be discovered, but no. Diego rapidly composed himself and we continued talking as if nothing had happened.

We got into the car and started down the same road that the bus had taken before. We spent some moments without speaking and I took advantage of the time to look discreetly at him. He was not handsome, not at all. But he had something more appealing: the force of his attention. When he spoke to me, or looked at me, he made me feel that I was the most important thing in his surroundings. It worried me and gave me pleasure in equal parts.

In the distance I saw trees: a woodland that seemed to cross over the highway and obscure its course. I felt a light confusion. It wasn't clear how we were going to pass through on the highway. As we got closer to the mirage I wanted to ask, but reading my thoughts, Diego said:

"Does the road surprise you, Mrs. Lopez?"

Yes, it did surprise me. We turned into a smaller road that was invisible from a distance, and entered a narrow gravel path, barely wide enough for the car. I couldn't see how we had left the highway and gotten there.

"I designed it especially this way. The entrance to the house is on a curve, in the middle of a group of trees, as you have no doubt noticed. Coming from the west, it's almost impossible to see it and from the east, completely impossible. If you don't know where to turn, you will always miss the entrance.

"Did you do this on purpose?", I asked.

"Yes. I need a way to be out of the limelight from time to time. I need quiet and space to concentrate on my work, and outside there are always people who need things from me. The house provides me with a refuge when things get hectic."

Gathering my courage, I asked him:

"So this is the only entrance?"

"No. There's another." Diego let several seconds pass by, as if he were deciding whether to tell me or not.

"There is a wall around my property. It's eighty hectares".

"Eighty", I said, impressed.

Diego continued: "I didn't put any other gates in the wall, but my wife liked to go for walks and it bothered her to feel closed in. She asked me to make another way out, and I did, to make her happy.

Diego got pensive, remembering.

"Rosa was like that. She noticed all the details, she wanted honesty in everything. She felt like the house, to be an honest place, needed more than one entrance. She asked me to put up the numbers on the gate, just as they are on the main entrance. When I told her that no one would ever see them, she laughed, like she enjoyed the paradigm."

"So…."

"The gate is on the other side of the hills, on the opposite side of the property, very far from here, and well hidden. There is no way to find it from the outside unless you know where it is."

"Are you sure about that, Mr. Alba?", I asked myself under my breath.

We travelled down a curving path for several minutes to then enter into a long stretch bordered by rows of tall trees whose trunks were an astonishing white color.

"They are eucalyptus. *Eucalyptus viminalis*. They get to forty meters tall."

I felt his gaze rest intently on my face.

"Are they native to here?", I asked, gibbering like an idiot.

"No. They aren't."

Diego stopped to think again.

"The history of the house is very interesting, if you'd like to hear a bit of it...?"

Of course this was interesting to me; everything related to Rosa was interesting to me, and when I nodded, he stopped the car suddenly. He turned and said:

"Good. Nearby there is a little house where we can stop for a bit."

I felt a brush of fear.

"And then we'll go to the main house, where you can meet my children and Mrs. Poncia, the housekeeper. They were with me when...."

I waited for him to finish. The mention of his children calmed me, and my desire to know everything about Diego and Rosa surged ahead.

"When....?", I suggested.

"When my wife died."

With these simple words, a crack opened in the façade of Diego Alba, and that gave me the courage to continue.

"Very well, then".

"Speaking about Rosa is going to be difficult for me", he confessed. "It would be better to leave that discussion for tomorrow, if you don't mind."

"That's fine, Mr. Alba. I have three days available for the investigation", I said, focusing on making my voice as serious and cordial as possible.

The little house was up a hill; an enchanting site next to a pond with lily pads and ducks floating serenely in it. There was a carved stone fountain that looked very old, from which Diego filled a pitcher of water. It was sweet and very cold. There were biscuits on a plate that came from nowhere. We sat down in the open air and Diego began to speak.

"I came to Mexico for work eight years ago. One day when the meetings were over, I went to visit the ruins. I spent a long time there, walking from one pyramid to the next. My head was full of the history of the people who lived there before: their art, their gods, their ideas. I felt a very strong impression of a past that was continuing in that present moment. I got anxious, somehow. I decided to walk away and I saw a path that led to the northeast. Suddenly a great somnolence came over me, or a kind of confusion perhaps. I continued walking in this trance for a long way beyond the limits of the archeological zone. After about an hour, I came across this path, this same path that leads to the house."

"What happened to you in the ruins, Mr. Alba? Why did you feel that way?"

Diego looked at me with a grave expression.

"Sometimes when the impression of something is very strong, I am overcome. Does that ever happen to you, Mrs. Lopez?"

I felt like telling him that yes, those things happened to me too, especially in these moments when he was talking, when I felt his presence so close to my own.

"Almost never. But continue, please."

"So, I continued walking until I came across the skeleton of this old house."

"This same one where you live now?"

"Yes, and no. I fell so in love with the house and its grounds that I tried to buy them. I had been looking for a while for a place to get away from the art world and from politics; a place where no one could find me."

Diego gazed at me, focusing his most intense forces on my face, enveloping me in his story.

"But there were some problems. It was nearly impossible to discover who was the owner of the house; the records of the title had long since vanished. I had to hire a very good lawyer who was finally able to unravel it."

"I see."

"Then I reconstructed it."

"You had it remodeled?"

"I did it myself. The house was in ruins but the outline remained. I remade the walls and roofs, adding some rooms where they were needed. So, it's not exactly the same house."

Diego closed his eyes, remembering.

"I spent a year doing that. I didn't paint. I didn't go anywhere. I worked for twelve hours each day, falling into bed exhausted each night."

I didn't say anything, loathe to interrupt his reverie.

"There isn't a corner of this house that I don't know. It has been my refuge. Here, I've spent the happiest days of my life."

Was he referring to his time here with Rosa? I wanted to ask him that, but I stopped. I would have to be patient, and hope that Diego would say more.

"Then, in middle of the reconstruction, I noticed a pool of water in the patio that filled and emptied various times each day. I dug there and discovered a natural spring."

Diego stopped, thinking.

"Discovering the spring seemed to me to be a sign of something. A signal, a communication."

"Of what, or from whom?"

"From the past. Or the future. I don't know. But now comes the most interesting part. During the construction, in a half-torn-down wall, I discovered the remains of another structure; a structure much, much older than the colonial house, in a completely distinct architectural style."

A cloud passed over the sun, and I felt the momentary shadows like a symbol of fear, of a great disquiet. Diego's story spoke of a history that was deep and deeply mysterious.

"Who lived here in that time?", I asked.

"Come with me", he said.

He stood up, took a few steps and indicated that I should join him. I got up from my chair in a fever of anticipation.

"Do you see it?", he asked, looking out across the hills.

"No. I don't see anything."

I looked in the direction he indicated, but all I saw were the tops of the trees and the pathway through them.

"What is it you want me to see?", I asked.

Diego came very near me and spoke quietly into my ear.

"Look. It's the pyramids."

I felt the warmth of his breath on my neck. I breathed in the fragrance of his body, which vibrated near me. Suddenly I caught sight of what he wanted me to see. Above the treetops shone the angled rooflines of the archeological zone. The pyramids. I felt a shiver run down me. I stayed a long while there, paralyzed by the force of the past.

"You live in a very mysterious house", I told him, trembling.

"Well, not so much", he responded.

With this, the spell was broken.

"I feel like we've taken up a lot of time", he continued. "You probably would like to rest a bit."

It was a warm day, and I felt the sun coming down strongly. Without warning I felt extremely sleepy. Inexplicably, in the car I fell into slumber.

21

Leonora
The Plan III

It's curious how an unexpected drowsiness can come upon a person. I couldn't have spent more than a few minutes in the warmth of the car, but I know that I fell asleep. And when I woke up, what I saw was like a dream.

Before me appeared a house so beautiful that it seemed like it was from a fairy tale. It was large, with white walls that curved around with the harmony of an entire town in miniature. The exterior stairways carried your eyes from one level to another; the arches formed into walkways that revealed other arches, other passageways; the patios led to other patios, and there was an abundance of doors and windows; some wide open and some well shut, that invited or prohibited the passage of the spirits.

Around the house were large lawns shaded by enormously tall trees. The road we were on curved around to reveal two wings of the house that extended out the back, and at the end of one was a tower, higher than the second floor. Many of the windows were framed in wrought iron, harmoniously bent into complicated forms.

We passed through the front door; made of thick planks in a vaguely Arabic style, and we entered an interior patio. I couldn't see very much because Diego was hurrying me along. He didn't walk fast, but he did not let me linger to observe. We crossed the patio and entered a darkened room.

"I'm sorry you took the trouble to bring an electric typewriter", he said. "But we don't have electricity here."

He relieved me of the heavy typewriter and put it on a table that appeared out of the gloom.

"But we have these." Diego showed me an oil lamp. "And a lot of matches", he said in a jovial tone.

He lit the lamp and I could see that we were in a kind of library, or office. There was a sofa, a large desk with a leather chair from the last century, its feet in the form of a lion's paws. One wall was a bookcase that went from the floor to the very high ceiling.

Diego went to the windows and pulled the velvet curtains. Suddenly the room was filled the afternoon sunlight. The walls were of a lustrous wood that shined in the golden light; the floor were red tiles that gleamed as well. The floor was partially covered with a thick Persian rug in the hushed tones of nature; greens and blues. At the back was visible a door that led to a bedroom and a bathroom.

"I hope this suite is to your liking", he said.

"Thank you very much Mr. Alba. I'm sure it will be fine."

We bid one another goodbye with the usual polite words, but before we could finish, I heard a sound coming from far away. It sounded like the song of a little bird.

"Maaaaaa...."

Diego turned his head towards the sound, listening intently.

"Mamaaaa…". You could hear now the voice of a child, as well as the sounds of footsteps approaching rapidly.

"Mama! Mama!"

A girl of eight or nine entered the room and threw her arms around me, throwing her cane to the side.

"Mama!"

There passed a moment that did not go forwards. We were paralyzed.

"She is not your mother, Miranda", said Diego finally. "She is Mrs. Lopez and she's come here to do some work."

The girl let go of me as if I were a lighted candle. She stooped to feel around for her cane, and quickly stood up and moved a good distance away.

I didn't know which of the surprises was the greatest: her appearance or her mistaking me for Rosa. The child was a living replica of my sister: the same face, the same long, wavy hair, the same voice. But I was even more astounded by the second fact: Miranda was blind. She carried a cane like any other blind person.

No, this couldn't be. Such a great misfortune! My poor niece had no other family but this man with all his secrets. And now, on top of that, she was blind? I was rendered mute by the astonishment.

Then I realized something else. Was my ruse going to be uncovered by her confusion? Would Diego discover that I was not who I said I was, because of Miranda's misperception? Once again it was a problem with my voice. Surely Miranda recognized her mother's voice in my own. Would this reveal "Mrs. Lopez" to be a fraud? A criminal, a person who came into his house to steal away his secrets, a person who entered his refuge to rob him of it?

I felt smothered by the weight of my doubts, by a mountain of fear. I tried to think about Rosa, about my duty to find out the truth about her. I tried to erase all my ethical concerns and concentrate solely on that. This gave me strength.

"We need to leave Mrs. Lopez for a while, Miranda. She has to rest. Tomorrow she will want to talk to you, so let's go out now."

Speaking to me, he added: "We have dinner at nine o'clock. Mrs. Poncia will come for you."

With this, they left the room.

22

Leonora
The First Interview

"We didn't want to wake you for dinner", said the older woman who appeared at the door to my room. "You were so deeply asleep."

Before me was a very strange looking person. She had long, grey hair, which fell in loose folds down her back. Her upper lip was distinguished by a thick moustache, and her eyebrows made one single line across her brow. Her eyes were deep-set, but her mouth was large and protuberant. Her lips were vaguely greenish. Her eyes were of such a pale blue that they seemed transparent. Everything about her made me deeply uneasy.

But just under the surface vibrated something very alive in Mrs. Poncia. Beneath her pale skin beat a carnal force, a kind of intelligence that came from the mud, from the earth. I didn't know at that moment that I was meeting the person who later on would embitter my time in Diego's house, who would poison my life and that of Adriana, like a root that comes from the mud to drag us down into it.

But I wasn't aware of that then. I only felt a confusion that inhibited me from responding to her comment.

It was day. I remembered that the evening before, Miranda and Diego had left me in my room. I had lain down for a moment on the sofa, where I had an exhausting nightmare, which I couldn't remember. It was dark by then, and I was felled by a terrible tiredness. I couldn't think clearly. I couldn't find the oil lamp and I had no matches to light it with anyway. I took off my clothes letting them fall where they may, and collapsed into bed.

The night was a series of dreams and wakefulness, all mixed up. I had more nightmares. One I remember well. In the dream I was wandering around Diego's house, lost, and worse still, I couldn't see. I squeezed my eyes shut and then opened them wide, trying to regain my sight, but I couldn't. I felt around for the objects near me, without finding them. The dream was certainly a response to the fright I experienced at Miranda's blindness. To be blind, even in a dream, is a horrifying experience, capable of making anyone crazy.

"Thank you Mrs. Poncia", I finally managed to say. "I wasn't feeling well last night."

"But, do you feel better now? Should I call a doctor, or tell Mr. Alba?"

"No. It's not necessary. I feel fine now."

But I didn't feel fine now. A lethargy pursued me that I could not shake. Mrs. Poncia had brought my breakfast on a tray, and she put it down on a table near the windows.

With the coffee I began to feel better. I looked out the windows at the garden. There were no flowers, but vast expanses of green lawn. And above me, the canopies of the enormous trees. In the distance I could see woods, but no other structures. The ambience was one of profound tranquility; it felt like another kind of dream. The city, with its noise and traffic and its busy people, faded completely away.

"If it's all right, I can come back in a little while for the interview", interrupted Mrs. Poncia. "Mr. Alba has told me what this is about." She looked uncomfortable.

"But I don't know how I can help you", she continued. "I really don't know what happened to Mrs. Rosa."

"I understand Mrs. Poncia. I hope it's not too difficult for you to speak to me, but it's very important that I get your help."

"Yes, of course." With this, she left the room.

Rapidly I showered and reapplied the makeup that changed me from a woman of twenty- one, to middle-aged. When Mrs. Poncia returned, I was ready.

"Let's talk about Rosa. When did she arrive here? Were you already working for Mr. Alba then?"

"Well, I couldn't really say. It's that…."

We spoke all morning but I couldn't get anything of substance from her. She avoided directly answering my questions very successfully. What she did want to emphasize was that she had been working for Diego for many years; that he had great trust and confidence in her.

The tiredness of the previous day came back. My arms weighed on me as I tried to take notes. I looked at the first of the pieces of paper; I hadn't written anything. I asked Mrs. Poncia to leave.

The midday sun came in through the windows and a breeze brought me the fragrance of the lawn and the tall trees. As soon as I was alone, I lay down on the sofa and while I listened to the harmonious tinkle of the fountain in the patio, I fell into a profound sleep.

23

Leonora
The Second Interview

I awoke with the firm knocking on the bedroom door. It was Mrs. Poncia with a snack and Miranda with a huge book in her hands.

"Mr. Alba has asked me to bring this", she said. "We don't usually have a meal at midday because of his work; we have dinner in the evening instead."

After that brief nap I felt very refreshed, very alert. And there before me was my little niece. I wanted her to hug me again, as she had before, but of course this was impossible.

"I brought you a book, Mrs. Lopez. It's the story of Don Quixote de la Mancha", she said.

I looked at the book. It was enormously thick, with thick covers.

"I'm going to read you a little while you have your lunch. I'm really happy now that I can read the story. It's the same story that my mother used to read me when she put me to bed."

She opened the book and placed her fingers lightly on the page, but didn't begin to move them.

"We never got to the end. My mother said we were very lucky to have this book because it was so long, and it would last us a long time."

Miranda had completely abandoned her embarrassment of yesterday. She was as lively and talkative as a spark of fire, as pretty and delicate as the tinkling of the water in the fountain that was audible from outside the room.

While I ate, I listened to her, with her beautiful voice so similar to that of my sister.

> *In that time, Don Quixote sought out a peasant, a worker and neighbor of his, who was a good man but very silly. He spoke so much and so persuasively, promising him so many things that the poor man decided to leave everything behind to become Don Quixote's shield-bearer.*

Miranda moved her fingers lightly across the page. "Sancho Panza is my favorite", she said.

"Why?"

"Because he is very loyal to his captain. And he helps him believe things."

"True things or false things?", I asked her.

"That doesn't matter. It doesn't matter at all", she responded.

I was perplexed at her answer.

"And, who taught you to read Braille?"

"My teacher, Mrs. Barbara."

As if she heard her name, a woman came to the door.

"Excuse me. I'm Barbara. I was wondering if I could have a moment of your time."

Directing herself to the child, she said: "Miranda, can you go out for a minute? Wait for me in the living room."

As Miranda went out, Barbara began.

"I needed to speak to you urgently. It appears you haven't begun your interview with the child?"

"No, I haven't. But, what is this about?" I indicated that she should sit.

"Let me explain. My husband and I run a school for the blind in Morelia. Mr. Alba has contracted with me to teach his daughter to read and write in Braille. My work at the school doesn't allow me to come up here more than twice per month, but I have come today because it's really important that we speak."

"Go on."

"Miranda is under medical treatment from a psychiatrist: Dr. Leocadio, who has come today as well."

In effect, a distinguished gentleman appeared and knocked on the open door. He introduced himself and began to speak.

"It's a delicate situation, Mrs. Lopez. I know you have to interview her for the investigation, but in my professional opinion, this could be very dangerous for her. She is, how shall I say it? In a precarious psychological state. Any question about the death of her mother could provoke another crisis."

"And, what does Mr. Alba think? I don't understand why he mentioned nothing to me of this before."

Dr. Leocadio and Barbara looked at one another.

"Mr. Alba is not in agreement as to her treatment", responded Barbara.

"Miranda was present at the death of her mother; she saw the accident as it occurred. Since then, she hasn't said anything at all about that day. She's erased all memory of it. And she lost her sight", explained the doctor.

"She's suffered a tremendous trauma", added Barbara. "We think that asking her anything about it could worsen her condition considerably."

I was quiet, absorbing the information.

"The treatment is long and we have to proceed very cautiously", said the doctor. "We still are not at the point of being able to speak with any seriousness about her mother. We've achieved some things, but I'm afraid that your investigation will traumatize her once more. I don't want to lose the progress we've made."

I felt very sad. Sad for my little niece. And frustrated by the blockage of my plans. First, Mrs. Poncia who evaded all my questions, and now Miranda. But I had no choice. I couldn't put the psychological health of Miranda in danger simply in order to satisfy my own desires.

"I understand perfectly, doctor. I won't ask her anything about that. But I have a question for you both: what is her blindness due to?"

Once again, the doctor and Barbara looked at each other.

"Well, that is the question", he responded. "I believe that it's a result of the trauma."

We fell silent, each one subsumed in the grave events that had occurred in the house of Diego Alba.

"But in any case, I would like to get to know her a little", I said. "If you permit it."

"I don't see any problem", he answered.

"Not at all", added Barbara. "In fact, I think it would do her a lot of good. The family receives very few visitors; I keep telling Mr. Alba that she needs to meet people, have friends, grow socially. The poor child is very alone here."

Barbara went to the door to call for Miranda, and more quickly that I could imagine, she entered the room.

24

Leonora
Don Quixote de la Mancha

I was with Miranda all afternoon. We talked about her favorite books, her doll named Minx, her lessons with her teacher, about her conversations with the kittens and the chicks that lived in the area behind the house.

"Do you have other dolls, Miranda?", I asked her, remembering the Barbies and Kens that I and my sisters played with as children.

"I only have one doll. The other ones disappeared when the soldiers from the other tribe came and took them away."

"How did that happen?"

"Mrs. Poncia explained it to me. When the tribes fight one another and kill each other, the soldiers want vengeance."

"Ah."

"And if they don't find other men soldiers, they kill the women and the girls. Or they take them away to their own tribe."

I believed that Miranda was speaking about fantasies that didn't have to do with reality. Now I know that everything would have turned out differently had I paid better attention to her fantasies. But I did not.

It was getting to be late afternoon when we left the library and went into the patio. The long rays of the sun fell on the objects there, illuminating them with a fiery light, making the very air burn with a fiery glow. There was a profusion of flowers and vines that climbed the walls of the patio, or spilled from the many flowerpots of all sizes. Overhead, the wooden beams that crossed over the space created a melodious rhythm of sun and shadow. We walked on polished clay tiles that lent their red gleam to the visual scape. I saw a fountain, in the shape of a modern fountain, but covered with colored tiles, all broken and re-positioned in a lovely design. There was also an enormous table with a variety of chairs and benches around it. On the table were crystal vases of all shapes, filled with exotic cut flowers whose fragrance filled the air. There were light sweet scents, and heavy, fruity scents.

Seated in a shaded corner of the patio was Diego. He was drinking what I imagined was wine. I remember that the bubbles gleamed when, as he raised his glass to drink, suddenly the sun's rays passed through the golden liquid. When he saw us, he stood and motioned us to come closer.

"Papa!"

Miranda went towards him, her cane making a slow tac tac across the floor.

Diego helped her sit down at his side and directed his gaze to me. In that moment I heard something that I had failed to notice previously: Miranda called Diego "Papa". What had Rosa told her about her real father? How had she explained it?

"Ah, Mrs. Lopez. You've arrived just in time… the end of a working day. How does your investigation go? I hope the conversations have been useful to you."

"Somewhat useful, Mr. Alba."

He served me a glass a wine without asking and indicated that I should try the olives on the platter. Miranda ate them one after the other, very carefully putting the pits to one side; something I thought would be difficult for a blind person to do.

We began to speak. Light things, easy thing. Others not so much. He showed me what he had been working on as we came in: a sketch of the famous feathered serpent of the indigenous people.

"I found many such carved tablets when I renovated the house", he explained. "Now the feathered serpent is my totem."

I didn't know whether to laugh or take him seriously. His totem?

"The house is full of totems, Mrs. Lopez. They are hiding, waiting for their master to come near so that they can take ownership of them."

There was something in Diego's voice that erased all notion of smiling at his comments.

It got to be evening and Diego lit an enormous candelabra that hung from the rafters of the patio. I drank the wine and breathed the fragrance of the flowers, those flowers that only release their scent at night.

"Is it possible to see the pyramids from here?", I asked him.

"Only from the tower", answered the child.

"Yes, only from the tower. Or the little house on the hill. If you'd like to see them again, we could meet in the tower tomorrow", suggested Diego.

Suddenly we could hear other voices coming from the interior of the house. Several people came into the patio: Dr. Leocadio, Barbara, Mrs. Poncia and a boy of some six years. It was Cecilio, the son of Diego. I had no idea of his existence; Rosa had never mentioned him.

Mrs. Poncia served us dinner and it was delicious. There were dishes I didn't know: sweet and spicy, with little seeds on top; soft creamy things with crunchy things alongside; cold things with hot ones near them; meats with a sauce of spicy chocolate on top; and again, the wine that had the color of honey. In Brussels I was used to drinking wine to accompany myself in the solitude; here I drank it from the pleasure of the company. Each time my glass was empty, Diego refilled it. I felt very well.

"I don't know if you've noticed the objects made from obsidian that we have here?", Diego asked me.

"Obsidian?"

"Yes. It's a volcanic glass that the indigenous warriors commonly used to make their weapons."

Diego looked intensely at me. "The history of this area is deep and long, almost impossibly old. Think about it, Mrs. Lopez, when Columbus arrived here, there had already come and gone several entire civilizations; whole societies coming into existence, flourishing, and dying away. One after the other; one on top of the last; piled up in a huge encyclopedia of human activity."

The conversation of the painter made me distinctly uneasy. I felt the presence of other people, other histories. I remembered the pyramid that he had shown me; how mysterious it had seemed rising up above the tops of the trees.

Diego continued talking.

"Piled up... their great deeds and their horrors, their vengeances and their acts of love. I believe, Mrs. Lopez, that the past never truly disappears."

His words made me shudder. I wanted to bury my past in the deepest tomb possible. I looked for a way to change the conversation, but nothing occurred to me.

"Obsidian is what the Indians used for their arrow heads and the tips of their spears, as well as for making objects of art. I have also used it to make things."

Diego took out a wooden box and showed me a set of paintbrushes resting in their velvet nest, that gleamed with the blackish green light of that stone.

"Those are the brushes that you gave my mother, isn't that right?", asked Miranda. She felt around for one and used it to brush her cheek with the soft bristles.

"I do what I can so that our present time never loses sight of the past", commented Diego.

A moment of deep silence came upon us.

When we finished dinner, Miranda wanted us to listen to her play the piano. I was amazed: this blind child of nine could play the piano. I asked her if she took lessons, and she replied that she did not, but wanted to, very soon.

We entered the living room: a vast, high-ceilinged space decorated in the same style as the library: furniture from the past century made of dark, polished wood; leather chairs, paintings both of Diego's and other artists, another huge candelabra with dozens of candles. I stopped in front of an arresting painting: my sister Rosa seated in profile, more beautiful perhaps than in real life, kept in perpetuity in a fine, heavy frame. A cry of delight nearly escaped from my mouth and I barely was able to suppress it. I went to join Barbara, a little apart from the others.

Miranda sat down at the piano and from there flowed an enchanting music. It started slowly, as if to make the listener stop and wait, torturing the listener with the anticipation of the next notes. The sounds floated on the air. I recognized the melody but I couldn't remember the name. It was a famous piece, but at the same time, a very simple one. While the child played, I whispered to Barbara about how it was possible for Miranda to play like that. She answered that Miranda could hear a piece and improvise on her own until she had mastered it.

"There are people who have the gift of music", she said. "And it doesn't matter if she is blind."

"But, is she really blind?"

"That remains to be seen."

We went to join the others and continued talking. Each time Diego addressed me, I felt the warmth of his words, the force of his personality, the focus of his attention. I didn't understand fully what was happening to me, only that I had entered some other kind of world, some other kind of communication.

It was midnight when the evening ended. Miranda asked me to accompany her to her room. She took me by the arm in the most natural way possible and with her white cane, we went walking through the house. It made me happy that she had become so easy with me, and I longed to tell her who I really was.

As we walked in the shadows, I very quickly became disoriented. In the darkness it was hard to see where we were going and the oil lamp illuminated very little. We got to her room and she showed me her Barbie, Minx, who later would play a role in the solution to the mysteries of the house, but to whom in the moment I paid little attention. I told her goodnight and was leaving when Barbara came in.

"I wanted to talk to you for a moment, if I could", she said, walking with me down the passageway.

"Of course. What is it?"

"I have to ask you a favor. I know we hardly know one another, but you seem to be a very nice person."

I waited for her to continue.

"As you've no doubt seen, there is a tremendous need for a professional teacher here in the house. Miranda and Cecilio have no one but Mrs. Poncia."

Barbara sighed with sadness.

"And Mr. Alba travels a great deal. He is away from home for weeks at a time. I can only come twice per month and those few days are too few to give the children the education they need. They are very isolated here, as you can imagine."

"And, I suppose that the school in Comala is not prepared for a blind child?"

"No, of course not. Besides, Mr. Alba would be in opposition." She sighed once more.

"But they have to study!", I said with consternation. I thought of my poor niece, with such yearnings to study, to learn things, without the ability to put that into practice.

"Precisely", she said. "That's why I am working to get a private teacher here, despite the resistance of Mr. Alba. I think that, if I were to present him with the right person, he would change his mind and accept it."

"The right person?"

"Yes. And that's why I want to ask your help. As you must know the city very well, I imagine that you would know how to contact the agencies that handle this sort of thing..."

Her voice diminished without finishing the sentence, as if she were losing the impetus to struggle on.

"This teacher, what requirements would she need?"

"Well, she would have to be well prepared, of course, but she would need something else as well."

"What?"

"The ability to convince Mr. Alba of her necessity in the house."

From her purse, she took a small piece of paper with her telephone number on it.

"Please. I don't have the chance to go into the city and take care of this because my work in Morelia takes up almost all my time. Can you help?"

"Of course. I will do what's in my power."

We said goodnight and Barbara rapidly disappeared into the gloom. With my oil lamp firmly in my hand, I set off for my quarters.

Something happened then, that I did not understand then, nor ever.

I started walking in the direction of the patio, knowing that from there I could locate my rooms easily. But I didn't arrive at the patio. You might say it was the wine I drank at dinner and throughout the evening, but I know it was not. It was the house. It made me get lost on purpose. I walked through, and up and down corridors, passing by rooms that I couldn't really see, but could only sense from the feeling of space as I crossed in front of their open doors. I passed through areas that I didn't remember seeing before; I turned back and turned back again, second-guessing my orientation constantly. Everything seemed senseless, strange, and I became completely confused. I thought of my nightmare from the night before, when I walked blindly through the house and how afraid that made me feel. I heard voices, or thought I heard voices: nasal, rough tones that I didn't recognize as language.

I decided to return to Miranda's room and begin again, but I couldn't find her room either. I don't know how long I wandered, but it felt like an eternity.

Finally, finally, I found the patio and from there, my rooms. I shut the door with trembling hands and locked it. In a bit, when I had recovered, I went to my briefcase and took out some paper and a pen. I sat down at the desk, and with the weak light of the oil lamp and with my feet resting on the lion's paws, I began to write. I set down everything that had happened to me since arriving in Mexico, up until that very moment. They were such strange events that I didn't want to forget any one of them.

The sun had come up and Mrs. Poncia was at the door with my breakfast on a tray, when I was finishing. Today was an important day; I was going to interview Diego.

25

Leonora
Diego Alba

The spiral staircase was in a lamentable state: all broken down and wobbly, but Diego went up it at top speed, carelessly, almost with a crazy happiness. He asked permission to go ahead, saying that there was something he needed to make sure of ahead of our arrival.

We went into his office at the top of the tower. There were windows all around which looked out on the gardens, and from one of them, I could see the top of a pyramid. I felt once again that shiver of uneasiness. The little house where we had stopped the other day was nowhere in sight; covered perhaps by the tall trees. I felt like I was in the middle of an immense solitude.

"I suppose you have some specific questions?", he began.

I forced myself to concentrate.

"We will need the details of the accident."

"But, surely that information is readily available in the police report? You must have read that."

I had a moment of confusion and panic. Of course, a representative of the insurance company charged with disbursing the funds from an accidental death, would have access to that information.

"Yes, of course. But...."

"Excuse me for interrupting, Mrs. Lopez, but something occurs to me. Who is the beneficiary of the life insurance policy, if you don't mind my asking?"

This answer I had well-prepared.

"Her father."

"And, he still lives in Brussels?"

"I suppose so, but I couldn't really say."

"Well, then. Let's begin. What can I clarify about the accident?"

"Can you show me where it occurred?"

Diego became thoughtful. "Yes, I can. But the place is not in the same state as it was then. I am continually changing the studio. There are paintings that are in different states of progress: some finished and packaged for transport, some ready to be taken to my gallery in the city, others just begun."

"I understand. But in any case...."

I felt my heart beat hard, felt the blood flow strongly in my body. Finally, I was going to see where my sister spent her last moments.

We went down the spiral staircase and began navigating the multitude of corridors. We passed through arcades in the open air, we entered and exited through glass doors, doors of metal, wood, doors that were merely like curtains, with pull cords rather than handles. We passed over thresholds and through darkened rooms where you could only see the benches along the wall, and others where the gargoyles near the ceiling glared down fiercely on us. In some rooms, screens divided one section from another, always with the elegant, heavy furniture of the last century, or the last centuries. There was one room that resembled the cloister of a convent, with its benches and stained glass. At one point we walked along a wall whose stones were coming loose from the plaster, and then alongside another that was faced with tiles from the middle ages. The house seemed like its own universe; a place where I was a small, lost person.

Finally, we entered the studio workshop of the painter. It was incredibly full of things; there was hardly enough room to walk. There were a multitude of paintings, with sketches stuck all over the walls, there were an infinity of easels stacked on the floor and leaning against the walls; on the tables were his mountains of crumpled paper, his rags, his spatulas, his paints; all the many, many materials that he used in his art.

"Here it is."

We stood for a moment, my gaze taken up by the multitude of things there. Diego brought to my attention a shelf covered completely in bottles of all shapes and kinds, full of paint.

"I mix my own paints, as all artists do", he explained.

Everything he said, he said in a very special way. It was if the tone of his voice, his gestures, the way he looked at you, everything about him, was focused solely on you; as if he waited for your answers with the most careful attention; as if everything you said was of utmost importance to him. Diego Alba had the ability to make me feel unique, desired, beautiful, even. I wished he would touch my hands again, as he had when we ascended the spiral staircase. I wished he would talk again, whispering in my ear as he did when he was showing me the pyramids. I wished he could see me without this gray hair, and this makeup, without the ugly clothes that I was wearing; I wished I could be my usual self, with my usual appearance.

"So, this was where she died?"

"No. But it was here that the accident happened."

"Who was present in the house at that time?"

"Only Miranda and myself. She was playing with her dolls while I was working. On the table were the many bottles of pigment that I use. I employ a lot of rare ingredients, plants and soil that I collect from the property."

Diego swallowed hard. "Some of them are toxic."

As he said this, I had a premonition. I both wanted and did not want him to continue.

"That day, on the table was a pitcher of water flavored with melon, that Mrs. Poncia had made. It was the same color as the liquid that I use for mixing paint, and the jar was identical. Without noticing the difference between them, Rosa drank from the wrong pitcher."

"Did you see her drink it?"

"No. I didn't see her. I was working. But I guessed what must have happened."

I didn't say anything. Diego turned away from me, and I could see his shoulders heave up and down as he worked to contain his emotion. We stayed this way for a long moment.

"The effect of the poisoning wasn't immediate", he said with his back to me still.

"Are you saying that your wife did not detect the taste of the liquid?"

Diego turned back to see me.

"That is what I don't understand. I didn't understand it in the moment, and I still don't understand."

We remained this way, each of us deeply lost our own thoughts.

"And then, what happened?"

"She went to her room. She said she was very tired and wanted to rest."

"And you? What did you do?"

"I stayed in the studio. I continued to work."

Again, we fell into a deep silence.

"And, what was your wife's state of mind in those days? Would she have had a reason to commit suicide?"

I asked him this hoping that the surprise question would cause him to reveal something he may have kept hidden.

"We were having a bad time", he said.

It was clear that he was having difficulty speaking, and only with a great effort was he able to continue.

"I didn't have a lot of trust in her."

"Why?"

"Rosa had her issues. She had a past in Chile that still affected her. And then there was the thing with her father."

"What do you mean?"

At this point Diego closed in on himself, as if he realized he had revealed too much.

"It really is not pertinent, Mrs. Lopez. What happened was an accidental poisoning. It was an accident whose mystery we will never fully understand. That is what the police concluded, and there isn't really any more to say about it."

"But if it is a case of suicide, the policy is annulled. The beneficiary will receive nothing."

Diego forced himself to remain in control of his state of mind.

"No one has been able to confirm that. And when I told you that Rosa and I were having problems, I told you that in confidence. If you insist in repeating it, I will deny it categorically."

Diego looked at me fully in the face.

"Look, Mrs. Lopez. I want Rosa's father to receive what is due him. And I will do everything in my power to make this happen."

I couldn't avoid hearing the threat in his tone of voice. I felt an actual fear. But on the other hand, I was glad to hear that he wanted the policy to be honored. For a moment I forgot that all this was a fabrication. Yes, Rosa's father should get the money; it was fair.

"I'm sorry, Mr. Alba. I didn't mean to insist."

With this, the awkwardness in our conversation fell away and we returned to the cordial feeling of before. Diego accompanied me to my rooms, telling me that he would be out of the house for the rest of the day, but that evening there was to be a small gathering of people for dinner. I understood that he was suggesting that I wear something more formal.

With my heart cast down, I realized that I had nothing else better to wear, nothing other than the boring attire of a middle-aged woman at work. I felt then a kind of rage at myself, an anger for causing myself to suffer in this way, wishing with all my forces that I had a pretty dress to wear, a pretty dress for Diego Alba to see me in.

26

Leonora
The Ants

The dinner took place in the large patio. The guests were friends and associates of Diego; the food was as delicious as ever; the wine was abundant.

But I didn't feel at all happy. The conversation varied between the topics of art and the business of art. They spoke of people whose names I did not recognize, even though it felt like I should recognize them. The conversation was full of ideas whose importance I could only guess at.

Barbara was there, as was Dr. Leocadio. I chatted with them when the conversation went in areas unknown to me, and Diego paid me hardly any attention at all. His focus was directed to an elegant women named Esmé Moreau. She was French, and from the moment I heard her speak with her charming French accent, I lost the little interest I had in remaining at the party. I felt as insignificant as the ants that crisscrossed the patio floor.

What I really wanted to do was retire to my room and start writing. As soon as I could, I excused myself. Seated at the enormous desk, with the soft leather of the chair against my legs and my feet resting on the lion's paws, I started to write. It was important to put down everything,

everything. I felt like Rosa was there with me, reading over my shoulder, that it was important to her that I do this.

When I finished, I wrote a letter to Nikita, describing what was being created in my mind, what my next step was going to be.

The next day Diego took me to the plaza in Comala and waited with me for the bus. We spoke of the children, a topic that I introduced on purpose. I asked him about their studies and he repeated more or less what Barbara had already told me.

"Do you think I'm making a mistake by not sending them to the school in the town?", he asked.

"I don't know if I can answer that, Mr. Alba. But what I can tell you is that your daughter is a wonderful child. She has a quick and lively intelligence."

"I know."

"She took a great pleasure in getting to know me, and I her. She was with me all afternoon."

"Oh, really?"

"Yes. I think it's really important that she be able to have the doors opened to her."

"But the school here is terrible. And being blind...."

"There are other ways of educating her."

"I know, I know. Barbara tells me the same thing."

At that moment the bus drove up, but Diego had one last question.

"And your investigation? Are you satisfied with the answers you received?"

"Somewhat, Mr. Alba. Somewhat."

27

Leonora
Luz María Mendoza

The appointment was for four o'clock. At 4:20 I heard a voice. Coming towards me was a figure I recognized, walking quickly and calling a name.

Miss Mendoza? Luz Maria Mendoza?

I had practiced the name, trying to familiarize myself with the sound of it, and with the story of my past: I am from Bloemfontein, South Africa, daughter of a Spaniard and a South African mother. Diego will have a difficult time informing himself about me from such a distant place. Nevertheless, I hope I don't have to talk very much about my supposed past: I was only in Bloemfontein for a few days once when I was ten, on a visit to a friend of my mother's.

Miss Mendoza?

Luz Maria Mendoza was the name of a singer of country songs, whose poster I saw on a street near our hostel. Now I too am called Luz Maria Mendoza, and that's the way I presented myself to Barbara when I spoke to her by phone, deepening my voice, letting her believe that I was calling from the agency for domestic servants. Barbara, very happy with the rapid solution to the problem of the untutored Alba children, had arranged an interview with me and the painter for the following week. I was going to meet with Diego in the plaza in Comala, like a *dejá-vu* of the last time.

"I understand that you're looking for the position of teacher", commented Diego. "How many years of experience do you have?", he asked, seated next to me on the bench. He looked me carefully up and down, examining closely my face.

"Four. With a family of two children. The girl was eight and the boy was five."

"Ah. It's much the same situation here. But I warn you, Miss Mendoza, that my house is quite isolated; quite far from the city. Does that worry you?"

"No, I don't think so", I answered. I let my voice vary a bit, as if I were indeed somewhat worried, but there existed no doubt in me. I was taking the first step and my heart beat hard.

Diego took out the resume and looked over it; the resume I had sent to Barbara, that she had received presumably from the agency. Once again I had gotten good use from the typewriter I bought.

"I see that in addition to the usual subjects, you know French. My daughter speaks a bit of French", he said, but then he stopped speaking, as if the conversation were painful to him.

"Your daughter?", I asked.

"Yes. She's nine and Cecilio is six. Miranda's mother has just recently died and with my work….."

"How long has it been since….?"

"Nearly a year."

"I understand. Children need a lot of care, on top of the academic work."

"Yes. And with the special situation…."

I waited for Diego to finish. I wanted to see how he would explain Miranda's blindness.

"Miranda is blind. But she compensates very well. She walks around by herself, knows to dress herself, eat by herself…."

Diego spoke as if he were trying to convince me to take the job, but I needed no convincing; I wanted the position with all my strength.

"It would be useful for me to meet them", I said.

"Of course."

We got into the car, passing through the same streets and roads as before. I paid good attention to the entrance of the house, trying to see it ahead of time, but I couldn't. We passed by the little house where Diego had explained about the pyramids, and I felt a terrible nervousness.

Waiting for us in the same library where just a few days ago the middle-aged woman from the insurance company had been writing her report, was Miranda once more.

"Papa, is she my new teacher?"

"We will see, my love."

From a distance we heard the shouting of a child.

"That must be Cecilio", commented Diego. "Miranda, go and see what he wants."

To me he added: "Miranda is the only one who can deal with him."

I thought about how Rosa and I were as children: how we played together, how she took care of me, how she could comfort me as well or better than my mother. And now, this little girl knew how to comfort and care for this other little boy just the same.

I hadn't said anything to Diego about Adriana. I feared risking his acceptance of me, with the mention of a possibly inconvenient addition to the situation.

But as if he were reading my mind, he asked: "Are you here alone in Mexico?"

Diego put his gaze upon me like a pair of x-ray eyes. I know that the years have changed me, that I no longer look so much like Rosa, or as Rosa would look now if she were alive, but I still worried that there might remain some family resemblance. Would Diego suspect something?

I decided to throw caution to the wind; I felt that this was the decisive moment, the moment in which I would begin to recapture the family that I had lost. I could hardly breathe.

"I'm the guardian for my younger sister."

I saw the Diego was surprised, even as he tried to hide it.

"Your sister? How old is she?"

"She's fourteen."

"Ah." Diego looked at me with a frightening intensity.

"A... A... Amelia is a very tranquil girl. She could be a good friend to your daughter."

I nearly gave away the game by speaking the true name of Adriana.

"Yes, Papa, oh please!", exclaimed Miranda.

My hands trembled. Diego let several seconds go by without saying anything.

"Very well. Does the job meet your requirements, Miss Mendoza?"

We hadn't spoken of the salary. It didn't matter. The plan was going to work. I couldn't speak for the amazement.

"Miss Mendoza?", he asked me again.

I nodded, unable to trust my voice not to tremble.

28

Leonora
A Guide for the Blind

I discovered many things in my first days as a teacher in the house of Diego Alba; things that at first disquieted me, but with the passage of time I became more used to. I suppose that that is how we survive as humans; we must accept strange, new things in order not to fall apart.

In the first place, the house was not as it appeared at first. That is, it was not solid. It was more like a labyrinth: full of dark passageways, stairways that led to locked doors, some rooms with one door and others with many doors; there were rooms you could see from the window of another room, but that you couldn't get to, seemingly disconnected from anything else; there were long halls and dark corners whose purpose was not at all clear.

Besides the architectural complexity, the house had a sort of spirit that you could feel when you passed through an opening, or went through certain doors out into the gardens. It was a feeling that the house was thinking, judging you, perhaps refusing you. I often felt like the uninvited guest, an interloper that the house was trying to reject. It might have been for the stories that Diego told me about the history of the house, or maybe the comments of Mrs. Poncia regarding the warriors who still lived nearby, or maybe from my own fearful imagination, but I was very affected by the house. I even had a return of the nightmare that I had had the first night, when I wandered blind through the rooms. It was if the house were trying to disorient me on purpose.

I was given a small room at the back that had its own door to the outside. It was near the rear patio where Poncia washed the clothes, where the chickens pecked at worms and the cats slept in the sun. I didn't know what use the small room once had had, but for me it suited us perfectly. There was even a desk, similar in style to the desk in the library, with its high-backed chair and carved wooden legs. But, like many things in the house, this little room had its dark side as well.

The first night we were there, Adriana was sleeping while I was busy putting away our clothes. It was late and everyone was asleep. Suddenly I heard whispered voices that were coming from behind the wall, just behind the bureau. I couldn't imagine what this could be. I abandoned the clothes and crawled into bed. In the shadows of the night I didn't dare investigate.

But in the morning, with a lot of effort, I managed to move the heavy bureau and saw the crack of a door in the wall. The door had no handle; it turned on an invisible hinge and opened with a push. I opened it a few centimeters, but got so nervous that I shut it without looking in. I pushed the bureau back into place. Remembering once again my dream, I asked myself, if I were to go down that path, where in the world would I end up?

Then, there were the problems associated with Cecilio. He never spoke of his mother, who I supposed had once been Diego's wife or companion. I wanted to know more about her, but it was impossible to investigate. The child was terribly mischievous and Mrs. Poncia always defended him. If for example, we found a broken glass or food thrown on the ground where Cecilio and Adriana had been playing, she always said it had been my sister who had done it. I knew that it wasn't Adriana, but I had no way to defend her.

Poor Adriana! She hardly understood anything at first. It was very difficult for her to become accustomed to this new life. She asked for her mother constantly, asked for Nikita, for our father. I was constantly afraid that she would ask me, in the presence of Poncia or Diego, why I called her Amelia with them and Adriana when we were alone. I tried to explain it to her the best I could. She never stopped asking why we didn't go anymore to the *Gran Place* to eat *gaufres* and drink hot chocolate. She asked why she didn't go to the *Lycée* anymore. She cried a lot, complaining of headaches, stomachaches. I didn't know how to comfort her, but at the same time, I knew it wasn't she who was committing all those mischievous acts in the house. It felt like Mrs. Poncia had something against her, or was even jealous of her, because of the attention that Diego paid her. Because Diego always treated Adriana well. He always made the effort to understand her despite her incoherencies, trying to untangle the meaning of her words.

Also worrisome was the attitude of Miranda towards her Barbie doll, whom she called "Minx", this doll with the long legs, the tiny waist and the pointed bosom. As children, Nikita, Rosa and I played with our Barbies too, but at the end of the day we put them away and played with other toys. But Miranda carried her doll around constantly, never leaving it alone for a second, day and night.

According to Miranda, Minx could see. She had opinions about everything. She even knew what was going on without being present. Minx talked to Miranda in the night, telling her things that the child was too embarrassed to repeat to me the following day. Minx had a beautiful voice and could sing. At times Miranda couldn't pay attention to the lesson because Minx needed her. And whenever I asked to see Minx up close, Miranda refused to let me. I was never able to examine the doll, not even in the few moments when she was out of Miranda's hands, because the child had an excellent intuition, and would arrive just as I was getting close. When I asked her how she had gotten Minx, she said that the doll was a gift from her mother.

Another thing I noticed in those first days was that the painting of Rosa that hung in the living room, disappeared. When I first saw the empty space, I stopped before it, hardly able to stifle the cry of anger and sadness that came from my mouth. I tried to repress my tears but some fell anyway, and my anxiety rose further when I sensed Poncia passing behind me. Since I supposedly had never seen the painting, I had no way to inquire about its absence now. Those were very bad moments.

What did give me a lot of pleasure was teaching the children. Being with them compensated a lot for the doubts and frustrations that I felt in those days. We held class in a Socratic style: asking and answering questions orally, discussing the nuances of the problems. Miranda and Cecilio captured the instruction incredibly fast. They were enthusiastic learners, always asking for more homework, more information. They had an enormous curiosity, and were not satisfied with the simple lessons. They wanted to know where, and why, and when for everything.

At the end of the first week, Miranda proposed that we put on a small theatrical based on a story she was reading.

"What is it called? What is it about?", I asked.

"It's called *Marianela*. It's about a poor little girl who is the friend to a blind boy. He is very handsome and she is very ugly."

When she said the word "blind", I stopped short.

"They live where there are a lot of mines. The boy is from a rich family and goes to school, while she is poor and has never gone to school."

"Ah."

"And, she's an orphan. Her father left the family and her mother drank aguardiente because her work in the mines was very hard. One day she drank too much and the foreman fired her."

I felt my heart beating fast, with fear and fascination. *Marianela....* I recognized the name. But what a coincidence that it had to do with blindness. It felt so morbid that Miranda would read this book.

"So then her mother got really sad and threw herself down a deep mine hole."

"She committed suicide?!"

"Yes", said Miranda calmly.

She continued talking without noting my perturbation. I couldn't help notice the similarity between the story and real life: a blind child, an orphan, and a mother who poisons herself from sadness. How in the world had Miranda found this particular book to read? Who had given it to her?

"Marianela goes everywhere with Pablo, who is the blind boy. They wander around in the dangerous mountains. They are best friends", said Miranda.

"Do they fall in love?", I asked.

"She does. But Pablo has to marry his cousin, who is very beautiful. Then a doctor comes and operates on Pablo. Now he can see."

"And when he sees Marianela, I suppose that he puts her aside", I remarked.

"Well, yes and no. Pablo loved her while he couldn't see her, but as soon as he sees his beautiful cousin, he forgets about her. He goes crazy for the beautiful cousin."

"And then, how does he treat Marianela?"

"He still loves her, but he doesn't have time to tell her because she dies in that same moment. She dies in the exact moment that Pablo sees her for the first time."

"She dies of sadness?"

"Of sadness", affirmed Miranda. "The ending is really nice."

I was horrified at the thought of acting out scenes from this book.

"So, you'll help me, Miss Mendoza, to write down the dialogue?"

I didn't know what to say.

"Come on, it will be nice. Besides, my father will be very happy to see it."

In that moment, something occurred to me. Maybe Diego would reveal something about Rosa's death, upon seeing and hearing a story so similar to the real one. I told Miranda that we could do it.

"Good. Miss Mendoza, you will be Marianela. I will be the cousin Florentina. My father can be Pablo and my teacher Miss Barbara can dress up as a man to be the doctor."

All this Miranda said in the same voice as Rosa's: very efficient, organized, very sure of herself.

That afternoon we came together on the patio, with its fragrant flowers, beneath the pretty designs of sun and shade, to write down the tragedy of a blind boy.

29

Leonora
The Kiss

Barbara was enchanted with the idea of the theatrical. The characters were interesting to her: Marianela, the poor, ugly girl who loves the blind boy; the beautiful cousin who will soon be his wife; the helpful doctor who restores his sight and sets in motion the tragic events. For her next visit, we would have everything ready.

Miranda had chosen for me the role of the ugly girl, but that was just fine. I wanted my niece to triumph in anything she tried to do. For herself she chose the part of the beautiful cousin and she put her father, Diego, in the role of the blind man. The irony didn't escape me; the fact that the painter, who perhaps sees the best of anyone, would play the role of the blind person.

Miranda wasted no time in explaining it to him.

"It was Miss Mendoza's idea", she told him. "Papa, she is so clever!"

"But, but…. " I stammered.

"Oh, wonderful", he said, not letting me finish. "I'm very anxious to see this play. When is the performance?"

"In two weeks, at my next visit", said Barbara. "At night. It will be very beautiful in the candlelight."

"And who will be the audience?", asked Diego. "We need someone to applaud us, don't you think?"

He thought for a moment.

"I'll invite some friends", he said.

"And I will bring some students from the institute", added Barbara.

The next day at breakfast, I came into the kitchen at the same moment as Diego. He looked like the cat that ate the mouse.

"I didn't sleep a wink last night, Miss Mendoza", he said smiling.

"I hope it's nothing serious", I told him.

"On the contrary. I was studying for my part in the play. I know it now by heart."

"That's wonderful. I think Miranda will be very happy to know this."

Diego became serious.

"She is very much improved, now that you are here."

"Yes?"

"Yes. Before you came, she spoke very little. Well, she spoke a lot to Minx but very little to us. She spent most of her time alone in her room."

"What did she do there?"

"She read. Since Barbara taught her to read Braillle, she turned into a recluse. But that's all changed now, thanks to you."

I looked down to hide the happiness that I felt, but Diego's gaze upon me made me raise it.

"I never thought that such a change would be possible. To have you both in the house, has brought back something that was sorely lacking", said the painter. "I know it's been a short time, but I am very, very happy to have you here."

I didn't respond, I couldn't for the emotion I felt.

"And I see that Miranda is very enthusiastic with the play, as am I."

"Thank you Mr. Alba, for your kind words. I also feel very happy to be of service."

The night of the theatrical was cool and fresh beneath the moonlight, and the fountain made a lively tinkling sound. Diego had drawn a window frame as backdrop to our stage, and through this painted window was a view of distant hills. Poncia had helped me bring a sofa from the living room into the patio, which would serve as the couch for the poor Marianela as she lay dying. Poncia was grumbling about this, but got happier when Diego gave her the part of the nurse, helping the doctor.

In the days before the play, Miranda and I had talked a lot about it.

"Do you believe that the love between Pablo and Marianela is a true love?", I asked her, curious to hear her interpretation on this complex idea.

"I think it was a true love. Because it was a pure love."

"Then how did it change so quickly? Why did he stop loving her?"

Miranda was uneasy; almost at the point of crying.

"No! He always loved her. He just didn't have time to tell her."

"Ok, ok. It's all right. Look, let's rehearse again", I told her.

I thought about the reaction of my niece, her naiveté, about how one's desire to see things a particular way causes one to see them that way, and not another.

When everything was ready, the performance started. Diego said his lines very well, and I did too, if I may say so.

But in the second scene, something happened. When I, (or rather Marianela) extended my hand to Pablo for him to kiss it, Diego took off on his own. Instead of returning my hand to the coverlet, he kept it and kissed it again. Then again. I felt his warm lips on the back of my hand, I felt the ardor of his emotion translated upon my skin.

> *"Nela, Nela, my love. How wrong I've been! I doubted you, with no reason. I thought the worst, I thought badly, badly. The love you showed me was real, and I didn't see it. Doctor! She's not responding!*

Miranda didn't hesitate with the change in the dialogue and the action.

> *To die like this, without cause...it can't be!*

Until the end of the scene, Diego did not let go of my hand. I felt like he didn't want to let it go, that it was an effort to do so. I was completely perplexed, but the audience applauded nicely at the end.

Then, when everyone had gone, Mrs. Poncia came up to me.

"Take good care, Miss Mendoza. Mr. Alba is still grieving the death of his wife. You wouldn't want to...."

In that moment Cecilio joined us and she stopped. What was she going to tell me? That I leave Diego alone? That I stay away from him? Or, more frighteningly, was it a threat? A warning that the same thing that happened to Rosa could happen to me? I couldn't tell if this was a ridiculous idea or not. So many things had occurred in the play that I didn't understand: why Miranda had insisted that the idea was mine; what Diego was thinking when he changed the action and the dialogue; what was the significance of the emotion he showed? I had wanted to see if the play solicited some behavior on his part, some clue about what happened to Rosa, and it did. But I didn't know how to interpret it.

At least, the kiss that he placed on my hand remained. That kiss that burned my skin, that filled me with desire, the kiss that I felt that cool night, remained with me.

That night after the play, I dreamed of pyramids, of death and of the dead. And in the morning when I tried to write it down, no words came to me. I couldn't describe what happened; it was only images, sensations.

30

Leonora
The Storeroom

One night Diego asked me to go to the storeroom; a room half underground, with small windows very high up covered with thick curtains that admitted little light. The storeroom smelled of onions, of dust and of old things. I was looking for white wine. He asked me to bring it to his work studio, where, after dinner, we would possibly spend some time in conversation.

But the wine was not where it was supposed to be. I looked in the nearby shelves, but it wasn't there either. I went further, turning corners senselessly. I no longer was looking for the wine, but rather to control the panic which threatened to overtake me.

In a forgotten corner I saw something I didn't understand. It was a thin, rectangular object, wrapped in dirty rags. I uncovered a part. It was the portrait of Rosa that had gone missing not long after I arrived at the house. I could only see a small part of the painting, but it was enough to give me strength. Gleefully I tried to uncover the rest of it, but it was well stuck in between other boxes. I pulled on it but it wouldn't move. I pulled again and it came out of its hiding place, but oh my God, there was a huge scratch that extended from one side to the other. My sister's face looked out at me, unscathed and with the same tranquility as ever, but I couldn't look at her for the anguish I felt.

I heard someone enter the storeroom. I felt the steps, slow but firm. I looked up to see the person I least wanted to meet at that moment.

"Can I help you with something, Miss Mendoza?", asked the gravelly voice of Mrs. Poncia.

I didn't respond. I couldn't think of anything adequate to say.

"The storeroom isn't the place for paintings", she said, as if she were explaining this to a five-year-old.

"I didn't put it here!"

"And look what you've done", she said, indicating the ugly scratch.

"It's that…."

Mrs. Poncia took the painting, wrapped it up again and put it back where it had been.

"Let's not talk about this. I will take care of the wine", she said.

With that, she left. I felt terrible for losing the opportunity to be alone with Diego, and all because of horrible Mrs. Poncia.

As soon as dinner was over I went again to the storeroom. Even though I was afraid to take the painting, I wanted to do it. The possibility of looking into the face of my sister whenever I wanted to, whenever I was having a bad moment, made me very happy.

But when I got there, the painting was gone. Not even Mrs. Poncia, who was an expert in the movements of the house, could have done it. There wasn't time.

I felt sick at heart, weak, squashed by the power of Mrs. Poncia. Looking at the empty space where the painting had been, I began to cry. I felt a current of frigid air flowing across the floor, across my feet. They froze. I felt so alone, so helpless and forlorn there in the house of Diego Alba. But I could see no way to help myself. I evoked the image of Rosa, asking her to help me, to lend me her cleverness. The current of cold air ceased.

31

Leonora
Mrs. Barbara Barr

The days passed, the months passed. Nothing unusual like the acting in Marianela, nor the frightening occurrence in the storeroom, happened again. Diego travelled, sometimes spending a few days or a few weeks away from home. Barbara came regularly, as well as Dr. Leocadio. I prepared the children's lessons, we ate, we slept. Life had a certain rhythm, a certain style. The only thing that really made me anxious were the stomach pains that afflicted me and Adriana. I thought it was probably due to the ingredients that Poncia used in her cooking, but since no one else seemed affected by it, I said nothing.

And, what did I feel for Diego in that time? Every night when Adriana fell asleep, I would sit at the desk in my room, big and black, with polished wood, in the high-backed leather chair with its lion's feet at the bottom of the legs, and I would write. I filled page after page from the stack of paper that I had brought from the city, each sheet with its logo of the insurance company at the top. There, I put the contents of my heart, the deepness of my feelings. And after reading it over, I realized that I was beginning to fall in love with Diego. I longed for his conversations, his way of gazing at me. I missed his attention when he was gone.

Diego did not act with me like a common employer. He spoke to me of the things that interested him, things that happened on his travels, discussions he had with other people. As for me, I don't think I'm mistaken to think that I formed for him a kind of center as well. He would ask my opinion about his paintings; and with time I gained the confidence to tell him that I liked some things, disliked others, that images painted in a different way would be more pleasing. Diego never became annoyed. On the contrary, he was very interested.

It was the same with the children. Every day I waited anxiously for dinner where we would come together in the patio, or in the dining room if it were chilly, where Diego would listen carefully to the details of their day, of their academic progress. He was vitally interested in the subject matter, the material that I used to teach. Diego was interested in everything, even the most trivial matters.

And there was something else that occurred regularly during that time. The kiss that he gave me during the play was repeated. Every time he would leave on a trip, he would take my hand, in a very theatrical way, and he would kiss the palm, or the back, with all the tenderness and passion that he showed me on that evening. And upon his return, he would do the same. With the passage of time, that kiss took on the dimensions of everything; that kiss spoke to me, it listened to my lamentations, it laughed with me, it encompassed all my emotions and his; that kiss that began the evening of the play, ended up becoming a symbol of everything that went on between us.

One day Barbara arrived later than usual. After dinner, she and Diego went into the living room and closed the door. I could tell they were arguing.

"Luz tells me that Miranda has not been out of the house for two months."

Her voice sounded furious.

"I was out of town. What do you want me to do?"

"Why didn't you tell me you were gone? I would have come more often!"

"I don't have to be accountable to you, Barbara." Diego's voice was smooth, controlled, quite the opposite of his words. "You insist on holding a vigil over my daughter, and you do this on your own initiative. You and I both know that I don't like it, but for reasons that we both understand, I have to permit it."

"It is not healthy to keep her closed up here, Diego. She needs to go out into the world, meet people, have new experiences. Her world is very limited here, and you are at fault."

Diego responded: "The children are learning very well here with Luz. They are more advanced than children of their same age, much more advanced."

I was very happy to hear Diego defend me.

"I don't doubt that Luz is a very good teacher, but it's not sufficient. Miranda needs to have friends her own age; she needs to be around other children, and have interactions with other adults as well. How is it possible that you don't see this?"

"And how is it possible that you don't see that your comments on this subject are unwanted?"

Diego's voice showed no sign of anger, which was his custom when he became angry. His attitude of calm and control provoked his adversary to a state of even greater anger. The more he was calm, the angrier the other person became. I had witnessed that before whenever Diego would chastise Cecilio or Mrs. Poncia over some difficulty in the house.

"I also found out that Dr. Leocadio hasn't been to see her in over a month. The agreement was that he would come every two weeks and that he would pass me his notes", continued Barbara.

"I wasn't home, I repeat." Diego breathed deeply. "Besides, you know that I disagree completely with the need to submit her to psychological treatment."

"Diego, you promised me that Miranda would lack for nothing."

"And I am complying with that."

Barbara didn't say anything for a long moment. Finally, she murmured in a disdainful voice:

"You trample the memory of Rosa." With this she left the room, slamming the door behind her.

I was so overwrought that I could hardly breathe. Rosa! What could Barbara know about my sister?

The following day, I was dying to ask her, but I didn't know how to begin. My situation as the teacher did not permit me to ask those kinds of questions. But she sought me out herself. She came to my room after dinner, looking upset, looking like she needed someone to unburden herself to.

"Luz, you have come to love Miranda, haven't you?"

"It would be very difficult not to love her. She is enchanting."

"Well, I want to ask a big favor of you. I want you to call me if Dr. Leocadio does not appear for his visits. He should come on Thursdays, in the afternoon, and I need to know if he comes, or if he doesn't."

"Of course, Barbara. But, can I ask a question? " I had decided rapidly to simulate a certain naiveté.

"Do you think he can cure her?"

"Oh, Luz."

Barbara suddenly looked tired, sad. "I'm going to tell you something, but it isn't to make you lose respect for Mr. Alba."

I nodded. I went to shut the door of my room. I didn't want anyone to hear what she was about the describe. Barbara settled herself, getting ready to tell a long story.

"When I was twenty-five, I went with my husband to Brussels, to continue my studies in the education of the blind."

My heart leapt to hear the name of my childhood city. She continued:

"We stayed for two years, and I met a woman there, a very important woman to me. She was married with four children, but we didn't speak much about that. It wasn't until much later that I even knew it."

Barbara stopped, letting some moments of silence pass by.

"Her husband had a high position in the U.S. embassy, but we didn't talk about that very much either. What we most liked to discuss were the ways to educate the poor, the blind, the disadvantaged. She had a big heart for them."

I couldn't believe what I was hearing. Barbara was talking about my mother, about my family!

"She was a great friend of mine. I came to love her very much."

Barbara stopped speaking, as if the action were painful.

"Then, when I found myself in a difficult situation, she helped me.

"How?"

"The details don't matter. Suffice to say, my friend got me out of terrible mess. If it hadn't of been for her, I might have landed in jail, or worse."

Jail?! I thought quickly. Some criminal thing? Could it be that my mother used the fact that my father was ambassador to get Barbara out of her "terrible mess"? I was dying to ask her.

Barbara sighed deeply. "One day we met in the *Gran Place* to drink coffee and eat *gaufres*, which are the cookies that are common there."

I felt the tears in my eyes, and I made a superhuman effort to not let them fall. In that moment I could smell the coffee and taste the *gaufres*; my memory was that strong. A bittersweet feeling came into my mouth, for all the things, both good and bad, that had happened in Brussels.

"That day my friend told me that her eldest daughter, who was living in Chile, had separated from her husband. Can you imagine my surprise to know that she had an adult child? I never imagined that she could be old enough. She told me that her daughter had a daughter of her own, a little girl six years old. They had been living in Chile, but something very serious happened and they had to leave."

"What happened?"

"I don't know. I only know that it was an emergency. In any case, the daughter, Rosa, and the granddaughter left Chile and went to Mexico."

"Why Mexico?"

"It had something to do with the government of Chile. Something political. My friend didn't want to clarify it, which was unusual. I had the impression that she was obligated to keep me in the dark."

"What could have happened to her daughter in Chile?"

"I couldn't tell you. But it was clear that my friend was extremely upset, extremely worried for her daughter and her granddaughter. I was about to leave Brussels and return to Mexico myself, so she asked me to do something for her."

"What?"

"She asked me to get information about Rosa."

"How were you supposed to do that?"

"She knew that my husband and I were planning to open a school for the blind. Think about it Luz, they say that God works in mysterious ways. At that time, we were planning to open the school in Mexico City, where her daughter was. She suggested that I try to meet her, try to become her friend, gain her trust, if possible. I felt very indebted to my friend and I wanted to do anything I could to help her. She had helped me so much before."

Barbara stopped to catch her breath.

"But it wasn't in the capital that we started our school, but in Morelia. My husband knew people there who could facilitate it. But I get ahead of myself. I want to tell you what happened before I left Brussels."

My heart started beating so hard it felt as if it were leaving my chest.

"My friend discovered that her husband, the diplomat, had been unfaithful to her. She was so distraught that she killed herself."

She didn't kill herself!!!, I wanted to scream out.

"So, I was carrying in my conscience the promise that I had made her, and that now I could not carry out. The promises you make to someone who has died, are sacred, you know", she said softly. "But there in Morelia, and very busy with the starting of the school, I couldn't get into contact with Rosa."

Barbara paused, collecting her thoughts.

"Until one day it occurred to my husband to put a work of art in the foyer of the school. And who do you think came to paint the mural? Diego Alba, the husband of Rosa. I tell you, God is certainly in the details."

"Incredible", I said weakly.

"I knew Diego from before. We met in Brussels."

Upon saying this, she looked uneasy, as if she wished she hadn't mentioned that.

"I hadn't the slightest idea that he had married the daughter of my friend", she said after a painful pause. "Diego wanted us to take a look at his daughter, or rather, the daughter of Rosa, whom he had adopted. He said that she had recently suffered a loss of vision. By way of exchange, he did the mural."

"A mural for blind people?"

"It's a special kind of mural. It's made from tactile materials; as much to touch as to look at. Diego is very clever. In the midst of all that, we found out that Rosa had died."

"How did you find out? Did he tell you?"

"No. But one night, when he had been drinking, it slipped out. You know how he is."

Yes, I knew very well how Diego was when he was drinking.

"I felt so bad. Here was the same Rosa, the Rosa I had promised my friend to keep an eye on, now she was dead! I couldn't find out anything concrete about her death. But in that moment, when Diego and Miranda were there at the school, I was given another opportunity to do the right thing."

Barbara continued: "With what Diego told me, I drew my own conclusions. Think about it Luz, God had put in my path the very same person that I needed to honor my promise! If it were already too late to watch over Rosa, at least I could watch over her daughter."

I waited for Barbara to speak again. I didn't want to ask her anything, or take her away from her story in any way.

"I didn't have a lot of confidence in Diego with regard to his care of Miranda, but I told him about knowing Rosa's mother and about the promises I had made to her. I told him I had a heavy charge weighing on me and that I intended to deal with it to the best of my ability."

"And, how did Mr. Alba react?"

"He kept on painting the mural as if nothing had happened, as if he didn't even hear me."

Our conversation had left me a bundle of nerves. I wanted in that moment, to confess everything to her: who I was, why I was there, but I didn't dare. I wasn't prepared for the chaos that would ensue if I were to do that.

"One night I dreamed about my friend. It was one of those dreams that you can't believe it was only a dream, it was so real. In fact, I felt like my friend was speaking directly to me; asking me to take good care of her granddaughter, in fact, to bring her up in the institute along with the other blind children. I woke up with the firm decision to do exactly that."

"And?"

"Diego refused completely. The only thing I managed to accomplish was to submit her to the first round of examinations before they left."

Both of us fell into a profound silence. Finally, she took up the thread again.

"During the time Diego was in Morelia with his children, I became very close to Miranda. She is like a daughter to me, the daughter I never had. I knew that attending the institute would help her enormously; I was ready to do anything for her."

"But Diego refused", I said.

Barbara sighed sadly. "Yes. I had to let her go. But now I do what I can. I contracted with Dr. Leocadio, who is a specialist in infantile trauma."

"Like the trauma that Miranda suffered when she watched her mother die?"

"Yes. Luz, he believes that her eyes function perfectly well. The problem is somewhere else."

I didn't know how to respond. I had had the same suspicions, but I didn't want to acknowledge them. I didn't want to admit that Diego was wrong in not wanting Miranda to be analyzed or be treated by a psychiatrist. I didn't want to admit it now either. I didn't want to think badly of him. I nearly went crazy with this ambivalent situation.

Once again I felt an intense desire to confess all to her. But if I did it, this would convert me into an enemy. To tell her who I was would be to betray Diego. I didn't want us two to form an alliance in opposition to him. Not that. I couldn't destroy the hope I had that one day, Diego Alba would confirm what, exactly, he felt for me.

32

Leonora
Nikita Comes

I had been in the Alba house for a little more than a year, when I received a letter from Paris. Nikita had decided to abandon her university studies. She didn't explain anything—a custom she surely must have gotten from our father. She said she wanted to come to Mexico, to stay with me for the time being. For the time being? Well, it didn't matter; I was delighted, even though I had no idea of how to broach the idea to Diego.

But, like many things, Diego solved it himself. In an apparently casual conversation, he asked about my childhood in Bloemfontein. I had spent nearly every moment since I got Nikita's letter, creating a believable story; a believable set of lies. Nikita would now be called Nancy. To Diego, I told a few details about that South African city, and I also casually mentioned that my sister would like to visit me here. I said she was changing directions in life and looking for a new path.

"Why not?", he said. "There are unoccupied rooms here. Besides, she could help you with the children."

Diego looked a bit askance at me.

"The three sisters together. That should make you happy."

Nikita arrived confused, nearly catatonic. I explained her invented history, the story of our past, but she paid me little attention. I found her to be depressed, but there didn't seem to be anything I could do for her.

What finally made her come out of her melancholy were the visits of Dr. Leocadio. By his third visit, her depression had lifted. She came out of her room to greet him, dressed and made up like I hadn't seen her since her arrival.

"Hello, Dr. Leocadio. I'm Nancy Mendoza, the sister of Luz. I have a Master's Degree in Psychology from the Sorbonne, and I would love to assist you in your work here, if you need."

A Master's Degree in Psychology? I knew that Nikita had not finished her studies; she was far from finishing.

Dr. Leocadio was surprised, naturally, but he soon recovered. Nikita was very beautiful in those days.

"I could use someone to take notes during my visits with Miranda, in fact. If you could help me with that, I would be very appreciative."

So it was that Nikita started attending the sessions, with the responsibility to write down everything that occurred there.

Some days passed. One night while Adriana was asleep, and I was starting to fall asleep, I heard once again those sounds in the wall from behind the bureau. Someone or something was knocking softly. The sounds came closer, and the bureau, the enormous, heavy bureau, began to move. Someone was trying to enter through the hidden door.

I was stiff with fear.

"Lea!", I heard an urgent whisper. "Open up!"

I hurried to inch the dresser away from the wall, to see my sister squeeze through the swinging door and into the room.

"You didn't know about the passageway, did you?", she asked with a certain tone of triumph in her voice. "Come on. There is a passage that runs between my room and yours."

This was, effectively, the case. We entered a narrow space that was nearly completely dark, and even with the oil lamps, you could see very little.

"How did you find out about this?", I asked her. "How did you dare to go in?"

"I heard voices. I wanted to know where they were coming from, who was speaking. Come on, let's investigate where this passageway leads."

I didn't want to investigate. I wanted to return to my bed and bury myself in the covers. But Nikita wouldn't let me.

We walked slowly, reaching out to touch the walls on either side. We went for a distance I couldn't calculate. I thought again of that night, that first night I spent in the house, when I became disoriented after leaving Miranda in her room, and the hours I spent, lost, in the house.

Finally, we came to the end of the passage and Nikita began to knock softly on the walls, looking for another door. It was difficult, but we eventually found the door into the storeroom; a cold space with metal shelves from floor to ceiling, filled with canned food, salt, dried beans. There were also towels, plates and silverware; all kinds of supplies necessary to live for a long time. What need did Diego have to store all this? The storeroom also made me uneasy because of the cold wind that blew in along the floor. It felt like a place with its own will, a place that did not like me in the least.

"See? It's possible to go all over the house without anyone knowing. There must be more passages...."

"But, what's the need for all this?", I asked.

"Silly! You've been here a year and you still don't know? Don't you know how Diego is?"

I was quiet.

"He made these passages so he can wander anywhere in secret. He has the need to listen to conversations that don't include to him, to know things that are not his concern; he wants to know everything!"

We returned to my room, groping our way down the narrow hall.

"If you keep going, you come to my room. Come on."

I didn't feel at all like going, but it was as she said; soon we got to her room. She had left the swinging door partially open, otherwise we never would have found it. The passageway was like a labyrinth, a dark and secret set of tunnels, and if you didn't know they were there, you could never find them.

"Don't say anything to Adriana about this", she said.

"Of course not", I said, a bit miffed.

I sat on the edge of her bed.

"What's wrong Lea?", my sister asked anxiously.

I didn't know what was wrong with me. Where had that intrepid young woman gone, that woman who came to Mexico with nothing a year ago? How had she changed into this nervous, timid creature?

I didn't sleep well that night, nor during many others.

33

Leonora
The Stud Horse

We entered a long period in which things did not change very much. We seldom left the house, only when Barbara would come and take us out if Diego were on a trip. Diego, for his part, travelled frequently; he went to London, to New York, or often to meetings in other parts of Mexico or the Caribbean. Sometimes he would return very tan, or smelling of cigars, or with a carton of books, or with several paintings rolled up under his arm.

In his absences, Nikita and I went through the house, looking for evidence of Rosa, but we could discover nothing. It was impossible to look through everything; the house was too immense and too full of things. The house kept its secrets very well.

In my first days and months in his house, I asked Diego very often about Rosa, using as a pretext the idea that knowing something about her would help me teach Miranda, but he evaded all my questions, just as Miranda did. It was if the two had agreed to hide from me everything related to my sister. So, in the face of so much obstinance, and with the passage of time, I stopped asking.

And poor Adriana. She remained as backward as ever. It made me sad to admit it, but it appeared there was no remedy. She had learned to read in Brussels, but she read monotonously, with no enthusiasm or understanding. She had a huge capacity for memorization, but later when I asked her about the meaning of the text, she couldn't answer. It was as if she lacked all intuition. She couldn't synthesize what she learned; she could only repeat it. And her hearing remained as impaired as ever. If she were not directly in front of the person speaking, able to see the person's face, she appeared not to hear anything. I asked Dr. Leocadio if he would administer a hearing test on her, and he did, but found nothing wrong with her ears. The problem was deeper. With great delicacy he told me he could try to treat her, but it would be very expensive. He told me how much, and even using all my savings it was impossible.

There were also difficulties between Adriana and Miranda. They did not get along well. Miranda had little patience for my little sister. She preferred to read over playing games. And Adriana had no ability to involve her in games anyway. She would become infuriated when I would give praise to Miranda for her academic work, and I would have to invent some kind of prize for her as well, to pacify her.

With Cecilio, Adriana did play, but often the games ended in shouts or tears. Cecilio took tremendous advantage of her; despite being much younger, he was more astute. There were uncountable instances of me finding them playing together in some far away corner of the house, and I would overhead Cecilio maliciously tormenting my sister. He led her to believe anything at all, with the goal of taking away a particular toy, or getting away with any trick.

And the stomachaches and the headaches continued. Adriana at times would refuse to eat the food the Mrs. Poncia prepared, and asked me to do it. Then Poncia would get angry and suspicious and she would hide the food that I needed. She knew that I was afraid to go into the storeroom, so when I would ask for this or that item, she would tell me it was there, in order to force me to enter. All these various problems, with Adriana, with Cecilio, with Poncia, all these issues kept me very busy.

Now Miranda. There are so many things to say about a her that I could spend an entire day doing that without repeating myself. At the other end of the spectrum from Adriana, Miranda had tremendous powers of intuition. She astounded me with the ideas she expressed, the mental connections she made between things. For example, once she said that Minx and Sancho Panza resembled each other.

"How?", I asked.

"Both of them are very loyal to their friends."

"That's true."

"And they believe the things that their friends tell them, and that makes the things true."

Truth and fantasy, how did these work in her mind? In that time, I didn't put a lot of importance in how she thought about this; I merely marveled at her powers of synthesis. It wasn't until many years later that I looked back and regretted my lack of attention. I should have questioned her more closely, but I did not.

She was an avid reader; *La Celestina, Lazarillo de Tormes*, the stories of the *Conde Lucanor*; the old classics in Spanish were what we found in the bookstore for the blind. The appetite of this little girl for fiction knew no end.

And every day she played the piano better. She listened untiringly to the wind-up gramophone, listening intently in order to then re-create the notes on the piano. She always began her practice sessions with *Für Elise*, that simple melody that always gave me a shiver down my spine.

Miranda did her school lessons very competently: history, math, sciences. She was coming along well in English and French as well. The only thing that preoccupied me about her academic progress was her inclination to ask me things, sometimes via Minx, that I didn't know and I would have to do my own investigation in order to answer her correctly. She asked me once how magnets work, exactly. Another time, it was why things fall when you let them drop, instead of rising up; why it's not possible to leap into tomorrow just as you leap from one place to another. She, or more often, Minx, would not be satisfied with the simple answer; they wanted to know the reason, the complete reason.

But what intrigued Minx the most were colors. She wanted to know what colors were like; if it were possible to taste them, or distinguish them by the touch of the hand. Diego had told her that blue was the most dangerous color and she wanted to know why.

To these questions and many others, I worked to fashion an explanation that was adequate, but often I had to just invent something because it was just too perplexing. And every time I did that, I sensed that she knew I was fabricating. It was impossible to hide from her something she really wanted to know.

And Diego? How did he act towards me? What did I feel for him? How did we live there, in that labyrinthine house in the country, he and I, and all the others?

To go straight to the truth: I loved him, and I loved my life there, despite its difficulties. I really, really loved him. I was desolate whenever he travelled; I was desperate for a word of friendship from him; I died of jealousy when I thought about the things he shared with other people. I loved him, Diego Alba, the famous painter, the burly man of big gestures, I loved him without being able to show him one drop of my affection.

I knew very well how I had gotten to that state. Diego had captivated me with his way of being, his appetites and his abilities, just as Rosa had been captivated by him. I fell in love with him for his laugh, his deep voice, his care for the children (including Adriana, who was not related to him at all). I fell in love with his paintings, the majority of which he let me see; human figures, or geometric shapes, with vivid colors, sensual forms. I fell in love with his big hands, his vigorous walk, his imagination. And on top of all that, I felt the power of his ability to love; that is, if one day he were to fall in love with me, it would be explosive.

But I couldn't let myself express any of that. I repressed it. I fell quiet, did not speak. I paid no attention to my interior voice, to my own desires. Why? Because the memory of my father's deception still burned. Because I was very afraid to give myself over to anyone. Because I was changed and damaged by the lack of a father to look over me, that man who had abandoned us. Because of the fear of what my mother would think about me now, about the string of lies I've told, the falsity of my story in order to gain entrance into Diego's life. Because I didn't have the advice of a mother or of an older sister. Because of Rosa. Because I'm stupid, blind and introverted. Because of all this.

I had begun to go a little bit off track, there in that complicated house, on the outskirts of a city I hardly knew, living a peculiar life in a very irregular fashion. It was reasonable to imagine that I was having trouble knowing myself. Nikita didn't help me much, not because she wouldn't but because she was suffering with her own problems. She had abandoned her studies and all that that entailed - independence, freedom, a future profession – in order to join me. I, for my part, felt for Diego a profound sentiment, far from any logic, far from any reason, and more powerful than either.

As for Diego, he always treated me well, spoke nicely to me. I was certain he enjoyed my company, that he liked to talk to me, to know my opinions about things. We conversed a lot. Nevertheless, he always kept a part of himself hidden. He never spoke about the past, about his life before my arrival. That was a prohibited topic. Nor did he reveal everything about his character; he always guarded certain aspects of his personality. At times, in the middle of an animated conversation about art, or about an upcoming trip, topics about which he normally would talk freely, he would stop, as if he regretted letting me see what he would say next, as if he were on the brink of telling me something he shouldn't. You could say that on the one hand, I knew Diego Alba very well, but on the other, I hardly knew him. I remember that that period as one of continual desperation. I was living in an almost unbearable tension.

And Nikita. Now, Nikita.

At first we only spoke of the most trivial things. We didn't talk about the past and I could hardly get an idea about her life in Paris. Nikita showed little interest in the occurrences in the house apart from her sessions with Dr. Leocadio. They were the only things that solicited a response in her. Whenever the day of a visit grew close, the night before Nikita would paint her nails, wash and set her hair, cover her face with creams, and she would go to bed early in order to get up early and finish her beauty regime. Her process of artificial attractiveness was very complicated.

When Nikita first met Dr. Leocadio, she had told him that she knew how to take dictation, and in this way she could write down the conversations so faithfully and quickly. But in an unguarded moment, she confessed that she didn't know it at all and to hide that fact, she simply wrote down more or less what she remembered, or invented things so that the sessions followed some sort of logic.

It was during this period that the story of the stud horse happened.

The Alba's house had what we called "the corral"; a large open area at the rear of the house where Diego liked to put his canvases that were too big to fit in his studio, while he was working on them. The corral had high walls and complete privacy. The only entrance was through the studio, so if Diego came in and locked the door behind him, it was impossible to see what happened in there.

Or so we thought. One day when I was running after the children, I discovered that it was indeed possible to see what happened in there. An unoccupied room had a window very high up, all covered in dust and cobwebs, where, if I stood on a tall chair, I could see a part of the corral. That day, I sent the children away and took a look.

Diego was there, standing, rubbing himself. He had not lowered his trousers and the smooth fabric outlined a penis, how did I put it in my diary? Grandiloquent. That seemed to be the correct term. I can still see it now, in all its parts, all its curves, in its magnificent state of tension. I watched for a while, but then, getting embarrassed, I got down from the chair.

One day there arrived at the house an enormous cardboard tube with a huge canvas rolled up inside it. When it was extended, it covered the entire studio. So Diego constructed a special easel and set it up in the corral. There he stayed for several days without leaving. When he had finished the easel, he came to dinner, telling us that the painting was going to be entitled "The Stud Horse", and to paint it he needed a real horse.

He wasted no time in finding one. What he brought back was a beautiful creature; huge, with a shiny mane and hard, defined muscles. The children were in a delirium of delight with the horse, who, actually, was not very tame and with whom we had to be very careful. Whenever he set off galloping around the corral, his testicles would make a rhythmic whapping sound as they were flung from side to side. Even Miranda asked what the sound was, and Diego nor I knew how best to answer her.

"That's his balls, silly", said Cecilio. Diego laughed, but I was annoyed. I was sure that she would ask me again later. Besides, Miranda was so far from being a silly person! Cecilio's attitude bothered me quite a bit. He was always looking for ways to demonstrate his supposed superiority over Miranda.

So, we had a real horse in the corral, along with quantities of horse manure, which Poncia had to gather up and dispose of far from the house.

One night, very late, I heard movements from the corral, voices. I was afraid to wander about at night, but larger than my fear was my desire to see what was going on. I went to the studio, but the door was locked, so I went to my secret window and peered through.

There was Diego, in front of his canvas, painting in silence. Sprawled across the horse's back was a girl. She was nude, face down, with her arms loose and hanging down, and her face lying in the horse's mane. The horse was antsy and the girl kept sliding from one side to the other on its slippery back. Diego was in a bad mood, occasionally stopping to paint and saying "damn animal", and trying to calm the majestic beast. Various times the girl would sit up to complain or to reposition herself. She was very young, very pretty, with high, firm breasts and curiously large aureoles.

I couldn't see the canvas, but I was dying of curiosity. Then I died of jealousy as I watched the girl get down from the horse and come up to Diego, where he left his paintbrush to caress her body, paying special attention to her breasts, biting the nipples and leaving them red and inflamed. The girl moaned in pleasure. They left the canvas and the horse behind, and entered the studio.

This same thing happened five times. I know because I couldn't avoid hearing, in the night, very late, those same sounds, sensing those same movements, the same moaning. Five nights without sleeping, enduring the jealousy.

Diego never let us see The Stud Horse. As soon as it was finished, he rolled up the canvas, putting back into its mailing tube, and sent it off.

But that was not the end of the story. A few days later, Nikita came to my room.

"I HATE Diego", she said a propós of nothing.

"What do mean?"

She was furious; her eyes full of fire.

"He has a woman here. He sleeps with her, here. In the house."

"So?", I asked, trying to maintain a neutral tone in my voice

"Didn't you know that…. well… oh, why should I hide it from you? Diego and I have been, for some months….."

"For some months…?", I asked, my hysteria growing inside me.

"You know how Diego is."

"Yes, but what I don't know is how you are."

The effort involved in keeping my composure was enormous, nearly impossible.

"How I am? I am the way I am. I do what I want with my own body. Besides, at this point, who is going to care?"

I felt the walls of my world come tumbling down. Nikita, with Diego…..

"You should be ashamed of yourself", I said. "Diego is old. He could almost be your father."

Nikita seemed to shrink, as if to create a distance from her own words.

"Maybe that's why I got involved. I felt the lack of a father, and Diego took advantage."

"But you accepted it! You let him take advantage of you!"

I went towards her and grabbed her shoulders. In that moment, Nikita lost all her bravura and her anger. It was if the touch of my hands loosened the bonds of her prison. She began to cry.

"I'm so afraid. Diego does so many things to me. He nearly breaks me in two."

Her words made me burn.

"So, why do you let him?"

"I can't help it."

I waited for my sister to explain.

"He's always very gentlemanly at the beginning. He compliments me, he gives me pretty things. But then afterwards, my whole body hurts. I swear to myself not to do it again, but I always fall. I don't know what's happening to me, why I can't be stronger."

I knew why. Diego held the same power over me. I felt as defenseless as Nikita; as bereft of free will as she was.

"Let's leave here", she begged. "Let's go to the city."

I didn't know what to tell her. The salary I received was growing in the bank, but it was far from being enough to start anew. Besides, I didn't want to leave Miranda. I didn't want to leave Diego.

We were a long time in my room, both of us crying; one with tears on her face, and the other with tears in her heart.

34

Leonora
Nikita Speaks

On the one hand, I had nothing I needed to forgive Nikita for. Her relations with Diego were her own business; I had no claim on him. I am simply the teacher, nothing more. The only thing I could rightfully do was to chastise her for giving herself to a man she didn't love.

But on the other hand, I felt my insides twist, thinking about what they had done together. Those hands that I wished had caressed me, had caressed her; that mouth that I wished would kiss mine, had kissed hers instead. My own sister. It was a thousand times worse than with the woman and the stud horse. To have her in front of me, living here with me, where Diego could still find her, was intolerable.

But she was in such a bad state, that I couldn't hold on to my ire for long. She was crying as if her life were ending; completely undone.

"You don't know about the things that happened to me in Paris", she said between sobs.

I was confused. I couldn't imagine what had happened there to hurt her so.

"Tell me, then."

"I need something to drink. I feel faint", she replied.

In my room I kept some bottles of white wine. I hurried to open one and served her and myself a full glass. After downing the glasses, I poured us two more.

"After what happened with Papa, I was happy to escape from Brussels, happy to go to Paris. I was ecstatic with the idea of studying at the Sorbonne. Can you imagine? Such a prestigious university. In Paris. The city of love. Everything so beautiful."

Nikita sighed.

"But the classes were difficult, more difficult that I had thought: chemistry, biology, physics. I didn't get good grades. I didn't feel capable of doing the work."

"Why didn't you ever tell me?"

"Because I knew that you were having a hard enough time in Brussels, with Adriana and with your work and all. I knew your life was hard and I didn't want to add to that."

"Oh, Nikita!", I cried. I hugged her, suffering once more the effects of our family's breakup. "You should have told me."

"There's more. I met a boy. He helped me with my studies. We fell in love."

Now it was my turn to sigh.

"You shouldn't have let yourself become embroiled with someone so soon. So much had just happened, the things with Papa and then our mother."

"It was precisely what happened with Papa that sent me in that direction. I was so needy. And there he was, in my path."

I served her more wine. White wine doesn't do any damage, which is what Diego says.

"What happened then?"

"What had to happen. I got pregnant and he gave me money to end the pregnancy."

"Oh no!"

"He didn't want to marry me, he didn't want to be a father, and a few months later, he left me, saying that he couldn't stand listening to my regrets any longer."

Nikita started sobbing again.

"I loved him….. but….. I ended up….. hating him. I hate him. I hate him. Just like I hate Diego."

"Forget about that boy. He isn't worth the tears."

I felt a great relief then, because now I could forgive Nikita completely. Not just that, but the stifling silence that had surrounded her since her arrival in Mexico, was broken. We talked all night, remembering things about our family, analyzing the past, crying, drinking wine, crying again. I found myself close to her once more; sisters in blood and in spirit. But we had so much to cry about, so many losses, so much pain.

35

Leonora
Between a Rock and a Hard Place

Nikita had recuperated by the next visit of Dr. Leocadio, but I had not. I felt so emotionally unstable that I considered becoming his patient, or at the very least, asking for some medical advice. I couldn't sleep. I couldn't eat. The only thing that made me feel better was teaching the children. But I did it mechanically, hoping that none of them would notice.

With regard to Diego, what can I say? We had dinner together every evening, we spoke, we interacted, but everything happened under a barely-concealed fury. I know that Diego noticed, but he never remarked on it, nor changed his manner. I even began to believe that the incident with the stud horse, with Nikita and all that, didn't affect him at all. But then I observed him several times, very late at night, in the corral doing strange things. He would stand at a distance from the canvas, load his brush with a quantity of paint, and throw the paint wildly, where the colors would crash against the cloth with a loud sound. Diego was like the tyrant in the Greek myth: Poseidon with his trident punishing the waves.

As for me, I felt trapped, tied to a thing that did not belong to me. For Diego I felt a furtive love, more intense perhaps, for being hidden. There was no one I could talk to about this; I could hardly admit it to myself. Jealousy ate me up from inside if I thought about Diego with other women; women I didn't know or would ever know. Whenever he was away on a trip, I imagined that he was thinking of me, just as I was thinking of him. It's easy to imagine that the universe works on the basis of some kind of balance, some kind of yin and yang. But part of me knows that it is not true. And I know that Diego has many other places in which to focus his attention.

Then I scolded myself. I had little evidence that he cared for me; that anything that he did meant anything. Diego had never promised me anything more than housing and a salary. Why did I persist in holding out hope of something more? It was unreasonable.

Yes, clearly, reason had nothing to do with it. I thought about Rosa, my able and capable sister, so organized, so logical. She had fallen under the sway of Diego as well. And then something terrible happened to her. In my mind reigned a chaos. Fear and love mixed. But always, always, I ended up remembering the kiss that he had given me on the hand; that kiss never lied.

Little by little, with the passing of time, I recuperated somehow. Diego went away for several months; this helped me reestablish the rhythm of the days. Nikita, too, became more tranquil, and stopped pleading with me to leave the house. The visits of Dr. Leocadio and her work with him helped her reestablish her self-esteem.

At night, when I sat down to write, to note everything that had happened that day, I always asked myself the same question: in some way, did I have a relationship with Diego? Many people would say no. Many would say that he is a womanizer, that he's selfish, incapable of loving anyone but himself, dedicated solely to pleasure and sin. But they don't see him here, talking to me about his art, an artist in the fullness of his talent, of his craft; they don't see him with the children, interested in the most minimal details of their day, in their happiness. They don't see him when he kisses my hand; they don't see the tenderness he shows me then.

It was during this time that the children were studying the Greek myths. I had read out loud to them the story of Odysseus; of the sirens that called to him, trying to get him to abandon his quest, of his sailing the seas between two monsters, unsure which was more dangerous, the storm Charybdis or the beast Scylla, she of the eight heads and a great appetite for eating sailors. Miranda, with her keen intuition, asked me once:

"Miss Luz, you are between Scylla and Charybdis, aren't you?"

"What do you mean?"

"In between two dangerous things. Two things that could harm you", she said, as if explaining something to an idiot.

"And what are those things?"

"Oh, you know what they are."

She wouldn't say any more. In that moment I felt bothered, annoyed, annoyed with the world and with myself. When in that moment Nikita asked me something simple, I nearly yelled at her in reply. Blinking rapidly, she asked, surprised:

"What's wrong with you?"

"I'm sick of this. All this. Even you."

"Me!? What have I done?"

"You, well…."

"Look", she said, "we can't be on the outs. We can't argue. Miranda and Adriana need us." Then she hugged me hard.

"I know you're hiding something", she continued. "And I know that it's weighing on you. Tell me what it is. You'll feel better."

But I couldn't tell her. To speak to her about my feelings for Diego would serve only to distance her from me. For Diego, my sister felt only disdain, hatred, distrust. To imagine that I cared for him would cause her to see me differently. She would lose trust in me. No, not that. Never that. Once more I felt trapped between the sword and the shield, between Scylla and Charybdis, besieged by the danger of revealing the truth about myself.

Then, some days later, my sister saved my life.

In the dark of the early morning, she came to my room through the inner corridor to tell me that she had found the portrait of Rosa. She spoke out loud, but you could hardly hear her for the sharp whistling of the wind. These kinds of summer storms passed occasionally, and they always made me uneasy. The air became violent; as if the spirits of the land surrounding Diego's house, which were under the dominion of Mrs. Poncia, were trying to break us apart, to separate us from the house, making me and Nikita into intruders.

"It's in a cupboard in the storeroom."

"How did you find out where it was?"

"Last night I was passing by Diego's studio, and I saw him and Poncia wrapping it. By the amount of padding they put on it, they must plan on mailing it."

"Could you see the address?"

"Somewhere in Cuba. Then Poncia took the package to the storeroom, put it in a cabinet, locked it and said some words in her idiom; her usual spells. Let's go get it."

Nikita had been saying for some time that if she found the painting, she would take it. The idea made me afraid; surely Diego would notice the theft. And the spells and witchcraft of Poncia... I knew them well. Over every item that she used in her daily work, she would murmur some words. I had heard and seen her do this countless times.

"Let's go", repeated my sister.

We went to the storeroom and Nikita took a key from her pocket. She opened the cupboard and there was the package, the address in Cuba marked clearly on the front. We looked closely.

"Lea, doesn't it make you uneasy to know that Diego is still involved in socialist politics? I mean, Rosa got into that and look what happened. She lost everything she had in Chile, even her husband."

We looked at the address. Surely Diego had dealing with the Cubans, with the communists. I mulled over Nikita's words.

"Do you believe that Rosa committed suicide?", I asked her.

"No. She had a very strong character, too strong to give up that easily."

"And, I suppose that Diego loved her, right? If he loved her, she wouldn't have had a motive to do it."

"Diego doesn't love anyone but himself", my sister said dryly.

"He loves the children. Miranda. Cecilio, even Adriana."

"What he feels for Miranda is something else. Something like an obsession. And with regard to Cecilio and Adriana..."

Our conversation came to an abrupt halt. From outside came a sound that seemed to come from the center of the earth; a guttural, deep groan. Then there was a tremendous shock. The whole house shook, then the sound came again; a terrifying, god-like noise.

"It's the wind!", shouted Nikita. "We've got to get out!"

She ran, but I couldn't move a muscle. I was paralyzed by fright.

"Run!", she screamed. When she saw that I didn't move, she came back. Pushing and shoving she moved me to the door that led outside. We ran a short distance and as we turned to look, we saw one of the enormous eucalyptus trees fall. And as it fell, it dragged another one down with it. The two fell squarely over the storeroom, where just moments before, Nikita and I had been. I couldn't breathe; the air was trapped in my lungs.

Then the wind died down a bit and we came closer. The leaves were still trembling, like little birds all trying to escape their cages. The roots of the trees, which extended a great distance from the trunks, had brought up a tremendous amount of earth, leaving great holes, and uprooting the foundations of the house. The storeroom now was roofless, invaded by millions of branches broken in millions of ways.

Mrs. Poncia came up to us.

"So you see what happens when nosy people go where they shouldn't", she said with an unpleasant smirk.

She customarily treated us very disrespectfully, and we were used to it, but the rudeness of her words now left us astonished.

"It was the wind, Mrs. Ponica, which is a natural force", said Nikita, after a moment.

We didn't tell Diego that we had been in the storeroom. It wasn't important. And now, Rosa's portrait was buried there, possibly destroyed.

Diego took five days to clear the area, and as soon as he could, he began reconstructing the walls. He worked at an accelerated rhythm, as if he had something burning inside him, or some kind of fear, or panic, barely controlled. While he worked, Nikita and I tried to find the painting, but it was useless. We had to pretend to be innocently going about, but Diego knew that something more was afoot. Nor was it possible to ask him anything: he had the painting under lock and key precisely to keep it away from prying eyes.

The near-recuperation and then the loss of the painting saddened me enormously. When it disappeared the first time, I resigned myself, but now, to have it so close and lose it again filled me with a desolating sense of loss.

And that Diego would so casually send the painting away? The portrait of someone you have loved should occupy a very special place in your heart. How could he do this? Besides, despite the fact that he painted it, the painting really belonged to us; to me and Nikita, and especially to Miranda; Miranda who hardly had time to know her own mother and who would cherish a portrait of her, if she could only have it.

36

Leonora
A Bridge to the Past

One evening, late, Nikita came to my room.

"I have to tell you both something", she said. Adriana was sleeping, but sat up when she felt Nikita come in.

"To Adriana, too?", I asked. But immediately I realized, by her expression, first of happiness at being included, and then of sadness, that I had hurt my sister's feelings.

"Of course to Adriana too", she said. From a paper bag she took a small plastic bag. Inside, were some cookies resembling the *gaufres* that we used to eat in Brussels.

"But, how?", sounded in chorus my voice and Adriana's.

"I made them. With Poncia's help."

I felt the little hairs on the back of my neck rise up at the mention of Mrs. Poncia, to think that she was in any way involved in the confection of the cookies. But surely Nikita would not have permitted any culinary intervention. So, we ate the *gaufres*, one after the other. But not long after,

Adriana began to whimper. She dug her fists into her stomach, as if she were trying to keep the pain from spreading.

"Give her the medicine that Barbara got us", said Nikita.

I gave her the pills, trying to quiet my worries. Whenever I spoke to Nikita about my fears regarding Mrs. Poncia, she laughed at me. My sister doesn't believe in the supernatural.

While we waited for the medicine to take effect, Nikita spoke, first of light things, then when she saw Adriana was better, she began.

"I know that Diego had something to do with Rosa's death. Something definitive."

A long moment of silence passed.

"What?"

Adriana no longer was whimpering, but rather writing at top speed in her journal, looking at us intensely as we spoke.

"I found this."

She showed us a small metal box, decorated with painted flowers. I recognized it as one that had been in our house in Brussels. Our mother had kept recipes in it. From the box Nikita took out an envelope addressed to María Luisa Fernández, #30, Rue de la Science, Brussels. It was in the handwriting of Rosa. The envelope had stamps, but it was clear that it had never reached its destination. Nikita took the letter from the envelope.

"Where did you find it?"

"In the kitchen. In Poncia's things."

Adriana and I waited, hardly breathing. Nikita began to read.

"It says here that Rosa distrusted Diego. She was afraid of him, afraid that he didn't believe that she had divorced in Chile.'

"Divorced? Rosa never got divorced from René. I don't understand."

"Nor I."

Nikita thought hard. "Could it be that Rosa lied to him for some reason? Did she hide René's death from him?"

I shrugged helplessly.

–This is all too confusing, Nikita.

Paying no attention to my protest, she continued: "Then, here it accuses our mother of having recognized Diego when she came here to Mexico, at the Hotel Geneve. She writes that it appeared that mother knew him from before."

"Maybe they had met? Diego travels a lot."

"Why hide it, though? No, Lea. I think that Diego and our parents were involved in something that they didn't want Rosa to know about. When Rosa started to investigate, Diego felt like he was going to be found out."

"Are you saying he killed her? That is crazy."

Nikita shook her head.

"What did Diego tell you, exactly, about the day of the accident?", asked Nikita.

"That Rosa drank a substance that he uses for painting, believing that it was melon water."

"Did he see her drink it?"

"Not exactly. But he surmised that it happened that way because of the similarity of the liquids and the bottles they were in."

"Do you see?", she said triumphantly. "He didn't see her. Her death could have been due to something else completely. Something that had nothing to do with what she did or didn't drink. Besides, it's ridiculous to think that Rosa wouldn't have detected the taste."

"Diego said that the results of the tests proved that it was a poisoning."

"Bah! We're in Mexico. There is corruption at all levels. He could have easily paid to have the results changed, or changed them in some other way, what do we know?"

"That Rosa distrusted Diego doesn't mean…."

Nikita didn't let me finish.

"Yes, it does. If I were the judge, I would say that there is enough evidence to proceed."

"These are just guesses, Nikita", I told her, anguished. "We can't be sure of anything. We don't have all the information."

Nikita tilted her head to one side.

"There is a person who could fill in the gaps."

"Who?"

I had no idea about whom she was speaking. Nikita waited a moment, wanting me perhaps, to say something.

"Papa."

"Papa!"

"Yes. A lot of time has passed now. Maybe at this point…"

"At this point, nothing", I said heatedly. "He abandoned us, Nikita! No, I'm not willing to forgive him for that."

"It's not a question of forgiveness, Lea. Don't mix the two things."

"For me it's one single thing. The distrust I feel for him makes everything he says - if indeed we could get him to say anything – to be a lie, an excuse.

"It's possible that there is a reasonable explanation for what our father did in Brussels", she said hopefully. "Maybe something related to the politics of his job, or...."

She didn't finish. The history of my father during those last years was impossible to know.

We finished the wine, but not with any happiness for the disagreements between us. Meanwhile, Adriana wrote at full speed, but later, when I tried to read her journal, I understood nothing. I had no way to know if Adriana understood what we had been talking about, or if for her, everything was as confused as her garbled drawings.

That night I dreamed that Diego was making love to me and it was one of those dreams that you feel in your entire body. I knew that I was dreaming, but not for that reason was it any less pleasurable. In the morning, I stretched luxuriously, not wanting to chase away the dream. But the delicacy was ruined by the interruption caused by Adriana. She was standing at the foot of her bed, nude from the waist down. She was crying. The interior door was ajar, but I was sure that I had closed it securely the night before.

Even in her most lucid moments, Adriana struggles to express herself; now it was impossible. I felt strangled by the enormous weight of the anguish I carried inside; unable to help my poor sister, unable to know what, if anything, happened to her last night. Last night, the night that Diego Alba made love to me in my dreams.

37

Leonora
The Portrait

We were still hurting from the loss of Rosa's painting; we were still recovering from the upset of the falling trees and the destruction of the storeroom; we were still trying to see if anything truly awful had happened to Adriana in the night; we were still plagued by doubts as to how Poncia had gotten ahold of the letter Rosa wrote to our mother; we were still struggling with all this, when Diego asked to paint my picture.

I didn't know how to answer at first. Through my mind passed an infinity of things: the girl from the stud horse episode, all that had happened with Diego and Nikita, what issues Diego had with Barbara, what really happened to Rosa when she died, and how, exactly, I felt about all this. Plus, there was this great unknown: I didn't know if Diego was aware of my knowledge about any of these things. We hadn't spoken directly together about any of them, but nor had he tried to hide them. In this way, the crevasse of secrets between him and me deepened.

"Look, I thought to position you in this way: with your back half-turned away but the face in profile; your body in the shade but your face in the light", he said.

This was the exact position of Rosa in her portrait. Surely he had not forgotten that? What did it mean that he wanted to paint me in the exact same way? I thought about Rosa and Diego, in their lives together as a married couple. To have your portrait painted is an intimate thing. Imagining myself under the gaze of the painter, just as he gazed at Rosa, gave me a certain uneasiness.

But on top of all that, I felt a tremendous happiness. To spend time with Diego was my most favorite activity. That he would paint me, that he would think about me in this way, that he would have the idea to paint me even, filled me with emotion. I fought to hide from him my overwhelming joy.

"If you allow me to see the work in progress", I told him.

I fought also, with the desire to tell him everything. Everything about my past, all. But then I reflected on the fate of Rosa, and of my mother, which reminded me that the world is a vast place, full of danger and mysteries, full people who lie and mislead, acts that shatter illusions. No. It was better for me to remain silent. It was better for me to continue to hide everything I felt for him. My job was to take care of Adriana and Miranda, to be a sister and a help to Nikita.

Diego spoke to me again about his desire to paint my portrait, and we went then to the studio. He put me in position. He moved my head about, inclining it first in one direction and then another. I felt his hands on my face, his skin on mine. I inhaled his fragrance, his heat.

Each time I sat for him was marvelous. I felt a nervous energy running up and down my body, the result of his penetrating gaze on me. I felt naked, as I had the very first time we spoke. I felt like an object of immense value: desired, appreciated. I felt that I was made of a finer material than just flesh and blood, fragile yet immensely strong, capable of absorbing the avalanche of concentration that he put on me.

While he worked he hummed songs that I also knew; melodies that Miranda played on the piano or sang. Miranda loved to sing wherever or at whatever time, and I often found myself humming those melodies as well. Hearing his voice while he worked simply added to everything. The experience of Diego painting me was something so sweet that I hardly had words to describe it.

He honored his promise and let me see the work in progress. I looked like myself, but prettier than in real life. Diego said it was one of his best works and it was obvious that he was very happy with it.

When it was done, he took it down from the easel and put it next to me, comparing the two figures. He smiled and took my hand to kiss it, even though it was only two o'clock in the afternoon and he was neither leaving nor returning from a trip.

"It's perfect Miss Mendoza", he said.

But perfection cannot last. When Diego returned to the studio later that day, he saw that the painting had been destroyed. Someone had thrown black paint all over it. The image of me, so pretty then, was now a blackened mess. Not just that, but the perpetrator had mixed dirt into the paint, causing a kind of mud to stick to it. The destruction was complete.

I went running to the studio when I heard his shouts. We looked together with terrified, angry eyes, at what was going to be a great triumph but was now nothing but an abject failure.

Cecilio came into the studio. We turned to see, but without really seeing him for the upset that afflicted us. Cecilio stood by the painting, as if he were waiting for us to say something.

"Do you know anything about this?", Diego asked him.

"Amelia and I were playing here, but I went out a while ago."

"And Amelia?"

"She stayed behind. I don't know what she was doing."

"Amelia would never do something like this", I started to say, but I quickly stopped.

Adriana did behave very badly at times, always complaining about the unfair treatment she thought she received. She was terribly jealous of the abilities of the other children. She recognized that she was not as talented as Miranda and Cecilio, but she didn't know how to change that. Adriana was stuck in a very small world, out of which she glimpsed the light that shone on others without being able herself to leave the dark. I began to doubt. Could it have been Adriana who destroyed the painting?

"Go look for her, Cecilio. Bring her here", ordered Diego.

When she entered the studio, I knew immediately that it had not been her. She came in with the kind of innocence that cannot be faked; not even the best actress in the world could have shown such innocence. Diego showed her the painting.

"What do you know about this?", he asked. Adriana looked intently at his face, deciphering his words as best she could.

"About what?"

"About this! This!"

"Well, it is a painting", she answered timidly.

Yes, it was a painting. Like many others Diego painted, neither more nor less unusual than any other. Adriana did not have the ability to understand that this painting, was in some way, different from any other. I looked at her hands; they were covered in black mud.

"What were you painting here with Cecilio?", I asked her.

From her mouth came words without meaning. I looked at Cecilio's hands. They were clean.

"And you didn't touch anything or throw anything?", I asked her desperately.

"No. No."

She tried to express herself; she was trying to say what was obviously very important, but she could not pronounce the words; it was only a mix up of sounds that were not even words at all.

"So, Cecilio left you alone in here?", Diego asked her.

"I went out", said the boy, interrupting. "I went to the kitchen. You can ask Mrs. Poncia", he protested.

Diego let loose a chain of vulgarities. He kicked the canvas, he shouted. But there was nothing more we could do. Cecilio would confess nothing and Adriana could not confess to anything.

When I went to the kitchen some moments later I saw a towel stained with black mud, as if someone had washed and dried their hands with it, but Diego was so furious that I didn't dare tell him. And what would I confirm, anyway?

The portrait never came into being, truncated like the love I felt for Diego, destined to never see the light of day.

It was then, after the episode of the ruined portrait, that Cecilio began to change. If before he obeyed Miranda or his father when they spoke seriously, now he cleverly squirmed away. If before, Diego would chastise him and the child would apologize, now his father's words had no effect. If before Diego would try and correct a misbehavior, all the while assuring him that it would make him a better person, now Cecilio was that person who cared nothing for the guidance of others. Something weakened in him; some kind of force took him over and began constructing the malleable, unstable center that came to define him later on. As a child, Cecilio loved Diego with an astonishing eagerness, to the degree that he imitated him in everything. He spoke like him, he painted his little pictures, he described things as Diego described them, using the same expressions; in everything Cecilio was the son of the painter. If before he demonstrated all of Diego's good qualities, now he demonstrated only his bad ones: rage, shouting, jealousy. He had changed from being simply a mischievous boy to an ill-intentioned young man. In my mind there was no doubt that he had ruined the painting, but I had to put those thoughts aside, together with all the other thoughts that caused me fear, those hidden things that made me anxious, a deep well of uncertainty that I could not see the bottom of.

38

Leonora
The Nuptials

The perversity of Cecilio continued unabated. He would look for Adriana supposedly to play, but really to make fun of her, to mock her. He would tell her that he loved her and that they would get married when they were older. He would take her far from the house and leave her there alone. When I would ask him, he would say he didn't know where she was, and hours later she would come back, sad and unable to answer my questions at all, not even in the fractured way that was her custom. When Cecilio would see her underthings hanging to dry, he would take them and make stains on them, and then put them out again on the line. The stains were horrible, just as if they were menstrual blood. He laughed openly when she tried to speak. Once, his attitude drove me so crazy that I grabbed his shoulders and began shaking him violently. I felt in my hands the force of the eagle from the door of the consulate, from the official seal of the United States; claws with arrows clutched in them, to defend the country. In that moment, Mrs. Poncia came in and shouted at me to let go of him. I felt such rage then, for them both, that I could hardly control myself.

From the beginning I had suspected that Cecilio was her son, but he never called her "mother" or "mama", nor showed her any kind of love that a son might show his mother. No one ever spoke of the mother of Cecilio, if she existed, and to think that perhaps Poncia and Diego had had a child together turned my stomach.

"Didn't you know that Diego goes often into the village, to her house?", asked my sister, surprised.

"For what?"

"Leonora! Don't tell me you are so naïve!"

It wasn't that I was naïve, but I refused to believed that this woman, she of the fleshy lips and the sunken eyes, this woman of rough character, this retrograde person with her evil spells and her malevolent beliefs, that she could attract someone like Diego, like my Diego.

So while Cecilio carried on in his alarming trajectory, Miranda became even sweeter, more understanding, more docile. Often we would go us four: Adriana, Nikita, Miranda and me, to the gardens for a picnic. There, in the fresh air, Adriana and Miranda would walk together, crouching down to smell the grass, listening to the birds' singing and trying to guess the kind of bird by its song, holding hands as they clambered about. In those moments Adriana could express herself very well. But at other times, when Miranda preferred to play the piano or read instead of interacting with my sister, Adriana would return to her usual state of incoherency. It made me feel like crying to see how the influence of something good could change Adriana so fundamentally, the same as how something bad damaged her so much.

The relationship between Cecilio and Miranda was very odd, I thought. Cecilio never practiced his black arts on her, and she treated him with kindness. That was perfectly good, perfectly normal. But at times their way of interacting bordered on something adult, something like romance. They pretended to be boyfriend and girlfriend; they created mini-weddings in which the bride and groom might have a fight in front of the altar, or they would flee as the ex-boyfriend appeared, or the ex-girlfriend. Miranda was a child with a great interest in melodrama; for her, her invented world of dramatic conflicts was as real as the real world. These incidents bothered me; they seemed abnormal.

The worst came when I came upon Miranda and Cecilio kissing. I wanted to correct this misstep, but when I commented on it to Nikita she said it was simple infantile impulses, with little importance. According to her studies on childhood psychology, it would be counterproductive to put much attention on it because if we did, the children would think it more important and consequently have more interest, rather than less.

I was so worried about all this that I decided to consult Dr. Leocadio. But this didn't bear fruit either. The doctor said he would ask Miranda about it, but later, he told me that she denied it completely. Dr. Leocadio was in agreement with me on many things regarding the children, and this time I could see that he was truly concerned. But his hands were tied. The situation with Miranda was always so delicate that to pressure her could cause more problems than they solved. There were many occasions in which Barbara, the doctor, Nikita and I spoke together about how best to proceed, but we rarely came upon good solutions. The frustration was exhausting.

As was the sensation of seeing how Diego acted with this woman, Esmé Moreau. Miss Moreau, Mrs. Moreau. I had no idea of her marital status, but I had never seen a Mr. Moreau nor heard him spoken of, so I couldn't be sure. She owned the gallery in the city where Diego showed his paintings, and she was as elegant as could be imagined. She dressed well and smelled of expensive perfume. Her voice was lilting with a light French accent, and I came to hate her. She had a sports car that she drove very fast, and you could always tell when she had arrived from the impudent spray of gravel from under the tires.

As the gallery owner it was natural that Diego would pay her much attention. They were in business together. But it was too much attention. Nikita suspected that there was more than business going on between them, but I didn't want to believe it. Every time Esmé visited, I felt very low, very insignificant. I also once had clothes from Paris, even though now they were long gone; I also spoke French, but now from lack of practice it was rusty. I too, had opinions about art. But none of that mattered when she was around. Now, I wore common clothes purchased nearby, I smelled of the common soap that Poncia bought in the village. I didn't know how to drive a car. I wasn't the owner of an art gallery in the city. Whenever Esmé was around, the change in my life since leaving Brussels came home to me in a terribly pointed way; I felt again the loss of all the possibilities I once had, and I confess that I cried tears of rage each time Esmé made clear her dominion over Diego. Meanwhile I, being being nothing more than the teacher, had no rights to him whatsoever.

39

Leonora
The Summer Storm

It was a day of tremendous winds and confusion that something happened with Adriana and Dr. Leocadio.

Adriana always liked to go outside when one of these summer storms passed through. She loved to see how the enormous eucalyptus trees leaned from one side to the other; how the leaves were shaken in the air that seemed to come from all directions at once. She wasn't alarmed by the groaning of the thick white trunks, as if they were trying to embrace one another, or get away altogether. I can see her now, standing in the garden, smiling and watching the storm unfold. She would gaze for long minutes as the whiteness of the trees would suddenly be illuminated by a shaft of sunlight coming unexpectedly through the cloudy skies. I didn't like those storms; they made me uneasy, especially after the disaster of the trees falling on the house and destroying the storeroom. But Adriana loved them.

She liked to place herself in a good spot, far from the house, and look at herself in a hand mirror. I imagined that she was working on her pronunciation; trying to say the words and phrases that gave her such trouble in conversation. It seemed she didn't want anyone to see her doing this, but I managed to observe her a few times. Nor was it possible to hear exactly what she was saying; the wind took her voice away. Possibly it was the chance to speak loudly without being overheard that so captivated her, or gave her the courage to do it. Or maybe it was the ability to watch herself in the mirror? I didn't know.

That day I saw her leave the house with a happy face. Later, I was passing by the open door of the room where Dr. Leocadio customarily had his sessions with Miranda when I heard something that made me stop short. It was the voice of Adriana, more clear and coherent than normal.

"My sisters say you are a great psychiatrist."

I stopped in the hall, eager to hear what more would be said.

"A great psychiatrist?", answered the voice of the doctor. "I don't think so. There are questions that I cannot resolve, and I don't think I ever will be able to do so."

His voice had a sad, resigned tone that I had not heard before.

"I know what you are referring to, doctor." Adriana was eighteen then, and even though she was delayed academically and socially, I noted something very adult in her voice.

"No Amelia. You don't know. And even if you did know, these are not things we should be discussing. Listen, I asked you here for a reason."

Adriana waited.

"I would like to do some tests on you."

"What sort of tests?"

I stuck my head into the room; neither of them saw me.

"A test of your senses. I want you to look at something and tell me what it is."

Without waiting for her reply, the doctor turned to the bookshelves and searched for a book. Continuing to speak with his back to her, he said:

"You know what philosophy is, don't you?"

Adriana didn't react.

"I consider myself more a philosopher than a psychiatrist, although I'm not very good at either of those things."

Adriana appeared not to hear anything. Dr. Leocadio turned once again to her, and held out the book.

"It's a book", she said.

"Open it. On the first page there is a quote. I want you to read it to me."

> *The truth is like air; it's everywhere at once but it has no fixed point. That is why a good philosopher always begins with the lies."*

Adriana turned and I could now see her in profile. She frowned.

"I don't understand", she said to him.

"Amelia, you can distinguish between lies and the truth, isn't that right?"

My sister didn't say anything. A long silence passed.

"Very well", he said finally. He went to the desk where he kept, in a locked drawer, the journals that held the notes for his visits with Miranda. He took out one journal.

"Is the test over?", asked my sister.

"No. You know what this is, don't you?", he asked, showing her the notebook.

"Yes."

"Have you ever taken one of these from the drawer?"

Adriana looked uncomfortable.

"Sometimes the drawer is open", she said with difficulty.

From outside you could hear the whistling of the wind and the crashing of the leaves.

"And have you ever read anything? Or written anything in them?"

The wind was so loud that I couldn't hear her reply. Suddenly, there was a series of lightning flashes that illuminated the room like the flash of a camera. Adriana startled and ran out into the garden. After a moment of being startled myself, I came into the room.

"Ah, Miss Mendoza. It's good that you've come in. I wanted to show you something."

Dr. Leocadio opened the notebook and showed me a page. The margins were completely filled with drawings and scribbles; words in English, French, Spanish, all garbled and poorly spelled; the drawings were incomprehensible meanderings of arrows, hearts, boxes inside boxes; all the strange hieroglyphics that my sister used to express herself.

In among the writings I could distinguish the names of my family: Robert Burleigh, María Luisa Fernández, Nikita, Leonora, Adriana, Rosa. There appeared our address in Brussels: #30 Rue de la Science. I felt a stab of fear. There, in all that mess, were some truths that were clear and plain; but covered now by a thick layer of lies. I felt a storm inside me, like the one outside; a dizzy sickness that nearly took me to the floor.

"It's obvious that Amelia has been messing about with things that she shouldn't", commented the doctor.

I held on to the edge of the table in order to remain upright. I tried to think: what could I say to distract him from the notebook?

"I've also seen that the drawer is left unlocked", I said, as dryly as I could, given my state of mind.

Dr. Leocadio looked surprised. We usually treated one another with the utmost respect.

"I understand that you want to defend your sister, but we should correct her when she makes mistakes."

I didn't say anything.

"I'll speak to Barbara. Perhaps it has been an oversight of hers", he said, trying to bring the conversation back to its normally courteous tone.

I felt bad to have spoken to him like that. He is a very good person, an ally, a person who only wants to help, the same as Barbara. Both of them always did whatever they could to make any situation more tranquil, solve any problems they could in the house.

"I should tell you also that your sister has sought me out several times. She seems agitated. She mixes up her languages and I can't understand her very well. I don't know French or English."

Oh heavens. What else had Adriana said to him?

Into the room at this moment came Mrs. Poncia with her cleaning buckets and rags. I cursed the bad luck that brought her there at that moment: unsure of what she might have overheard.

Poncia went to the glass doors that led out to the garden. With her back to us she stood to look outside. I looked too. There was Adriana, standing in a vast area of lawn, shouting into the voice of the storm. You could see the veins in her neck standing out.

"Savage child", said Poncia. Then she pronounced some incoherent words with a smile that crossed her face. The wind made a penetrating sound in my ears, as if to deafen us. Poncia let drop her bucket and went out into the garden. It seemed she was after Adriana.

"Dr. Leocadio, can you go out and bring Amelia in?", I said urgently.

He nodded and went out.

Thinking as quickly as possible given my state of mind, I went to the desk drawer where he had returned the notebook. I tried to still my hands, which trembled. With difficulty I managed to find the page where my sister had scribbled, and yanked it out. I wasn't sure what I would gain by this, but at least the names of my family and our address wouldn't be available to be seen by just anyone. Those truths wouldn't be in there, in the open, if later Dr. Leocadio went looking for any lies.

The next time a summer storm came through, I tried to prevent Adriana from going outside, but I couldn't. Nor the other times, with other storms. My younger sister appeared to me to be getting worse, but I felt impotent to help her.

40

Leonora
The Visitor I

Seven years had passed since that first night that I spent in the Alba house. You may ask how it came that we stayed so long there. Speaking for myself, I can say that I did not miss the outside world; what I felt for Diego sustained me better than any nourishment that I could find there. Additionally, my teaching work filled me greatly. It made me feel necessary and useful. It got to the point that I even felt uneasy with the thought of leaving. What usefulness would I have out there? What would I do?

As for Nikita, I would say that it was the same, except that she did not admit it to herself. From time to time she would come up with some plan to leave: we would go to the city and start a school for damaged children; we would go to Morelia and work with Barbara at the institute; we would return to Brussels and…. At this point I would always remind her that we had under our care, a young blind girl and another one with many psychological problems. And very little money. My salary from Diego was not great; it was not enough to embrace any of Nikita's plans.

So we stayed.

In those seven years we saw the children grow up, learn their lessons, mature. Well, to tell the truth, we saw Adriana and Cecilio grow, but what we saw in Miranda was something more complicated.

Physically, Miranda changed little in that time. At twelve, she seemed the same as she was at ten. By the age of fifteen, she was taller, but at an age when other girls are starting to grow into their shapes as women, she still had the body of a child. At sixteen you could see some small curves, but they were hardly noticeable.

If physically she didn't change much, emotionally she demonstrated an astonishing sensitivity. She intuited things, guessed things, knew things that she should not have known. For example, Diego had told me early on that, whenever he travelled, his custom was never to tell anyone of the date of his return. This was to avoid misunderstandings, because often his plans changed at the last minute. But Miranda always knew, down to the hour, the time of his arrival. It was if she could read his mind.

I felt like she could read my mind as well, that she seemed to know me better than I knew myself.

"What is it that you're looking for, Miss Mendoza? I think you want something but you cannot get it, isn't that right?", she asked me once when she saw me more subdued than usual. I didn't answer, fearing that she might guess what it was by my voice or manner.

It was the year that Miranda turned seventeen that a man named Fernando Blau came. He was a painter from Barcelona that Diego had invited for a study course with him in Mexico. He was to stay in the house.

Fernando was around thirty, handsome and very clever. He had become famous in Spain for his sculptures. Diego showed me a photo of one. It was a large, irregularly-shaped stone, formed into a rough sphere. The surface was rough, and marked with several tunnels that penetrated it, inviting the insertion of a hand. Inside, according to Diego, the rock was polished to a skin-like smoothness and carved into vaguely biological shapes: noses, or mouths, or genitals; a delight to the hands which the eye could only imagine. Now, Fernando Blau was coming to Mexico, so that Diego could teach him to paint.

He arrived with an enormous amount of stuff: books, notebooks, paints, brushes and other materials for his art. He came also with an attitude of superiority that was nearly unbearable. He believed himself to be an expert in contemporary art, among other things. With Diego, he behaved in a defiant manner; to listen to them converse was like watching a boxing match. At times Diego would win with a convincing answer to a question, at times Fernando would win with a question whose answer Diego didn't know.

At first it seemed as if Diego went out of his way to leave Fernando alone with me. He looked for any reason to exit the conversation or leave the dinner early, but not without telling us to resolve some question, or solve some little problem. Whenever Nikita was with us, Diego would subtly discourage her from continuing to be there, making her uncomfortable in that way he knows. He gave Fernando and me jobs that we had to work together on, projects of his own that for some reason or another he couldn't finish, but that we could, as a favor to him.

Nikita said she thought Fernando to be very charming and open. She gave me as an example, the fact that he spoke genially with everyone. With Poncia he joked and listened to her long discussions about the events of the village; with Nikita he flirted lightly; with Dr. Leocadio he spoke seriously about psychology; with me he conversed of the ties between art and mathematics, a topic I had long been interested in. But underneath all his pleasantries, there lurked a self-regard that seemed to put him above others.

But it was in Miranda and Cecilio that Fernando worked his most profound effect. From the first moment of his visit, Miranda fixated on him. She sought out ways to be near him whenever possible, she defended him from the insults and laughter of Cecilio. Miranda was only seventeen, and even though they didn't appear on the outside, inside her were stirring the desires of a grown woman.

One day I saw them together. They were seated on a sofa in a hidden corner of the house. Miranda had her doll Minx in her hands. I couldn't hear what they were saying, but I saw that she showed the doll to him. Slowly he took it and examined it carefully. As they continued talking, Fernando began to undress the doll. With slow, deliberate movements he first removed the blouse, allowing those terribly pointed, hard breasts to be seen. The skirt had a tiny zipper which he lowered. Miranda seemed not to notice what he was doing, until suddenly, perhaps upon hearing the zipper, she put her hands over his to stop him. She took back the doll, with a startled look on her face. Then, she turned it over to expose the chest once again. At the tiny waist there appeared a stain or a defect, but as she raised it up I could see that there was a miniscule hook that would allow the torso of the doll to be opened. I couldn't see very well, and Miranda quickly covered it up. I was dying to see what this was about, but I knew it would be hard to get ahold of the doll since Miranda had a sixth sense about its location which prevented any investigation.

During all this, Fernando appeared to be in a sort of trance, that only disappeared when Miranda put her hands on his once again. It was if the touch of skin woke him up. Then he moved to sit more closely to her on the couch. This made me very uneasy. Miranda was young, very naïve, while Fernando was older, came from a different world, and had surely been with one or more women in his life. Miranda had no defenses to save herself from an attack from this experienced sculptor.

They remained talking for a long time but I was afraid that if Fernando looked up, he would see my face pressed to the glass from the window of the adjoining room, so I left.

From that day on I tried to intervene whenever I saw them together, but I was not always successful. Moreover, Miranda became annoyed whenever I did that, and since she never ever got angry with me, I worried. I didn't want to alienate her.

With Cecilio and Fernando things went poorly. Cecilio was terribly jealous, which prompted his horrendous behavior. He stole things from Fernando's room and buried them in the corral, he ridiculed his Spanish accent, he dirtied his clothes which hung drying on the line, he spat in his plate of food when he thought no one was looking, he even left a perfectly formed turd just outside Fernando's door.

But Cecilio was always very astute. All these bad things he did in such a way that it was never possible to blame him specifically. He was always able to throw the blame to Adriana, and since my sister couldn't defend herself, she fell time and time again victim to his malicious tricks.

This topic came up daily between Nikita and me.

"Dr. Leocadio says that Cecilio doesn't like his father paying more attention to Fernando than to him. Also that Fernando's interest in Miranda bothers him and makes him anxious."

"So now he's analyzing Cecilio also?", I remarked.

"According to Dr. Leocadio, it's important to analyze the entire group; you have to look at the group dynamic in order to see the connections between the members. This helps to reach conclusions about the patient."

"And what does the doctor say about me?"

"You function as the mother that Miranda never had".

"She did have a mother", I protested. "Rosa was a good mother, I'm sure."

Mentioning Rosa always made me feel, on the one hand, brave and capable, as brave and capable as she was, but on the other hand, it made me anxious and worried. Something had happened to Rosa, there in that labyrinthine house, something that Diego didn't want to tell me and that the house prevented me from discovering.

"What else does the doctor say?"

"Well, he says a lot. But they are things that I shouldn't tell you. According to the treatment - which by the way, I studied in Paris - if you reveal anything to the participants in the group, it changes the dynamic. If you were to know certain things, you might change your behavior with regard to Miranda. And that is to be avoided."

"Besides", she continued, "it's not so much what the patient says but how the patient interprets what they themselves say. The patient can relate anything at all, and the facts or details don't really matter; what matters is what opinion the patient has about the facts. That's why the doctor continually asks Miranda what she thinks about her situation, how she herself interprets what she is telling him."

"And what does Miranda say? What opinion does she have of Fernando, for example?"

"I really shouldn't tell you", answered my sister.

"But Nikita! Don't be like that. How can you keep secrets from me? You know I love Miranda very much, that I only want to protect her from…."

"Maybe she doesn't need your protection", answered Nikita. "Miranda needs to live her life. She needs to feel the emotions that any person would feel."

"Miranda is not 'any person'", I said, annoyed. "She is innocent; a girl who knows very little about men."

"Lea, don't be so sure. You need to recognize that you don't know everything."

I left off discussing this with Nikita because I didn't want to add more fuel to the fire. I decided to find out about the psychology of Miranda by more subtle means.

With regard to Cecilio, I would have liked to hear what the doctor said about him, since every day his behavior was worse.

One day the doll Minx disappeared. I was completely convinced that it was Cecilio. Putting myself in the position of the psychiatrist, I deduced that he was inhibited in expressing his anger and his jealousy towards Miranda, and was forced to express it by stealing from her an object of great worth. Taking Minx away was the only punishment he could exert over her; since she never, ever treated him badly.

On the day that Minx went missing, Miranda tried to maintain a stiff upper lip.

"Minx knows where she is", she said. "She's not lost." But her voice trembled uncontrollably.

"Miranda, don't you think that at your age you should put your dolls aside?", Nikita asked her, but not unkindly. Miranda became instantly serious.

"Minx was a present from my mother", she said, in all the severity. "She is nobody's business but my own."

Later, Nikita commented to me on Miranda's ability to appear as a child and as an adult simultaneously. "She can choose between the two things… doesn't that seem strange?"

"Miranda is not a common person", I said. "And with regard to Minx, it could be that we don't know the doll's entire history, its real importance."

Nikita shrugged, as if my words made little impression on her.

We looked for Minx throughout the house but it was hopeless. The house was so large, with so many hidden parts, that we could look for a year without finding it. Worse still would be to look in Diego's studio, for the overwhelming quantity of materials in it. The studio was covered in one wall with floor-to-ceiling shelves; the topmost ones were so high that you had to go up a ladder to reach them, and for that purpose there was a rolling ladder that could be positioned where needed. Minx could be in one of thousands of boxes on those shelves.

I thought it might have been Diego himself that took the doll away. Many times I had expressed to him my uneasiness regarding Miranda's attachment to the doll, to the power it seemed to exert over her. Possibly influenced by my words, he could have decided to get rid of it in order to rid us of that power.

By the third day of the disappearance, Miranda had become inconsolable. She could do nothing but cry, or seated before a window, look out vacantly at a distant point, completely still.

"I feel like Minx is in danger, Miss Mendoza", she said in a nearly extinguished voice. "I feel like she's left the house; that she's wandering around out there; that she needs my help but she can't find me."

"Try to stay calm, Miranda. I'm sure we'll find her soon", I told her, but I was not at all sure we would.

On the fourth day, she was found. I found her in the kitchen garbage, that the next day Poncia would have taken to the village and disposed of. Somehow the doll ended up there and if it hadn't been for me, she would have been lost forever. It was never known how the doll came to be in the garbage, but Cecilio and Adriana tended to spend a lot of time in the kitchen, so naturally the suspicion fell upon them.

Both of them had a reason to get rid of the doll. Adriana was always exceedingly jealous of anything having to do with Miranda. She hated the doll and made that clear more than once, but it wasn't permitted to be openly angry with Miranda. Miranda gave no reason for anyone to be angry with her.

We had hardly recovered from that episode when Minx disappeared again. This time we found her quickly, but not before she suffered some damage. On her neck was an X cut with a sharp knife. I had a moment of unreasonable fear when I saw that the "flesh" around the cut was swollen and lightly reddened, as if the flesh was escaping from the opening. The wound appeared human, too human.

Minx. Is. A doll. Made of plastic. This, I wrote in my diary, trying to negate the importance that she had. But it wasn't that easy. I remembered the tiny mechanism in the torso of the doll; I imagined that Miranda had told Fernando what it meant, how it worked. I wondered if there might be something hidden inside the doll, but I had no way to find out. This impotence infuriated me, but my fury had nowhere to go.

When Miranda saw the damage on the throat of the doll, she said nothing. She went to her room where she stayed the rest of the day. We didn't hear anything all that time, which was very unusual. Her custom was to be singing, or reading aloud, or chatting; at all hours of the day and night you could hear her voice. But not that day.

I became alarmed and went to her room, but she refused to answer my questions. By hand signals she indicated that she wanted to be left alone. She didn't come out until the following morning.

"Minx is much better, Miss Mendoza", she said. "Look."

It was true. The X that had been cut into her neck had disappeared. In that moment I felt a tremendous fear for my own sanity. I wasn't sure what was real. Should I believe my eyes, or should I put my belief in reason, in logic? I had clearly seen the wound, and now there was nothing. The neck of the doll was as smooth and perfect as it always had been.

I tried to forget about what happened to Minx. I had no one to whom to direct my doubts, my questions, nor anyone capable of answering them. Nikita would never believe me. But the things that happen in life are not always things that you can forget about so easily. What happened to Minx stayed trapped in me, like a fish bone stuck in my throat.

Miranda, with all this, put even more focus onto Fernando. She increased the energy she put towards seeking him out, in speaking with him, embroiling and tangling herself into him. Things were going from bad to worse. Fernando started to return her affections just as ardently as they were expressed. They spent much time together. Talking. Playing the piano. Laughing.

One day I went to speak with Diego about something, only to find that he had left on a trip. He left, leaving his daughter at the mercy of this man who would clearly take advantage of his absence. I went into a panic.

I called Barbara but she wasn't at the institute until the end of the month. Nikita wouldn't help me. I had no option but to implore Dr. Leocadio to go to the aid of his patient.

I waited for the chance to talk to him with much anxiety, but he approached me first.

"Miss Mendoza, I need to propose something to you", he said. "I'd like to have a session with you in private."

"Of course. What about?"

"It has to do with Miranda's treatment. I need to corroborate some things, and if you are available….?"

"Yes, absolutely", I told him. Rapidly I abandoned my idea of going directly to him about the danger Fernando posed to Miranda. I thought there might be a better way to get his help.

We went to the room where he customarily had his sessions with her each Thursday. He indicated that I should lie on the same sofa where my niece rested.

"We're going to do a simple relaxation exercise", he explained. He took out a package of differently colored cards and he showed me a turquoise one.

"Look closely at this card", he requested. "Now, close your eyes and try to see it in your mind."

I did as he asked. After a few moments of concentration, I could see it clearly.

"Now open your eyes." He took out another card, it was pink.

"Close your eyes again and try to see both cards, side by side. Concentrate on the edges, finely delineated and aligned."

I listened to his even, calm voice. "Concentrate on the colors, vibrant and saturated."

I did as he asked again, and I could easily see the two cards, one turquoise and one pink.

Dr. Leocadio continued in this way until I had seven cards in my mind, each a different color. Then he said:

"The turquoise card disappears. The space where it was, is now black."

"Yes."

"Now the pink card disappears. Its space is black."

"Yes."

In this way, he continued instructing me to make disappear all the cards. Then he bid me open my eyes.

"Very good, Miss Mendoza. That's all for today."

What? In no moment did I feel that I had been hypnotized, but then I wondered.

"Doctor, what was it that you wanted to corroborate with me?", I asked him. I didn't want to lose the opportunity to see if I could get him to reveal anything he knew about Miranda and Fernando. He took a moment to respond.

"I wanted to see if you have the ability to resist the effects of the relaxation", he said finally.

"Why?"

"In order to see if I can rely on you as a source of true information. To corroborate certain things that Miranda has asserted."

"And?"

He hesitated again, this time for longer.

"If I answer your question, it will undermine the validity of the procedure", he answered.

I remembered what Nikita had told me, that it isn't so much **what** the patient says but their interpretation of it that matters. Now I was the patient, and I had to be more astute than he, if I wanted him to help me get rid of Fernando.

Later, something occurred to me. Hypnotizing Fernando might not be too difficult? Might it be possible to suggest to him that he should distance himself from her, leave the house, even?

Meanwhile his siege upon my niece continued unabated. He had, for the most part, abandoned painting to spend all his time with Miranda. I did what I could; I lengthened the classes, insisting in more studies, more extra work. But inevitably they would end up together despite all my efforts to keep them apart.

When Diego came back from his most recent trip, he was upset when I told him how things were going. But by the same token, he said he wouldn't judge Fernando until he had seen with his own eyes, any impropriety on his part. I noticed that their arguments at this time became more pointed, more heated. And for some months, Diego did not leave the house.

Fernando Blau stayed more than a year, and in that year, he evolved into a vampire; intent on sucking out the soul of my beautiful niece. He had everyone in the house bewitched, thinking that he was an amiable chap, relaxed and genial, when in reality he was a monster. What he did was more than horrible. One example suffices, but there were many more.

One night very late, Nikta passed by the open door to Miranda's room. From inside she could hear voices speaking softly.

"Minx wants to take off her clothes. She says she's hot", said Fernando.

"Minx says for you to take off your clothes too. She wants to see you", said Miranda.

"Minx can see?"

"Of course. Minx sees everything. Didn't you know that?"

Nikita heard laughter.

"And if you don't take off your clothes, she's going to punish you. She punishes everyone who disobeys her."

"Hmmm. I will need to behave myself, then."

Nikita heard that they laughed animatedly.

"All right. I'll take off my shirt, to keep her happy."

She heard light movements from inside the bedroom. There was a long silence and then:

"Now you."

"Not me. Minx."

"Yes, Minx. She should take off her clothes. All of them."

As Nikita told me the story the following day, I had to deliberately control my voice in order not to scream at her: why didn't you go in and stop what was happening?

"Because I was happy for her", she replied. "It's about time that Miranda experiences what any normal girl would like to experience."

"But this is beyond the bounds of decency! A crime!"

"It's no crime. That Miranda feels that she's in love with Fernando is not a bad thing. Lea, you know she loves him. And he loves her."

"What does Miranda know of love? And Fernando? He is a pig. He's taking advantage of an innocent child. This is blasphemy."

"Lea, calm down", my sister advised. I tried to.

"So, what happened next?", I asked when I could finally control my anger.

"I don't know. I didn't stay in the hall. But probably what happened was what had to happen."

I was furious with her, and something in me refused to believe that Miranda and Fernando had actually gone through with what they appeared to do.

"You're wrong. It's not possible. You're inventing, or you misheard. This is absolutely crazy."

"Ok. Believe what you want", Nikita replied, in a short voice.

And with that, the conversation ended. I was furious and the only thing that occurred to me in that moment was this: it was time to get rid of Fernando Blau.

41

Leonora
The Hypnosis

I waited for the moment to be alone with Fernando. Finally, I saw him enter Diego's studio, and I followed him. While he was busy, I looked for a book that I had scrutinized earlier: Salvador Dali. I paged through it: melting pocket watches, skulls changing into piano keys, banal beach scenes with boats in the background and an enormous lion's tongue in the foreground. Near the end I found what I was looking for: the painting was called "The Bather" and it showed a nude figure lying in the sand, with the different parts of his body grotesquely inflated and distorted, with a tiny head and enormous hands. It would serve perfectly as a reason to get into conversation with Fernando. I stopped for a second to give thanks to God, for taking care of the details.

"Ah. Dali. He is one of my favorite artists. He's Catalan, just like me."

"Really? I don't know his art very well." The hook was launched. Fernando couldn't resist the idea of teaching, of showing off his knowledge of art.

"Do you see this painting here?", Fernando indicated "The Bather". "It represents the beginning of Dali's fascination with the theme of masturbation."

Fernando was so happy to be known as the expert, and he spoke with increasing enthusiasm.

"In the case of Dali, his imagination tended to be based in the traumas or neuroses of his youth."

The conversation was going just where I wanted it to go.

"Dali himself has said that all his art, in essence, came from his memories. One of those memories was that of his mother fondling his penis. She licked it, he says. That's why, according to those who study these things, masturbation holds a prominent place in his paintings."

Fernando smiled.

"And, was that true? About his mother, I mean?", I asked.

"Who knows. He also said that it could be a false memory, but in any case it gives credence to his hypothesis of the duality in everything. The rational and the irrational."

"The irrational is the subconscious, isn't it?"

"You could describe it like that. Dali was very influenced by the ideas of Freud. But I imagine that you knew that."

"Oh, um."

I didn't want Fernando to think that he should stop lecturing me.

"By the way, Fernando, do you believe that the subconscious really functions in daily life? I mean, outside of art."

"Of course it does. It is the basis of all knowledge."

Perfect. Fernando was falling exactly into the place I wanted.

"But reason is a stronger force, don't you think?"

"Not at all. Reason is simply a skeleton. It's a construction that we are continuously working on. We have invented reason in order to have limits, to have rules and order."

"And the subconscious has nothing to do with rules and order."

"Precisely. Like in my sculptures. They are examples of the shock that results when the irrational meets the rational."

Fernando sighed.

"I'd love to show you some of my sculptures. I know you would be impressed."

I let him continue talking. That was what he most liked, to talk about himself and his art.

In one pause, I asked him:

"In your art, have you taken advantage of the ways to reach the subconscious?"

"You mean, like dreams?"

"Like hypnosis."

"Ah, I would love to try that."

"Would you like me to hypnotize you? Because I've done it many times. And it's always very interesting."

"Hmmm." He appeared doubtful.

"Once I did it with a stutterer."

Fernando looked interested.

"I put him into a deep trance. I had him retrace his past until he got to his childhood. At that point his speech changed completely. He spoke with the fluidity of any normal person."

"His defect disappeared?"

"Yes. Later I discovered that at age eleven he was operated on for appendicitis. The surgery was difficult and there were complications afterwards."

Fernando looked fascinated.

"So, his stuttering was due to the surgery?"

"It seems so. And once I knew that, I could uncover other things about him, things that were completely buried."

I let pass a silence, waiting for just the right moment.

"Would you like me to hypnotize you?", I asked him.

"When?"

"Right now."

"All right."

I took him to the room where Dr. Leocadio had hypnotized me and I had him lie down on the couch, while I sat at the desk. I took him through the process of the colored cards, and he seemed to fall into a deep, passive somnolence. I went slowly, to make sure that his trance was absolutely deep. When I judged it so, I began.

"Now you see that the red card is covered in blood. It's wet."

Fernando showed no change.

"Do you know where the blood comes from?"

"No."

"From a wound that you have on your hands."

Here, I stopped. I wanted the maximum effect from the suggestion. After a long pause, I began again.

"Now you see on the card the image of a woman. She is young, beautiful. Do you see it?"

"Yes."

"She is dangerous. She was the one who cut your hands."

Fernando did not respond.

"The image of the woman changes into fire. The card burns. You are very afraid. Do you know what you are afraid of?"

"No."

"You're afraid of being consumed by the image on the card. You feel flames on your hands. They are hot. Hot. You smell burning flesh."

I let several seconds go by.

"Now, when you hear me count to five you will slowly open your eyes. One, two, three, four five."

I counted slowly, calmly. I wanted him to wake up without feeling any panic. When I got to five, Fernando opened his eyes and looked at me, astonished.

"Is it over?", he asked incredulously.

"Yes."

"But, what happened after the turquoise card? I made it disappear, but there must have happened something more…..?"

Poor Fernando, he didn't remember anything. Now I had to wait. To wait and see if the suggestions would take effect.

42

Leonora
The Visitor II

As the days passed after the hypnosis of Fernando, I noted that he spent most of his time in his room, painting, one assumes. I was happy; I enjoyed his absence and didn't want to provoke anything by asking about him.

It was Adriana's birthday, and it started out very nicely. We were in the patio, which we had decorated with colorful paper banners, hanging in lines strung from the rafters above. There were flowers growing and blooming everywhere: orange, pink, yellow. On the long table were pitchers of water flavored with melon: red watermelon, green honeydew, orange cantaloupe. One pitcher was clear water with slices of lime and lemon: a beautiful play of colors. Hanging from above was a piñata, brought by Barbara from Morelia. It was a rooster, its tail an extravagant show of bright paper feathers, which burst out like fireworks exploding. We could hear piano music; Miranda was practicing a new piece that was very delightful.

On the table was a paella; the colorful ingredients in playful company with the colors and designs of the tiles; shiny like water or a clear, blue sky. Diego had made the paella, a process that I always loved to watch.

Whenever he cooked, he took over the kitchen as if he had lived his whole life there, putting the pans on the fire, stirring the ingredients with a rapidity and elegance that was astonishing. It was like watching a ballet. And all the while he would be humming a tune or conversing with whomever was around. He drank, and as the afternoon or the evening wore on, the alcohol would free him to sing in full voice, which wasn't always to everyone's liking since he was sometimes off key. But the rhythm was always perfect, and, taking advantage of the upturned pots and pans, he would strike them with wooden spoons as if they were drums, each with a separate timber.

Besides paellas, he also made delicious desserts; cakes and pies like the ones we used to eat in Brussels. What pleasure it gave me to see him, dressed in his apron, putting the chocolate to melt, adding the flour, the cream, the eggs, and then putting it all into the oven, to later take out a rich delicacy. Not even Mrs. Poncia, who was a great cook, could make such delicious cakes. One time I asked Diego about it, and he told me that everything Mrs. Poncia knew to cook, he had taught her.

In those moments I admired Diego more than ever. To be with him was like being on a giant merry-go-round that never stopped, that never slowed down in its manner of pleasing, with its music and movement. Diego was a force that no one could detain, larger than life.

But later, when I was alone, far from the studio or the kitchen, I burned with the desire to love him openly, that he would love me the same way. I imagined scenes where we were kissing, touching. I called to mind the time when Diego painted my portrait, how his hands moved my head, my shoulders, the sensation of his skin on mine, the fragrance of his breath. These memories sustained me, because in those days I was living in a continual state of enduring: enduring the desire, the jealousy, the frustration and the impotence. I saw no way of leaving my tower, no way of changing anything. To confess to him my love would be a disaster. He would be astonished, he might distance himself from me, even dismiss me from my job. I would lose what I most valued in life.

On the table with the paella and the pitchers of sweetened water, there was a glass plate nearly overflowing with a light yellow, creamy substance: crema catalana, made by Poncia in honor of Fernando. Fernando, the protégé of Diego, with a special dessert from his region of Spain. The thought was hateful. The party was not just to celebrate Adriana's birthday but to celebrate Fernando also. The sculptor was having an exhibition of his work, done during his time with Diego, in the gallery of Esmé Moreau. What fury that engendered in me! That he would be honored for his art filled me with distaste. That we would celebrate it on the same day as my sister's birthday made me furious. Poor Adriana, who was never first in anyone's thought, had to share her special day with him. Her birthday was one of very few occasions where she could be the focus of attention, and now the horrible Fernando was going to steal it away from her.

We were all in the patio, dressed in party clothes, with the champagne served, when we heard the words.

"I have a boyfriend!"

Words, just words, pronounced by a voice that was strong and happy. It was the voice of Miranda.

"A boyfriend?", asked Diego.

"Yes. It's Fernando."

The group became quiet. Fernando seemed very uncomfortable. After a moment of surprise, Nikita said:

"Congratulations, Miranda. Let's have a toast to the couple!"

"Fernando, wouldn't it have been wise to have spoken to me first?", asked Diego.

"Papa, we're in the twentieth century. Nobody does that anymore", answered Miranda smiling.

Adriana came up to Miranda.

"Congratulations", she said mechanically. She gave her a kiss on the cheek and quickly stepped back.

"Since when are you boyfriend and girlfriend?", I asked her.

"Mmmm. For a while. But we didn't want to say anything until the exhibition. We wanted the news to coincide with that. Now we know that Fernando's work will be out in the public for the first time, we have a good reason to go ahead with our relationship", said Miranda.

Their 'relationship'? No. There was not going to be a 'relationship'. Miranda was seventeen years old. What did she know about relationships? What did she know about the future, about exhibitions, about work, about the world? Nothing. She was too young still. Her place was here, in the house with us, with the people who knew how to care for her, to protect her.

The party continued. I noted that Fernando hardly spoke and never went to his new girlfriend's side to take her hand, or kiss her, or anything. It was if being called "boyfriend" had surprised and upset him. Good. Despite my fears, I tried to relax. The paella was indeed delicious and the crema catalana, exquisite. I drank the champagne and it was delicious as well. The birthday presents were unwrapped and the piñata broken open by a sure hit from Adriana. In all, it was a lovely party despite the distressing news from Miranda. We all went to bed very late, leaving the dishes for Poncia, who had left by then.

The next morning, I was the first to pass through the patio, where I saw an envelope propped up on the table in such a way that I couldn't miss it. On it was written "to everyone" in pen. I opened it to read:

Dear Friends,

I have so much to thank you all for. It has been an unforgettable experience to be a guest in your house, to work alongside you Diego, to live with you all and participate in your lives.

But the time has come for me to say goodbye. I know it will seem strange that I leave just when my paintings go on exhibit, but I have my reasons. It's urgent that I return to Barcelona as soon as possible. Forgive me, and please excuse me for not saying goodbye in person; I hope that this letter serves to do that in some way.

Sincerely,
Fernando

I ran to his room. It was completely empty. I had his letter in my hand still; I looked hard at it. There was something missing, something terribly important. There was no personal message to Miranda there. I knew she would be desolate at the absence. I returned to the patio, and I sat down to write. In the small space in between the last line and the 'sincerely', I wrote, trying the best I could to imitate his handwriting:

Miranda, my love. Forgive me. I will love you forever.

So, Fernando was gone. I felt a tremendous relief, a tremendous happiness. He would no longer be at the side of my niece, tempting her away. The hypnosis had worked perfectly.

The last person to awaken that morning was Diego, and when he read the letter he became furious.

"He leaves? Just like that? The ingrate. Who does he think he is?"

216

"What could have been his real reason?", Nikita asked me in private. "His leaving now makes no sense."

"And Miranda?", asked Barbara. "How could he deceive her in this way? Oh, the poor thing. She is going to suffer."

"It's better for her", remarked Cecilio. "Fernando wasn't the man of her dreams. It never would have worked between them."

"You, what do you know about such things?", Nikita protested angrily. "Didn't you see that Miranda was very much in love with him?"

"That doesn't matter. It makes no difference if she was in love or if she wasn't... he's gone", the boy answered with insouciance.

Everyone was nervous about Miranda's reaction when she realized what had happened. And the fears were justified. She cried all afternoon. We tried to console her but it was useless. She couldn't stop crying. At times she shouted in pure rage, her pride trampled upon; the loss of the first person who had ever told her he loved her, the first person whom she had loved romantically, wounding her deeply.

Finally, completely exhausted, she said she wanted to be left alone, and went to her room. There she stayed for a long time; none of us cognizant of anything she did. We were all wrapped in a melancholy that didn't allow us to move, or think, or do anything.

Now that I write this, now that I organize my memories of the past, I feel like hitting myself in the head for my stupidity. What did I imagine would happen with these silly games of hypnotism? Why didn't it occur to me that their relationship was already too serious for that? How is it that I didn't realize that what Miranda felt for the sculptor was stronger than I knew? How could I imagine that she would be all right afterwards? Because she was not all right afterwards.

All the next day, we walked around like zombies. It was hard to know what to think, what to do. That night no one slept well.

The next day was no better. And in the evening it became much, much worse. At around seven o'clock we heard Diego shouting from his studio. There, on the floor, like a bird fallen from its nest, was Fernando. The blood formed a pool around his head; his legs were bent in an unnatural way; one arm was twisted upwards, horribly distended and curved. He was lying under the rolling ladder; it appeared that he had fallen from it upon ascending or descending.

It was I who called the police. They came, took many photos, and measurements of everything in the studio; they investigated the rolling ladder and its movement. They were there until past midnight, until finally the workers from the morgue arrived to take away the body. During all this, Miranda was quiet. She stopped crying, she stopped speaking altogether.

Everyone had to explain themselves to the police, but she said she couldn't. Diego told them to return the following morning; that his daughter was exhausted and it was true. No one had eaten in the whole day despite the exhortations of Mrs. Poncia, who came and went continuously with trays of food and drink which no one touched.

It was one o'clock in the morning when Niktia came to my room.

"Who was it?", she asked with no preamble.

"What do you mean, who was it? He fell from the ladder."

"Didn't you notice that the handles that lock the wheels were not set?"

It was true. The ladder had stops that inhibited its movement, keeping it in the desired position, making it possible to go up or down securely. Moreover, the ladder moved silently on its track above and on its wheels below. Completely silently.

"Doesn't it seem suspicious?", she asked. "Think about it. Several people had a reason to wish ill upon Fernando. Cecilio hated him. Surely you recall all his nasty tricks."

"Of course I remember. But Cecilio is no assassin. That's absurd."

"And Adriana has always been jealous of Miranda. To take away her boyfriend would be the perfect way to hurt her."

"Are you crazy, Nikita!? Watch what you say!"

"Even Diego had a reason for wanting him to leave. In the first place, he didn't want Miranda to be close to him. What Diego likes most is to have everyone under his control, and even more if it has to do with Miranda."

"You're wrong. Diego would never hurt her."

"Additionally, Diego might have been jealous of Fernando. *Diego Alba*, the famous painter, now in competition with his protégé. He wouldn't want that. Painting is his forté, and now to have to share that with Fernando would be intolerable."

"Then why did he invite him here?", I asked.

"For heaven's sake Lea", she sighed. "At times you seem blind. Diego invited Fernando Blau here precisely so that he would become involved with you."

"What? Why??"

Nikita shook her head in exasperation.

"Because Diego feels sorry for you."

"Sorry!!??"

"Yes. Diego cares for you, in his way. He wanted you to have someone to love, for you to have some kind of normal life."

"I don't need his pity", I said scornfully. "I don't need him to worry about me", even though my heart was breaking inside to think that she might be right. I was engulfed in the need to explain, to justify.

"In any case, Fernando was leaving", I continued. "Everything was going to solve itself. There would be no motive to kill him", I said with as much reason as I could muster in my voice.

"It could be that Fernando had no plan to leave at all", she said mysteriously.

"But the letter?"

"Who do you think wrote the letter? Fernando?"

"What are saying?", I asked, unable to fathom what my sister was saying, unable to understand why she was saying it.

"If not Fernando, then who?", I asked.

"It could have been you. You've always been opposed to his presence here."

I was speechless. Babbling, I managed to squeak out:

"Are you accusing me of this horrible crime, this horrible, horrible crime....???"

"Calm down. I'm not accusing anyone of anything. I'm just saying that things are not easy to understand."

Nikita fell silent, meditating over her words.

"Think about something, Lea. Miranda suffered a tremendous disillusionment. What do people do who have gone through that?"

"I don't know."

"They seek vengeance."

"Miranda!? Miranda is a good person, an intelligent girl. She doesn't carry one vindictive cell in her body."

Nikita's face revealed the profound nature of her thoughts.

"There are moments in life when even the best, most intelligent person in the world goes crazy from grief. The passion that she felt for Fernando was, perhaps, deeper than we thought."

"Do you truly think her capable of murder?"

"I don't know. I only know that I, too, have passed through moments like that. And under these same circumstances, I might have done it."

"Nikita!!"

"Don't play the innocent, Lea. Everyone is the same. Passion is a terrible thing. It takes you out of yourself."

"You are completely wrong. I think the scare has affected you and you're not thinking straight. You should go to bed. Tomorrow everything will be much clearer."

43

Leonora
The Visitor III

Two days after the death of Fernando, Diego put up a post on the highway to mark the entrance to the house, and the swarm descended.

The parents of Fernando came and a sister, full of questions, of tears, and cries of woe. They did not cease talking all the while they were packing up his things. His family was as clever and talkative as he was, and they weren't satisfied with easy answers. They wanted to know everything; they wanted to do their own investigation. Meanwhile, the mystery of the whereabouts of his personal things continued. Where were they?

More police came, to ask more questions and take more measurements; going through the whole house paying special attention of course, to Diego's painting studio. They told us to take everything out of there, the whole enormous bulk of stuff, and put it all in the corral. They looked through all the private rooms, they looked in the corners of the bathrooms, the kitchen, the rooms that we didn't use. They investigated all the obvious places, but the house, with its infinite number of spaces, defeated them. There were many places they didn't touch, didn't see, even.

They took fingerprints of the rolling ladder, of the surrounding floor and walls, the windows; everywhere they could think to take fingerprints, they took them. They asked many questions of Miranda. To all their questions, she answered with great calm. It was if her interior was frozen, permitting her to maintain an astonishing tranquility. As did Barbara. Those two spent much time together alone, in Miranda's bedroom and even though I passed by the closed door an infinite number of times, I never could hear much of their conversation.

The police interviewed Nikita, Cecilio, Adriana and me. Separately. The tension was so high in the house that it was useless of me to ask each of them what they discussed with the police. No one could remember with any accuracy what, exactly, were the questions and what, exactly, they had answered.

Diego went from one end of the house to the other, grumbling and impeding the work of the police. He returned the boxes that they had removed; he interfered in their work, he distracted them with his comments and questions.

And me? I tried to maintain things in as normal a way as I could.

In the middle of this great mess, a group of people came: Esmé and another man, someone I understood to be the editor of an arts magazine. Diego took them aside, into the living room where they could converse in private. I was dying to know what they were doing, but I could gather very little.

In all, it was horrible.

Finally though, Fernando's family left, the police left, Diego's friends left, and little by little things returned to normal. Diego brought back all his easels and his paintings to the studio, he returned his drawings and his canvases, his brushes and his books, his cans of paint and turpentine, his jars and his buckets, his mountainous amount of stuff to their customary places. And the conclusion of the police? An accident. The death of Fernando Blau was an unfortunate accident.

It was when things had returned to normal that we received the greatest shock. Miranda tried to kill herself.

We found her in the drainage ditch that marked the edge of the property, the same drainage ditch that Adriana and I had followed when we had discovered the hidden entrance to the house the first time. We found her covered in mud, half swallowed by the dirty water, with her arms covered in blood. She had tried to cut her veins but she didn't do it correctly. She didn't know that to really die, you have to cut along the veins, not across them. Thank God she didn't know that.

"Or maybe she did it that way precisely to draw attention to herself", said Nikita. "I don't believe that Miranda would be make that mistake."

"Nikita, you are awful. Don't say things like that", I told her. "Your cynical attitude doesn't help at all."

Nikita looked abashed at her own words. "I'm sorry", she said.

The wounds in her arms were not serious, but it was difficult to clean off the mud that covered her hair and face. Somehow, the mud had gotten deep into her eyes and we couldn't get it out. Diego was in a panic. Mrs. Poncia went running to the house to bring water and when she returned, we tried to wash her face. There, in the dirtiness of the drainage ditch, we tried to clean her.

But Miranda was fidgety, crying and avoiding our efforts. She complained about her eyes, she cried and screamed. She wouldn't let us help her; she wouldn't allow us to clean the mud from her face. She said she wanted to die. She said her life was over, that nothing mattered anymore; she ordered us to leave her, that we return to the house without her.

Finally Diego had had enough. He picked her up and carried her back. He put her in her bed and stayed by her side. But he was not able to calm her.

"Miss Mendoza. Call Dr. Leocadio. Ask him to come as soon as possible", he ordered me.

44

Leonora
Miranda I

"I've spoken with her and she's better. She's stopped crying."

Dr. Leocadio had given his report, occasionally consulting his notes that Nikita had taken during his session with Miranda. At the end, gathering his composure, he added:

"But there's something more."

Everyone stopped breathing.

"Miranda is pregnant. About twenty weeks."

"What! How?" The words exploded from Diego's mouth. Dr. Leocadio looked uncomfortable. Surely the mechanisms of a pregnancy were well known by Diego.

"I haven't noticed anything, any change in her body", said Barbara. "I don't understand…"

"The baby is smaller than it should be", answered the doctor.

There was a moment of silence; each of us with our own thoughts.

"What kind of test did you do on her?", asked Diego.

"Urine."

"And, are those tests one hundred percent accurate?", he asked again.

"They are about eighty-five percent accurate", said the doctor.

"So there's a chance that she isn't pregnant?", Diego insisted.

The doctor looked tired and uncomfortable.

"I can repeat the test in a few days but I assure you, Mr. Alba, that she is. She has all the physical signs."

The doctor closed his eyes, thinking.

"What worries me is that the physical changes of a pregnancy can upset even the most stable person. Psychologically. There are hormones…."

"Miranda is healthy."

All of us looked at Diego, unable to swallow what he said. It was preposterous.

"She doesn't have any more problems or instabilities than anyone else in her situation."

No one said anything.

"Certainly, she's young. She's just suffered her first romantic misadventure; her first love has died in an accident and now she is expecting a child. But none of these things is capable of ….."

Diego didn't know how to end the sentence. Dr. Leocadio looked embarrassed by the lack of logic in his words. They customarily treated one another respectfully, despite Diego's lack of support of the doctor's treatment. It was some kind of gentlemen's agreement.

"I hope you're right, Mr. Alba. I prescribed a calming medicine, that will help her sleep. She tells me she hasn't slept since the boyfriend died."

"That was three months ago!", exclaimed Nikita.

"Surely she is exaggerating?", asked Barbara dubiously.

"Of course she is", said the doctor. "No one can go that long without sleep. But it's worrisome that Miranda doesn't recognize this."

"This is nothing more than youthful misperception. She is experiencing all the normal upsets of a person in these circumstances", said Diego.

"Today she tried to kill herself! What more proof do you need, Diego, that Miranda is not well?", said Barbara.

Diego didn't respond.

"Miranda needs a lot of care now. The baby is underdeveloped, and the mother must eat well, sleep well", said the doctor.

"I will make sure of that", I said.

But I could not make sure of that. Miranda refused to eat what we prepared for her. She would go for three or four days drinking nothing but tea; then she would trade that for apples; then something else. But it was never enough food, even for just her. The baby could not have been getting the nourishment it needed.

She stayed mostly in her room, coming out late at night to play the piano. She would shut the doors to the living room to muffle the sound, but she struck the keys with such fury that everyone could hear. The music was crazy; it hurt my ears.

"The baby is going to be born deaf", said the doctor on one of his visits. "Miss Mendoza, Mr. Alba trusts you; he values your opinion. Things are not going well here; Miranda is not behaving normally. Can you say something to him?"

But I didn't say anything to Diego. I knew it would have no effect. He was persistent in his belief that Miranda was fine. He didn't want to see the reality.

The only person who had any effect at all on Miranda was Barbara. Whenever they spent time together, Miranda afterwards would be more calm. When I asked what they talked about she answered:

"We don't talk. We pray."

Days passed and it appeared that the baby didn't grow. Or at least, I didn't see that it was growing. One day I went to her room.

"Miranda, my sweet. I'm so worried about you."

"Miss Mendoza, do you remember the story of Sancho Panza and Don Quixote?"

"Yes, of course."

"That they helped one another forge ahead in their invented world?"

"Yes."

"So, don't be worried. I know that all of you are like Sancho Panza for me. You are helping me get through in this invented situation."

I found no adequate response to her observation. What was "invented" about her situation? It made no sense.

While she was speaking, Miranda slowly unbuttoned her pajama blouse, to show her belly. It was round and firm, just as it was supposed to be.

"See? Everything is going to be all right", she told me calmly.

But it was very difficult to see how everything was going to be all right.

45

Adriana
I Remember

I remember everything. I remember the first time that Cecilio called me stupid. I remember the second time, the third time, the fifteenth time. I remember the circumstances of each time: where we were, what happened afterwards. I remember conversations that happened a month ago, a year ago. I remember the house in Brussels; the bicycle that I rode in the park across the street; I remember the big front door and the small back door of our building; I remember my parents perfectly. I remember everything.

And they call me stupid.

But one thing is to be stupid and another thing altogether to be unable to say what you want to. When I was a child my words would often come out of order. In my mind they were in the right order, but when they left my mouth they would be all mixed up. The first word would come in the middle and the last word would come first. People who didn't know me found it silly, or funny, but I found it enraging.

One day my mother gave me a really pretty notebook and she taught me how to draw the things I couldn't say. The notebook was pink and it had a horse drawn on it, with real threads to represent the mane. I remember combing the soft threads, arranging them first one way then another. In the notebook I sketched, as best I could, what I could not say. In that notebook I discharged all the fury, all the frustration that I felt. There were pages with deep impressions on them; marks from the pen pressed so deeply that they damaged the paper.

While my mother was alive, she could understand me at least. With her, I didn't have so often those episodes where my language fell apart. But that changed when she died. A few days after her death I was in the hall outside my father's office in the embassy. I stood outside the open door and I heard my father talking to a woman I didn't know. He was saying that because of my mental defects, I was not going to remember any of this; that I was going to be fine and not remember my mother at all.

But they were wrong. I was not fine at all. I remember my mother perfectly; her face, her voice, her way of treating me, everything.

In the absence of my mother I got worse. Now when I got into an incoherent state, I became infuriated, even though I knew that I should try to control myself. Along with the fury came a fear. I became afraid of talking because I was afraid of becoming angry. I didn't understand very well this association; I didn't know what was wrong with me, only that there was something terribly wrong with me, in fact.

When we got to Mexico, I hardly spoke. I was too afraid. All my sensations and emotions became a tangled jungle in my mind. I couldn't separate anxiety from anger, fear from hunger; all was pain.

But little by little I got better. I learned to write with letters, and I developed a system to describe things; a kind of shorthand that allowed me to express a lot with a few symbols. I filled notebook after notebook with my writings and in this way, the frustration of being unable to speak seemed to diminish somehow. Writing things down allowed me to understand them in a way that hearing them did not. It's curious, people think that they understand something as soon as they perceive it, but it's not always like that. Many times it's only when you repeat something that you truly understand it.

I filled many notebooks that my mother gave me and then my sister, but all the same, it was a tiring process. Faced with the impossibility of recording everything, I simplified my system even more, realizing with satisfaction that no one would ever be able to decipher my notebooks. When I reread my notes, I could fill in the details of everything that had happened; I could fill in the natural voids in my mind with the pictures. It's impressive the number of notebooks I have filled; shelves and shelves; full of mysterious stories that no one will ever read.

But now something has happened that I must write down in regular letters. There are not enough symbols to adequately express what I need to; I don't have the right kind of symbols to describe how I saw my sister kill someone.

A man had come to live with us named Fernando Blau. Everyone liked him; everyone liked to spend time with him. Supposedly he came so that Diego could teach him to paint, but what they most liked to do, he and Diego, was argue about art. Even so, Fernando painted a lot of paintings during his time here, and he gave one of his paintings to me. I thought it was the prettiest one he made. It showed a woman on a walkway alongside the ocean; she was walking with the wind blowing her skirt, and she had a man on either side of her, walking arm-in-arm. The woman looked a lot like me.

I loved to spend time with him. With Fernando, I could always speak normally, and I never had an episode of confusion or anger. I felt comfortable with him because he always took me seriously. No one else spoke to me in that way. If for everyone else, I was stupid, with him I was an interesting person, an intelligent person. He asked me a lot of details about my life; he was interested in all the details of my past. Lea told me never to say anything about our parents, about our lives in Brussels, and if anyone asked, I was to tell them that we were from Bloemfontein, South Africa and that our father was Spanish and our mother was South African. That was so absurd, and I didn't pay much attention to Lea. I told Fernando all about us: who we were, where we had come from, why we were here. Fernando was very curious about all of that.

So, we got along well. Even better, since he often would let me accompany him in his studio while he painted. I think, that of all the people in the house, he liked me the best. That's why it bothered me so much that Miranda interposed herself in his life. It wasn't fair. The horrible Miranda tricked him into spending time with her, just to take him away from me. If Miranda was not here, Fernando would have fallen in love with me. I know it. One time he tried to kiss me. The second time, I let him. The third time we were kissing for so long that I got nervous because I wasn't sure how it was going to end. He stopped only because he heard her voice as she came looking for him.

If I say that everyone liked Fernando, I have to amend that. Lea did not like him at all. She never said anything, but you could tell from her face, from her gestures. If you are silent and don't speak, you have time to observe many things, and I saw that Lea was very jealous of Miranda; jealous of the attention he paid her. And when I say I was jealous of that too, it's nothing compared to the jealousy that my sister felt. She died of jealousy. She was also jealous of the attention that Diego paid to Fernando. Lea wanted them both to pay attention to her. She went fairly crazy with jealousy. To be rejected like that made her immensely angry, but no one would ever discern that because she hid it very well. She hid all her emotions well. It was if she didn't know herself, or if she did, she repressed so many parts that her personality became cracked and started missing pieces. I remember that she flirted with Fernando, but that he preferred to be with Miranda; I remember how Lea would invent tasks for them to do that kept them apart; I remember how her face would harden when she found them together; I remember the strategies she used to interrupt their relationship.

One day I found out about the plan Fernando and Miranda had to run away together. Fernando couldn't bear not being able to make love to her, and she was the same. But then when they did make love, it wasn't enough. They seemed to me like panting dogs, seeking each other's faces and sniffing their hands; it was repulsive. I know they had sex in Miranda's bedroom. I saw that each time they did, on the day after, they both looked different, unmistakably different. It made me furious to know that they had been together, but I'm not crazy. Not crazy like Lea.

I remember that it was my birthday and the patio was so pretty with colored paper banners and a piñata. In the party, Miranda announced that they were a couple. Everyone was surprised except me. That night I slept poorly and I woke up at dawn. I saw that Lea wasn't in her bed. I went to the patio and I saw Lea there, seated at the table, writing something. She put the paper in an envelope and after she left, I looked at it. It was a letter supposedly from Fernando, saying that he was returning to Spain.

I didn't understand this. I didn't know why Lea would write such a thing. I carefully returned the letter to the envelope and went to his room. His things were gone. What had happened? Had he really left? All day he didn't appear, nor were there signs that anyone had come to pick him up.

Miranda reacted as we expected. She cried. She screamed. But her boyfriend had abandoned her. That made me happy.

I don't know what time it was, but the sun was setting when I sensed that something was happening in the studio. Very quietly I went there.

It was dark but I could see three figures standing there, and I guessed they were speaking to one another. I couldn't see their faces, but I could well imagine what they were saying.

"Where? Where is it?", said a man's voice. It was Fernando.

"On the top shelf." I saw that one of the figures indicated with a wave of their hand where he was to look for whatever he was looking for. I thought I heard Lea's voice.

"I need the ladder", said the first voice. That person moved the ladder in place, fixed the wheels in place and went up.

"I don't see anything", said the voice from up high. I heard him moving boxes around.

"No, it's behind the biggest box… yes, that one. You'll have to move it to one side", said a woman's voice.

"For God's sake, Fernando", said a man's voice. "Hurry up. I don't have the patience for this."

The woman said nothing. She waited until Fernando was well occupied with moving boxes, and then, when he had a big box in his arms and was coming down the ladder, she crouched and undid the stops on the wheels. I saw that she pushed the ladder to the side, just as he was about to take his first step. I saw how he fell to the floor. I heard his head crack open; it was a short, cruel sound. I saw how a pool of blood formed quickly around his head; how his arms and legs splayed apart like toothpicks spilled from the box; all broken and twisted. I saw how my sister ran out of the studio without saying anything. All this I saw with my own eyes.

I didn't say anything when the letter was discovered, or when the body of Fernando was found. I didn't say anything because the disappearance of Fernando made Miranda anguished, and I liked that. I liked to see her cry so desperately. It made me happy to see that she had lost something of such great value to her. I was glad that she was not going to leave the house with him, that she was not going to start a new life with him, that she was going to have to stay here, just as she always has, stuck here without the possibility of leaving.

I know I shouldn't feel this. I know that a human being lost his life. I know that Fernando didn't deserve to die that way; I know that his only mistake was to become involved with Miranda. I am aware of all that. And on top of that, his death made me sad because he was one of the few people who really understood me.

But Lea, my sister Lea.... she revealed herself as the monster she really is. I was happy over the misfortune of Miranda, but I am not capable of destroying someone in order to achieve it. I am not a monster, not a monster like my sister Lea.

46

Leonora
Miranda's Notebook

Some weeks after the news of Miranda's pregnancy, we woke up with the news that Diego had left on a trip.

"How can he leave Miranda in this state?", Nikita asked me.

"He thinks she's all right; that the thing in the drainage ditch was just a momentary panic", I answered her.

"Do you think she's all right?"

"I truly hope so", I said.

I wasn't thinking very well in that period. The fourth of September Miranda would turn eighteen and the words of Nikita came to my mind: repeated instances when she would say that we had to leave the house; that it was a madhouse; that we should go to Morelia; that we accept Barbara's offer to stay and work at her school. This way, Miranda's baby would be born in a good hospital and we would no longer be isolated, far from the civilized ways of a modern city. Her words swirled in my mind, without my finding form or logic in them.

One day Nikita and I had been in the storeroom, the room that had been destroyed two years ago when the trees fell on it, the trees bewitched by Poncia who sent them to destroy us, the intruders. It always made me nervous to go in there, a place always in the shadows, where there flowed an inexplicable current of cold air across the floor. Poncia said that the storeroom was where the spirit warriors gathered together when they were looking for vengeance upon the loss of one of their group.

"What spirit warriors?", Nikita asked her once.

"The ones who live on the other side of the hills", she told her.

Nikita looked at me with a laughing expression. Poncia's "fantasies", as my sister called them, were well known to us. But as much as we smiled at her manias, I secretly felt afraid of them. The Alba house held much history inside it, events that had never been acknowledged in any form but not forgotten either, nor absent. Nikita didn't share these fears; she didn't believe in spirits.

I was living in a distracted way; I was having a hard time making things concrete in my head. I thought about all the things that had happened in these last months, and all the things that had happened in my seven years in Mexico. I thought about how much I loved living in Diego's house; how much I loved being near him, listening to the comments that he shared with me when he returned from a trip; how much I loved sharing with him the events of the day; how much I treasured the kiss he gave me at regular intervals.

Suddenly something caught my attention; a reflection of light where there shouldn't be one. It was a suitcase. I knew that suitcase; it had metal borders and handle; it was Fernando's. I opened it. Inside, exactly as he had left them, were his clothes. I showed it to Nikita. Her face registered the extreme confusion that I too was feeling.

"Who could have put it here?", she asked.

One more mystery, one more question without answers. One more thing to add to the list of unexplainable things.

Returning to the kitchen, Nikita began speaking.

"Lea, I want to show you something. Something that will help you see what's happening here."

"Dr. Leocadio's notes?"

"Yes. You need to read them."

"Why?"

"Lea, they accuse you of so many things! They say barbarous things about you!"

"Who is 'they'?"

"Everyone. Diego, Miranda. And then there's what Dr. Leocadio puts down about you as well."

I felt my knees shaking.

"Come on. Let's go to the office."

During that time Barbara's visits came more often. If in the past she came every two weeks, now she was coming every Saturday. She would arrive at around noon and go directly to the office to read the notes. The doctor kept them under lock and key in a desk drawer. There, with the door closed, Barbara would read what Miranda said in private.

"It bothers me that Barbara reads the notes", Nikita has said once. "She shouldn't do that."

"Do you say that because there should be confidentiality between doctor and patient?", I asked her. "Because you are just as guilty as she is.

Besides, Barbara has her reasons for worrying about Miranda. We should be thankful for her care, for all she does for her."

I had told Nikita about Barbara's past in Brussels. About her friendship with our mother.

"Yes, I know. But she can't change the fact that this is a madhouse here. Crazy, crazy things happen, and you don't even realize."

"Like what?", I asked.

"You need to read what Miranda has written."

We had arrived at the office. Nikita closed the door and the windows, then opened the desk drawer where the notebooks were lined up and organized by date: the months and years all written clearly; all the important events that had occurred to Miranda. There they were: her reactions, her ideas, her fears, her daydreams and her dreams at night, her thoughts and opinions, her fantasies. One time years ago, Miranda had told me that for her, her doll Minx and Sancho Panza were alike because they facilitated the beliefs and the fantasies of their friends. I hoped that Miranda knew the difference between fantasy and reality. And then I thought about the page in the notebook that I had ripped out, the page where the names and address of our family in Brussels appeared, knowing that it was a reality that become invisible, existing only in Dr. Leocadio's memory; wishing that all that would recede into a fantasy, an unreality.

I chose a notebook at random: May-November, 1984.

"Not that one. The more recent ones are the ones you should read. Look---." Nikita took out another notebook: December 1987. "This is the first one that Miranda wrote herself."

"What do you mean, 'wrote herself'?"

"Dr. Leocadio had asked her to write down in Braille her thoughts."

"Like a diary?"

"More or less. Miranda knew that it wouldn't be a private diary. First she wrote it on her Braille typewriter, then during the visits she would read it out loud and I would transcribe it."

Nikita handed me the notebook but I didn't want to read it.

"Read it to me, Nikita."

"All right." She looked at me, perplexed.

Nikita started to read. There was a lot of description of how Diego acted, and then here were things about me; that I had come and put myself in the middle of everything; that I had acted badly in provoking him; that I had seduced him with my body; by offering him everything; that she had heard us fornicating..."

"Fornicating!", I exclaimed, astonished and horrified that she would think that, that she would use that term.

"That's what she wrote. Should I go on?"

"All right", I said dispiritedly.

Nikita continued. Miranda was furious with me and with her father. Unhinged with hatred. Minx told her what was going on in the house. Minx was also disgusted by these things. She said that her father was a pig and that I was a whore.

"I don't want to hear any more, please Nikita."

"That isn't the worst, Lea."

"I don't believe this! I never saw that Miranda harbored those feelings toward me!"

"Well, it's a question of paying attention", my sister said.

"Are you saying that you **did** notice that Miranda believed these absurd fantasies?", I asked her, incredulous.

"That doesn't matter now. Don't let yourself get distracted. You have to listen to what else is written here." Nikita showed me another notebook, the most recent one, dated February 2.

"The day that Fernando had the accident", I murmured.

"Yes", responded Nikita in a sadly severe tone. She began to read:

I know that my father doesn't like it that F. and I are a couple. But I never imagined that he would be capable of doing what he did. I'm going to put here exactly what happened to see if I can understand it, because right now I can't understand how my father killed Fernando and how it was that Miss Mendoza did nothing to stop him.

We were in the patio to celebrate Amelia's birthday. The party was really pretty and F. hardly left me alone for a moment. He had his arms around me, held my hand. My father seemed like he didn't like that, and even more so when we announced our news.

The party ended late and we all left to go to bed. I went to my room and in a few minutes F. knocked on the door. He came in and we kissed. He laid me down on the bed and we stayed there until dawn. Suddenly my father came in. He was horribly angry. He grabbed F. by the arm and took him forcibly to the painting studio. I followed.

"You're leaving right now, Fernando", said my father. "Get the ladder and remove your things."

F. was very nervous and didn't want to go up the ladder.

"Papa, Papa!", I called out in a panic. "What are you doing? You can't make him leave like that. Fernando is just about to show his paintings!"

"I don't give a fuck about his paintings", said my father.

"Mr. Alba!" I thought I heard the voice of Miss Mendoza, who had just entered the studio.

"Calm down. We should do this some other way."

"Things will be done exactly as I see fit", he affirmed.

I protested but my father was furious. He made F. go up the ladder. I felt him crouch down and release the stops that hold the ladder in place. I felt Fernando fall. I heard the shock of his body hitting the floor. I couldn't cry out from the fear.

Miss Mendoza took me by the arm and made me leave the studio. She took me to my room. I couldn't breathe; I couldn't get air into my lungs. I could hardly walk in the halls that I knew so well I could run down them without bumping into anything. I couldn't even cry.

She left me in my room. In the silence and the solitude, I could hardly stand the tension. Then I did start to cry. The tears came out like a fountain, but with no sound. It was like I was afraid to make any noise.

In a bit, Cecilio came to the window. Whispering, I begged him to go to the studio and see what was happening. The anguish was tearing me in two. Very soon he returned to say that my father had gone back to his own bedroom.

I was a disaster. I didn't know what to do, who to ask, who to confide in? Nancy? No. She is Miss Mendoza's sister and would be on her side, not mine. I felt an enormous fear. Fear of my father, of Miss Mendoza, of everyone.

"Cecilio, call Barbara on the telephone and beg her to come her as soon as possible", I told him.

"Right now?"

"Yes! Right now."

Barbara came in just a few hours, and I sat with her, in her lap, with my head on her shoulder, and I cried. She said that everything was going to be all right, that Fernando was going to be all right, that nothing had happened. She prayed that God would give us peace, that He would help us in the moment of confusion.

I asked her: "How is Fernando going to be all right? I was there. I know he fell."

"You might have misconstrued what you perceived, Miranda. In the dark it's difficult to know exactly what is going on."

"It's dark for me all the time, Miss Barbara", I answered her. "And it's precisely because of that, that I see what others miss. I have other ways of seeing beside with my eyes."

"Yes, of course. But what you must do now is sleep. In the morning everything will be much clearer."

I wanted to die. My father is an assassin. He murdered my boyfriend, the man I love, the man whose baby I'm carrying inside me. Minx told me that Fernando was bad luck for me; that he was going to ruin my life, but I didn't pay attention to her. She told me so often that I got sick of it and I put her in the closet so as not to hear her admonishments any more. But I know now that Minx was telling me the truth. Except that it wasn't Fernando who was bad luck for me, it was my father. My own father. Or should I say, my stepfather. I should call things as they are truly called, not as people tell me they should be called.

And Miss Mendoza, my teacher, who has cared for me so well, who is almost a mother to me, the cursed Miss Mendoza who did nothing to stop my stepfather; who did not intervene to prevent him from taking from me what I most wanted.

Here ended the notes written by Miranda. There was a long silence in the office. I had been left speechless, without voice, without words.

"Do you see now?", Nikita asked at last. "Do you see now why I tell you this place is a madhouse?"

47

Leonora
Miranda II

The due date for Miranda's baby was coming near. In that intervening time she mentioned nothing about my supposed participation in Fernando's accident. She was as loving and kind as ever. And I was the same to her.

"Could it be that Miranda has suffered some sort of mental mix up and she misinterpreted what happened to Fernando in the studio?", I asked Nikita.

"Or could it be that she has some other plan in mind, some other purpose in affirming something that she couldn't possibly know?", my sister responded. "Miranda knows that those notes are not private; they are read by Dr. Leocadio, and by Barbara."

"But what purpose would she have in making people believe that I was involved? I don't understand", I said, mystified.

"I don't know either. We should consult with Barbara and clear things up once and for all", said my sister energetically. In that moment I loved my sister more than ever. I felt, in spite of the difficulties that we had been through, the misunderstandings, and the disagreements of the past, that we were more united than ever: solid, together.

But when Nikita went to talk to Barbara, she avoided all our questions. She said only that Dr. Leocadio would know the truth, if indeed there was some kind of truth to the matter.

"One single version of the truth?", asked the doctor. "In questions of the human psyche, there is no such thing as one single version of the truth. There are various versions. It could be that one of them is more true than another, or that none of the versions are actually true."

"Do you mean to say that what appears in Miranda's diary is simply one more representation of the trauma that she has suffered, and that it doesn't signify what she actually thinks?"

The doctor said nothing, shaking his head. It was clear that he was as baffled as we were.

It was less than a week until the due date when the next disaster happened.

Miranda did not come to breakfast, which wasn't that unusual, but by two o'clock in the afternoon, she still had not left her bedroom. I went to see what was going on.

I found her sitting up in bed, covered up to the waist with the blankets and several pillows behind her back. She looked serene. Too serene, I thought. She had the appearance of a statue; her face blank and unfocused, her eyes unblinking, her hands crossed in her lap. Her face was white, very white and I couldn't see if she were breathing.

Next to the bed was the baby carriage that Barbara had bought for her. It was a thing of beauty, of exquisite quality, with its stainless steel wheels, its cushions and its little pillows, its parasol that you could tilt to one side or another to keep the baby out of the sun. I couldn't imagine where in Mexico she had found something like that; she must have had it imported from Europe because there wasn't anything like that here.

I saw a bundle of something in the carriage, and my heart fell to the floor. A number of ideas occurred to me; all of them horrible.

"It came in the night", said Miranda mechanically.

I hurried to the carriage. Halfway covered by the parasol was the baby, unmoving. I cried out in pain. Barbara and Nikita came running. The three of us looked at the scene without being able to react. The baby was wearing the little clothes that Barbara had bought. It was lying on the cushions in the same fashion as Miranda: covered to the waist with the blanket and its little hands crossed in its lap. But it didn't breathe, it didn't move.

"Miranda! What happened? Why didn't you call for someone?", I asked.

"It hardly hurt. I just felt some liquid between my legs. That was all."

I felt a sob that came from my chest and exploded from my mouth; a cry of pure anguish.

"Don't cry Miss Mendoza. I am perfectly well", she said. "Only that my breasts are leaking."

It was true. Miranda's pajama top was soaking wet.

Nikita went to the carriage to look more closely at the baby.

"It's beautiful." You could hear the tears in her voice.

I came closer as well. A more perfect baby you could not imagine: skin like velvet, long black eyelashes, a little bit of hair on its head, its mouth a perfect red rosebud.

"We should call the ambulance", said Nikita.

"No. There's no need. Anyway, it's too late. And I'm not going anywhere", said Miranda firmly.

"But Miranda, you need to be checked out. They need to look you over, see that you're all right", I said mournfully.

"I am not all right. But the doctors have nothing that will fix me. The illness I have is not in my body."

We looked at one another, us three women. None of us wanted to be the one to alert Diego.

"Miranda, was it a boy or a girl?", asked Nikita. Miranda didn't answer. We waited, but she would say nothing. The echo of her question reverberated in the room.

I started to remove the baby's clothing but Miranda's cry stopped me.

"No! Don't do it! It doesn't matter anyway."

Her cries managed to rouse Diego, and behind him, Cecilio and Adriana. In the midst of the explanation, the sobs and the exclamations I managed to undress the baby without Miranda noticing, but what I saw I didn't understand. It was impossible to determine from the baby's genitals whether it was a boy or girl. There was no way to answer Nikita's question.

48

Leonora
The Funeral

In Miranda's bedroom Diego made a huge emotional upheaval. He insisted that no one move, that no one do anything for the moment, which was met with unacknowledged resistance by everyone. It was a struggle to do as he asked; the natural inclination was to do something, anything, many things.

Nikita was able to leave the room and call for an ambulance. When it arrived, Diego went to the main front door to shout at them to leave. The ambulance men were apologetic, saying that they had had trouble finding the house, and for that reason they were so late in arriving, but now that they were here, they were ready to help in any way. They spoke so courteously that Diego calmed down, and in this way, he convinced them that their visit was unnecessary. So they left.

Miranda did not move from the bed and hardly spoke. I took advantage of her muteness to look at the baby. It looked like a plastic doll: its perfectly rounded arms, its little legs, the tiny half-moons of its finger and toe nails. I couldn't resist looking again at its genitals. Now I could see; it was a baby girl. There was no doubt. I wondered what craziness made me see it any other way.

Diego went finally to his workshop. According to Cecilio, he was going to make the casket.

Poncia was for the whole day organizing and cleaning in Miranda's room. The mattress was stained and no matter how hard she scrubbed, she couldn't get the stains out. The threads of blood ran in the current of water across the floor of the back patio. The mattress ended up being entirely soaked and we had to abandon it with the vain hope that it would somehow get clean and dry in the sun.

Then there was the mountain of towels that Miranda had used during the night: all wet and stained, as well as her pajamas, which were soaked in liquids from her breasts. Not milk; but an opaque substance that was slightly viscous. We were surrounded by liquids of all sorts. And during all this, the small creature in the baby carriage slept its eternal slumber.

At nine o'clock in the evening, Miranda came out of her room. She did not look very changed, but she hardly spoke and bumped into the furniture as if she had forgotten where everything was.

"The baby is in my room still. What are we going to do with it?", she asked.

She spoke in a completely neutral tone, the voice of a person unconcerned with anything at all.

"Your father is going to take care of everything", I told her. "Come and eat."

The patio was especially pretty that night, paradoxically. It was dark but the many stars were brilliant in the moonless sky, and the night-blooming flowers were sending their scent to every corner. I had set the table with large candles and the intense colors of the tiles shone like mirrors.

"Where is my father?", asked Miranda.

He came in that moment.

"Here I am."

"And where are we going to bury the baby?", asked Mrs. Poncia timidly.

"In the San Angel cemetery, in the village", answered Diego.

The following morning Diego told us to ready ourselves to walk to the cemetery.

"We're going on foot!" whispered Nikita to me incredulously. "This is like something from the last century. I don't understand."

"Nor I", I told her.

Diego, dressed in black, carried the tiny casket. Cecilio carried a lace cloth in which to wrap it before putting it into the ground; Miranda carried her doll Minx and I, a vase with water. Nikita had a bible in her bag; Adriana, a bouquet of flowers; and Poncia, just her parasol.

We left through the gate in the wall near the drainage ditch and began walking through the deserted streets. We walked and walked, seemingly without getting anywhere. It felt like an eternity. Occasionally people from the village would come out of their houses to watch us pass by; they looked with wide eyes but said nothing.

Finally, we got to the cemetery. There was no one there: no employee, nobody in charge. The grave was dug; it was much deeper than it was long or wide. It seemed more like a tunnel than a grave.

No one cried. Cecilio wrapped the casket in the lace cloth and Diego lowered it into the ground. He took the shovel and filled in the hole. When he had finished, Adriana put the flowers in the vase and we left it there; the sole witness to a silent funeral.

It was night time, very late, when Nikita came into my room from the dark hallway. Her voice was trembling, nearly crying.

"We are in an insane asylum! Don't you realize?"

"Lower your voice!", I told her.

"We have to leave here", she begged. "We can't stay here any longer. Everyone is insane."

"We have to stay here. Miranda needs us now more than ever. She's in a very bad state, but she's not insane."

"Not just her. I mean Diego too. They are acting like something from a gothic storybook, a horror story. Think of what has happened: Fernando's accident, Miranda's suicide attempt, the pregnancy, the birth, the death of the baby, the funeral. Everything."

"But now things are going to return to normal", I assured her.

"Oh my God, Lea. You can't be serious."

There fell upon us a deep silence.

"I've spoken with Barbara. She and I had a plan from before, from before Miranda was supposed to give birth", said Nikita.

"Again with that?", I asked tiredly.

"Yes. The plan was that we would leave: me, you, Miranda and Adriana, and go to Morelia. Barbara knows that she can take better care of Miranda there. Here is like a prison for her."

"And how did you plan on leaving without Diego realizing? In the night, like thieves?" I couldn't avoid a sarcastic tone in my voice.

"Miranda is nearly of age. She can decide for herself where she wants to live, how she wants to live", answered Nikita.

"And, is she in agreement with this plan?"

Nikita shrugged her shoulders. "She was. But now with everything that has happened, I don't know."

After a brief silence Nikita continued.

"But if Miranda has changed her mind, Barbara can change it back again."

Niktita's words made me burn with anger. They had ignored me and made their plans without even consulting me. I imagined their secret conversations, planning the future of my own loved ones: Nikita and Barbara collaborating against me.

"And don't you think that Diego will oppose you?"

"Of course he will. But the time has come for him to stop meddling in the lives of others."

"Don't believe it", I told her. "Diego will not stand by and do nothing. He's capable of...."

"That's what I'm afraid of. Of what Diego is capable of. And to live with that kind of fear is not healthy. It's not correct. Imagine what mother would say about all this."

Mother! I hadn't thought about her in a long time.

"She would insist that we know the truth, that we face it. She would say that we were wrong to hide away in this house, that we should go out and live in the normal world, like normal people."

That night I sat down to read over my journals from the last seven years; those sheets of paper with the logo of the insurance company at the top; filled with the occurrences of the house and the people who live here. But on top of the written words, or maybe underneath them, was another history, of other people and other ideas. I recognize that others have their own memories, their own versions of history, their own pages written with their own notes and by their own hand. I think it's possible that their histories and my own do not coincide. One supposes that there is one solid version of the truth, but as Dr. Leocadio said, it's likely that that unique version does not exist, has never existed in fact.

49

Leonora
A Momentary Truce

Three days of relative calm passed. Each of us stayed mostly to ourselves, licking our wounds. Diego didn't come out of his studio except to have dinner, and dinner was a tense affair. Poncia hardly spoke. Miranda stayed in her room, convalescing. Nikita and I hardly exchanged words. Even Cecilio stopped his normal tricks. The only person who seemed unaffected was Adriana. It seemed like she must know the significance of what had just happened, but it appeared as if she did not. She wandered about in her usual hapless way.

Nikita finally spoke.

"Have you thought about what I told you?"

"About what?"

"Don't pretend to have forgotten. About leaving."

"Well, no."

"What are you waiting for? Do you think that Diego will feel bad if we left?"

I didn't want to answer her. I thought to myself: what is a person's worst nightmare? Being abandoned. The fright of the empty space, to feel the absence of what was there before, to be left behind. There is no one to answer your questions, no voice to accompany your own, no one to sing in the afternoon, to play the piano. Nothing. That is the worst nightmare; and I didn't want to inflict that on Diego. That his daughter would flee from her own house? No.

"I think that all of us would feel bad."

"Lea, you're not seeing things as you should. Diego is a crazy person. Look what he has done to me. Look how things are here. Miranda is a girl who needs to be in contact with other people; she needs to live a normal life. You and I are buried here in a situation that does not suit us, and Adriana needs a special kind of education that we cannot give her."

"We're doing fine here, Nikita."

"No. You're wrong."

Nikita looked sad. "What can I say to you to open your eyes?"

I didn't respond, and she left without saying anything more.

The third day after the funeral dawned with a tepid sun that fought to get through the hazy clouds. I did not feel well, physically. My head hurt and I was tired in every cell of my body. The evening before, Diego and Barbara had been arguing until very late. I seemed to hear their heated voices all night long. Finally they stopped, and I fell into a heavy dream that didn't leave me until noon the next day.

The house was in complete silence. I saw that Adriana was still sleeping. I urgently needed to talk to Nikita. I went to her room; she wasn't there. Nor were her clothes, her things. I felt my heart lurch. I went next to Cecilio's room which was nearest. I tried to hurry but I couldn't; the air seemed thick and difficult to move through. There was nothing there but some old toys that he had long since abandoned.

I heard noises from a distant corner of the house: the striking of metal objects against others; the crashing of wood against the floor; the sharp crackle of glass shattering. I was too afraid to investigate because I suspected what was happening.

I went back to my room and I saw that what I thought was Adriana was nothing more than a bundle of sheets and pillows. I felt clumsy, stupid, like my brain had gone into a coma. And meanwhile, a catastrophe was being played out in another room.

What I wouldn't give now for answering my sister's questions? What I wouldn't give now for paying more attention to her words? Why didn't I tell her the truth about my reluctance to leave? Why? Why?

But then again, the 'truth'? What truth? There are many, and some are not at all true; they only appear that way to the person contemplating them. I know that not all mysteries are resolved in the end. Not all doubts are eased; not all questions answered; people are often not what they seem at first.

50

Leonora
The Escape

Diego was drunk. Blind drunk. It was clear that he had not slept the night before. His eyes were bloodshot and his voice hoarse from the argument with Barbara.

I found him in the patio, destroying everything around him. From his mouth came a string of curses. He was so absorbed in what he was doing that he didn't see me.

When he finally did notice me, his body shook violently, as if he were looking at something he never expected to see. He came closer to me, and looked me fully in the face, with an expression of anguish that I never would want to see again.

"I know who you are", he said in a terrible voice. "I know why you've come. I know what your plan is, I know why you've deceived me."

I felt completely naked, completely vulnerable. So many years of disguising myself as Luz Maria Mendoza, a teacher in his house; those years all wasted. So many happy years, years of usefulness, of working to take care of my sisters, my niece, now all turned to nothing. Diego grabbed me by the shoulders, his face only centimeters from mine.

"I know all about you, Rosa. Don't try to hide anything more from me because there's no point."

On top of the shock of everyone leaving without me, on top of the distress caused by Diego's state of mind, on top of my lethargy and my mental fog, on top of all that came a crushing fear.

Diego confused me with Rosa.

He wasn't in his right mind from the alcohol, but worse than that, he seemed to be operating in another time, in other moments, in circumstances that had nothing to do with me. I didn't know what to do, how to respond. He grabbed me harder and pushed me back until I was pinned against the wall, holding me there by force. Fear robbed me of all my strength.

"You deceived me", he said in the voice of a caged beast. "You told me you loved me. You married me. You said that Miranda would be like my own daughter, and she was." His voice was louder with each phrase.

"Rosa, Rosa! You threw it all away. You ruined it all!"

Diego's words hit my face like a series of slaps, and his fury seemed to feed on itself, growing progressively more violent.

"You are not the person I thought you were. And now you come disguised to my house. In an absurd disguise that I completely see through, that anyone would see through. You come to the house that was for us, for us to be happy in."

Suddenly Diego let go of me and hung his head.

"Why? Why did you do this?" His voice sounded broken, destroyed.

He raised his head to look at me once more. "You had everything you wanted here, everything you needed." He put his hands on my shoulders again, but this time with tenderness. He came close and bent his head to kiss my neck, drawing a line with his lips across it. Slowly, he unbuttoned my blouse and kissed my breasts. Even more slowly he took my blouse off, first one sleeve then the other, to kiss the white skin on the underside of my arms. He breathed deeply, as if the fragrance of my body gave him strength.

The thousand nights of repression, the thousand and one nights where I imagined this, knowing that it would never come true, began to evaporate. The millions of moments of frustration, the moments when I forcibly made myself stop thinking about him, about what I desired, began to disappear. I thought of the uncountable occasions in which I wished that Diego would touch me, would speak to me with words of caring, of love; all this sunk away in the exquisite sensation, of, finally, finally being able to have what I wanted.

I let all of me go, I gave myself over to him. I let go of the fear. And the shock of the morning's discoveries, the sadness at being abandoned. All that was erased. Everything further away than his face, his lips, disappeared. We were in a world apart, a place that we didn't recognize, a place where everything was pegged to a delicious anguish and desperation. It was then that Diego Alba made love to me like it was a matter of life and death.

When I finally came out of my delirium, it was evening. The sun had just set, and Diego was asleep. I got up from the bed, carefully and silently. The fear that I had managed to set aside earlier, come back with a crushing force. Diego was very confused. If in one moment he treated me with tenderness, in another he had been violent. In what state was he going to wake up in now?

I went through the house, wandering, without knowing what to do. It was very dark because there were no longer the people there who lit the oil lamps, the candles. No one there to prepare dinner, none of the customary smells of a coming meal; no sounds of piano, of voices, nothing. The house was moribund, dead.

A terrible anxiety permeated me. What would Diego do when he awoke and realized his error? I had seen him many times when he was angry over some problem of his own, or others. He got rough.

The more I wandered about, the more afraid I became. Nikita says that Diego is crazy. And now in the absence of everyone, he was worse. Much worse.

Without knowing exactly what to do, I returned to his room. Maybe he would recognize me, ask my forgiveness, return to himself. But, to what end? All the possibilities of how we were to interact after this, were ridiculous, grotesque. Should I continue as the teacher, as if nothing happened? Should we establish a relationship, him and me? What kind of relationship? No. None of these things seemed right. Nevertheless, something made me return to his room.

He was sleeping still. Some seconds passed while I looked at him, and then he awoke.

"You!"

His face was twisted with anger and pain.

"You!"

"It's me. It's Luz", I said desperately.

"Again with the false names? That game is over", he said, gnashing his teeth. He got up from the bed and started in my direction.

I ran out, back towards my own room. I don't know if he followed me. I shut my door and locked it, panting. I put some things in a suitcase; I don't know what. My hands were trembling. From a distance I heard something; I hurried even more.

From behind the bureau came a noise, and the bureau began to move. Someone was forcing open the revolving door. I left the suitcase, and grabbed my purse and the briefcase where I stored my journals, flew out the door to the hallway. I had one single goal: to get out. I ran through the gardens towards the gate, that gate that Adriana and I had discovered so many years ago, so many years ago when we knew little about Diego Alba. And from there, to the village where I could get a bus to the city. And from there, to Morelia, to throw myself once again into the new unknown.

51

Leonora
In Morelia

I had only been two weeks in Morelia when Miranda sought me out.

"Can I confess something to you?", she asked.

"What is it?" I saw that she was having trouble getting the words out.

"I… I'm not doing well here." She stood up straighter, as if to gain the courage she needed. "I know I should be grateful for everything that Barbara has done for me but…"

I didn't feel like having this conversation with her. I myself felt very beaten down, very unsure of myself. I had started my new life in Morelia without my clothes, without my books, my things; I had brought virtually nothing with me. And worse still was the thought of Diego. I was afraid of him, and afraid for him. What kind of madness made him confuse me with Rosa?

Then again, I had a tremendous desire to return to his house. The night we spent together had left me with a need that I hardly recognized as possible to endure.

"There is so much noise here. The sound of cars drives me over the edge. I can't think", she said.

It was true. The institute was in the middle of the city, surrounded by busy streets on all sides. And Miranda, lacking one of her senses, had the others much more finely tuned than the average person.

"And then, there's the piano. I want to play it but whenever I do, the students laugh."

"Who?"

"The students at the school."

Miranda started to cry a little bit. "I want to go home. I want to go to the cemetery. I need to see where my daughter is buried."

My poor niece; days and days here paralyzed, unable to process what had just happened. But now, she could.

"I don't want to be here." She started to cry harder.

"Miranda", I said as carefully as I could, "I understand your problems, but before we do anything, there's something I need to clear up with you. I know now is not the best time, but we must do this. It will not be easy."

Miranda looked attentive through her tears.

"I read what you wrote in your diary about the death of Fernando. I read what you wrote about me."

"I don't know what you're talking about, Miss Mendoza. I truly don't."

"I'm referring to the fact that you believe that your father killed Fernando, and that I was there but did nothing to stop him."

Miranda's whole body shook with fright and surprise.

"What? My father would never do anything of the sort."

"But I read it there, in the clear light of day. The words written there...."

Words written by Nikita, as she transcribed Miranda's diary. Was it possible? Rapidly I put in order the possibilities. It could have been Nikita who wrote all that, but why? Or perhaps it was Miranda and now she was denying it. Or maybe it was Adriana, who had already been caught once before interfering in Miranda's journals. Or maybe it was someone else entirely.

"You're right", I said. "Your father would never be capable of that kind of insanity."

Later, when I spoke with Nikita, I could hardly contain the desire to clear everything up with her, but such was my confusion that I hardly knew where to begin. I concluded that it was better to just remain silent for the time being.

Nikita had commented to me that Miranda's complaints about the school were unfounded. She said that Miranda refused to go to class, refused to eat in the dining room with the other students, that she refused to interact with anyone there.

"I like Morelia", affirmed Nikita with enthusiasm. "It's pretty. In the afternoon, people walk around the park by the cathedral, and in the plaza there are so many places to have coffee. It reminds me of the *Gran Place* in Brussels. You remember....?"

Nikita continued. "There is life here! We aren't stuck, drying up in the countryside like we were before. And Adriana is liking it very much too. When she is with Barbara, she's tranquil."

"What does Barbara say about Miranda's complaints?"

"She's very worried. She says that before, Miranda used to pray a lot with her, but now she doesn't want to. It seems that prayer has lost its effect."

"And Cecilio?"

Nikita's face darkened. "He has become an ally of Miranda. He wants to return to the house too."

Nikita and I were talking for a long time. Finally, she asked me:

"And you, Lea?"

52

Leonora
Diego in Morelia

It didn't surprise me when one day, in the courtyard of the school, Miranda said:

"Today my father is coming." For the first time, I doubted it. We had been there three months with no news from him. A total silence.

But it was true. Later that day he arrived in his unmistakable big black car. I saw it parked across the street, its windows darkened to keep out prying eyes.

The painter got out of the car and went directly to the director's office. After two hours behind closed doors, they came out, Barbara and her husband and Diego, and indicated that we should enter. We sat down as if entering a theater or a temple: anxiously awaiting the performance.

Diego, standing behind the desk and dressed in coat and tie, started speaking.

"During the absence of all of you, I realized many things. I realized..."

He couldn't end the phrase; a kind of paralysis took him over. I saw that Miranda had tears on her cheeks, and Cecilio was grabbing the arms of his chair fiercely.

"I've come to ask you to return, to beg you to return", he managed to say after an enormous effort.

"I have been very selfish", he continued. He sighed deeply. "I never thought about anyone else, in what they lacked, or what they were bothered by. I didn't take these things into account."

No one spoke. We were all suspended in the greatest void imaginable.

"But everything has changed now."

Diego loosened his tie.

"To begin with, Miranda needs instruction in the piano. I've contracted with a private tutor; an Italian who will start coming to the house as soon as we return."

"Papa!" Miranda's voice vibrated in delight.

"His name is Pietro Crespi. In Italy he worked in the opera. He's an expert in piano, violin and voice."

"Papa, thank you!", exclaimed Miranda.

"And for everyone, but I think Miss Mendoza will be especially happy, I've brought electricity from the town and wired the house for electric lights and power. Now, Miss Mendoza, you can use your electric typewriter."

I didn't say anything. Did Diego really think that electric lights were sufficient recompense for what he did to me a month ago?

"But Papa, you always said it was too far, impossible to do because of the distance."

"Well, now you see how things have changed.

"Well done, Diego", said Barbara. "It's time that your house entered the twentieth century."

"And for the teachers in the house, well. I know that you'd enjoy going out on your own. I thought a car would be useful. You can travel about on the weekends, go into the city, go shopping....."

Everything Diego said, he said with such a humble, abject tone in his voice that I felt very sorry for him. He had been at the top of the highest mountain, arrogant and powerful, and had fallen to the lowest rungs of childishness, simplicity. His inducements seemed pathetic.

Diego looked at me and Nikita. I didn't say anything and I knew that Nikita would not respond in that moment. She was never going back to the house in the countryside, ever. She had told me that several times during our stay in Morelia.

Miranda, Cecilio and Barbara were enchanted with this new Diego that we had before us. But I was not. It was clear that Diego remembered nothing about the night in which he confused me with Rosa; the night he made love to me like a matter of life and death.

"I've also come to realize some things", said Barbara. "Miranda is too old to be in school here. All the other students are younger. And she hasn't been happy here, isn't that right?, she asked her.

"No. It's not that. It's...." Miranda, always so polite, did not want to appear ungrateful.

"You don't need to explain, my child", she said tenderly. "I know you need to recuperate, and where better but your own home?"

There was a long silence in the director's office. Finally, Nikita spoke.

"Mr. Alba, there is one more thing."

269

"Anything", he responded.

"Well, thank you very much for the car. I'm sure that we will enjoy it very much. But I'm not going back to the house."

Diego looked heartily surprised.

"Although I think my sister wants to."

Nikita looked at me with a clever smile, and continued talking.

"But there is something else. Her salary doesn't cover what it should."

Nikita then named an extraordinary sum; a number that she chose from the air, like a balloon about to explode.

"Of course. How stupid I've been not to imagine that", responded Diego with all the *elán* of a courtier of the king.

Everyone began talking happily at once. Everyone but me. Nikita smiled like the cat that ate the mouse. She said to me in a low voice:

"At least this way you will save a lot of money for when you finally decide to leave that cursed house."

On the one hand, Diego's news made me happy, but on the other hand, I was disillusioned. During our time in Morelia I had entertained myself with constructing a story about Diego and me. In that story I told him who I was and everything about me; all the secrets and the lies and the cover-ups would disappear; and we could be together as free individuals. I was twenty-eight years old. It was time to leave behind the disguises.

But there was no indication that Diego thought of me in any other way except as his children's teacher. What happened that night that he confused me with Rosa, was long buried.

When I went to bed that evening after readying my few things to return, I set myself to thinking. The truth is there was no decision to make; I wanted to return. Then I reflected over the things that had happened since leaving Brussels. I came to Mexico with the objective of finding out what happened to my sister Rosa, and to take care of my niece. The second objective had been realized; Miranda was a charming young woman. Rosa would be proud of her.

But the first was stubbornly unsolved. I asked myself, what horrendous crime had Rosa committed to engender the fury of Diego in that way? What had she done? In these and other questions I was deep in thought, when I heard a soft knock on my door. It was Diego.

"Miss Mendoza. I have brought you something. But you'll have to follow me in order to see it."

I followed him to the school chapel. In the shadows I could see something resting on an easel. Diego turned on the light and I could see that it was a portrait; the figure sitting in profile, with her head in light and her body in the shadow.

"But… how?", I asked him astonished. "It was destroyed! How did you manage to restore it?"

"I didn't restore it. I painted it again. I remember exactly what you looked like when you came for the first time to the house."

"That was more than seven years ago…", I said quietly.

"Seven years is not much time. We still have many years ahead of us."

I couldn't stop the tears. The portrait was perfection. I had an expression of melancholy mixed with happiness, reflecting so precisely my sentimental interior. Diego had painted me exactly as if he knew me to my very deepest center.

"Do you like it?"

I nodded.

"Do you forgive me for what happened the last night we were together?" He indicated that I should sit down on one of the pews, and then sat next to me.

"I know that it was unpardonable. I'm a pig, a horrible pig. But I never wanted to hurt you. I was crazy. I hardly knew what I was doing."

Diego had never addressed me in such an intimate manner before.

"There's something that I need to explain to you", I told him. "It's something that you need to know about me, about Nancy and Amelia too."

There came a knocking on the chapel door. Diego looked up, electrified. Dr. Williams Barr came in, Barbara's husband and co-director of the institute. He seemed unaware of what was going on.

"Is there something I can help you with?", he asked.

"No, no", said Diego. "Thank you. We were just leaving."

Diego ushered me to the door; as he was so able to do…. guiding me without touching, making me go where he wanted me to go. It was one of his many talents; insisting on things without the person being aware of his insistence.

The moment of confessing everything to him had passed. I felt like I was drowning in sadness, in missed opportunities. I knew that the moment might not return very easily or very soon. And then, I realized that Diego really did not want to listen to me at all.

By the next morning we were in the car, on the way home. I thought about my sister Nikita; now she was independent, working in the institute for the blind, having a life that was free, her own life. We had discussed at length what Adriana should do: Nikita insisted that she stay in Morelia; I was just as firm that she should return with me. But in the end, Adriana decided on her own: she just quietly packed her suitcase.

As for me, so strong were my feelings for Diego that I put aside all reason, all logic. I was conscious of that, but I couldn't control it. I thought that once we were back at the country house, that everything would return to the way it had been; and I was both happy and sad. We would be together in that labyrinthine house, far from the upsets and anxieties of the world outside.

53

Leonora
Our Return

It was night when we arrived at the country house, returning from Morelia where we had been for some time. From far way you could see a point of light where there had never been any light before, small but brilliant. In middle of that great dark wood, there gleamed the electric lights that Diego had installed, as a way to convince us to return.

As we came closer, the lights got stronger. When we reached the point in the highway where you turned to enter the long driveway, I saw a post, at the top of which there was a lantern of wrought iron. The entrance was now perfectly illuminated. We passed through the rows of white Eucalyptus trees, every one lit up from the ground to the tops of their canopies. The leaves moved in the night breeze.

When we pulled up to the front door, we could see that the doors were wide open, spilling out a welcoming light, and once inside the patio, we saw that it danced with a lively play of light and shadow. On the table was our dinner. The vases were full of flowers, a multitude of flowers of all colors, all fragrances.

We ate. We drank. We toasted our return. We were happy; the prodigal sons returning to the fold. Diego talked and talked. He told us about the feat of installing the electricity, of bringing the wires such a long distance; a huge effort. We told him of our days in Morelia; Diego wanted to know each and every detail.

I found myself more quiet than usual, but Miranda was talkative. She was delirious with joy at returning home, delirious with joy at the thought of her piano teacher coming soon. Cecilio and Poncia were happy to be there, simply to be there. And me? Diego had asked my forgiveness for the night in question, the night he was drunk and crazy, and I had forgiven him. But things were not back to normal. I longed for a day when I could leave behind my disguises, my lies, but by the same token, the idea of revealing everything about me filled me with terror. Here, again in my old situation, I felt evaporating the courage that I had in Morelia, when I was about to tell him all.

After everyone had gone to bed, I went to the office to try out my electric typewriter. Oh, what a difference! It was astonishingly quick to write down my thoughts; so much better than with pen and paper. I could work so fast that in just a few hours, I managed to note down everything that had happened since leaving the house. I was quite happy with the typewriter. Just when I was finishing, Diego came in.

"What keeps you up so late, Luz?", he asked amiably.

I hurriedly put away my papers.

"I'm preparing the lessons for tomorrow", I told him, but Diego didn't pay much attention. It made my pulse quicken to hear him address me by my first name; he had never done that before. He came near and kissed my hand, as was his custom.

"I am so very happy to have you all here once again", he said, looking straight into my eyes. "You can't imagine what it was like in your absence."

I wasn't sure how to respond. My heart urged me to speak frankly to him, but my head counseled no.

"Miranda and Cecilio are very happy to be home", I told him.

"And you?"

"I am too", I told him cautiously.

"Luz", he started. "I think I have been very unfair. And very blind, if you will permit me the word. Seven years have passed that we have been together here, and in those seven years I have not allowed myself to feel what I really felt."

"What did you really feel?", I asked him, hoping against hope that he would tell me he loved me, and that I could say the same to him.

"I didn't permit myself to recognize many things. The memory of Rosa got in the way. And then, when everyone was gone... well, the shock loosened some things in my mind."

Diego continued, after a beat.

"I think the shock has allowed me to see things more clearly."

He came closer, without letting go of my hand. Once again, he kissed me; with all the delicacy of an artist painting the petals of a flower. He began at the wrist, drawing a fine line up the inside of my arm, up to my collarbone.

"Come. I have something to show you."

We went to the living room and in the place where Rosa's portrait had hung, there was my portrait. I felt a confusion, like a kind of nausea. For seven years the spot had been unoccupied, as if guarding the place in her memory. But no longer.

Diego had moved a big sofa, which normally was along the wall, to a position directly in front of the painting. He had me sit down and there, underneath my likeness, he made love to me. It was tender, rich, full of passion. I let myself go in the moment, trying not to think about displacing Rosa, trying not to think about the past at all.

Afterwards, wrapped in a blanket, Diego began to talk. He wanted to know everything about me, saying that my past was of great interest to him and he lamented not having asked me about it before.

"I have to confess something to you, Luz. You look a little bit like my deceased wife. You have a voice very similar to hers, and you have certain mannerisms that remind me a lot of her."

"Well, I…"

"And I think that's why I subconsciously kept my distance from you. I didn't allow myself to see you clearly."

"It's that…."

"But now I've erased all that. I've erased all the confusions, the mistakes about you, about who you are."

"Oh…."

"And now I want to know more. Tell me, in detail; I want to understand everything. Tell me about your childhood in Bloemfontein. Tell me about your parents, your family."

"Diego, I…."

"I want to fill that emptiness that I have about you. Because I can't bear it any longer. I feel like these seven years that we've been here, have been like a dress rehearsal. And now, only now, are we starting to actually act in the play."

"You mean…?"

"Do you remember *Marianela?*", he asked me. "That was the event that set in motion all my doubts. I went through a kind of crisis, but it didn't result in anything. For a while I would come close to the dilemma about my past with Rosa, but then I could go no further, and I would go back to all my old thoughts. Your presence, and what we did in *Marianela* provoked all that, Luz."

"My presence?"

"Yes. And since then, the walls that separated me from you only got higher. You reminded me so much of Rosa that I could not see the reality."

"What reality is that?"

"That I love you very much. For you. For your way of thinking, seeing. For your beauty and your character, for your work in the house, for what you've done for Miranda and Cecilio."

Diego stopped talking and took out a small box, opening it solemnly. He took out a ring: a band of white surrounded by two bands of black.

"I had this made for you. The black is obsidian and the white is polished bone."

I felt a moment of easiness. Bones of what? Or who?

Diego paused, then resumed speaking since I couldn't respond at all.

"The ring represents what you are for me: the light in the midst of the darkness, the white in tension with the black."

He put the ring on my finger. "I don't want you to be simply the teacher here. I want you to be my wife. I know that now. Before, I didn't but now I do."

Diego waited for me to respond, but I was too overwhelmed to speak, so I put my arms around his neck, embracing him. Again we made love, softly. Even as I fell into the throes of the sensation, I remembered Nikita's words: *Diego is a man who says what you want to hear, does to you what you want to have done,* and I wondered what it meant when she said that Diego nearly broke her in two when they were together. These thoughts were so upsetting that I had to work hard to banish them from my mind.

Afterwards, lying on the sofa Diego took up again his investigation.

"I'm going to know everything about you", he said smiling.

"Oh, not now. This moment is so beautiful. Tomorrow, Diego."

The ring presented a big problem for me. I couldn't wear it in Nikita's presence, if I was not going to explain how it got on my finger. Something in me just refused to explain anything to her. I felt, yet again, how hard it is to be between the sword and the wall; caught between two threatening forces: the lies and the truth. Both could ruin me.

The ring also really bothered Adriana. She looked at it fixedly as if by the force of her gaze she could make it disappear. Finally, she showed me something she had written in her journal, in plain language. "*If you marry Diego, Mrs. Poncia is going to kill you.*" I felt a tremendous shock of fear.

"What are you saying, Adriana?"

"For the wind. In the wind. The voices in the wind."

Poor Adriana. Her intelligence was fractured by the frustrations she experienced constantly, but there remained in her a bit of logic still. She was able to express something that hovered at the edges of my consciousness, something I hadn't been able to express to myself. But, how had she learned of what was happening with me and Diego? I suspected that Poncia had told her, because there was little in the house that she missed. What was the tie between them? Or **was** there any connection between them? Adriana was afraid of her, I knew that. But perhaps there was something else?

54

Leonora
The Following Days

In the days following our return, the house returned to its regular rhythm, as if it were trying to reassure me that my worries were unfounded. Diego spent most of the day in his studio, working. Poncia redoubled her culinary efforts and prepared exquisite meals for us. I was able to put aside Adriana's fears that Poncia might harm me. The piano teacher arrived and Miranda's music lessons began. The cloud of sadness that had covered her for these many weeks, lifted. She regained the verve and lightness that she had before the arrival of Fernando Blau.

And I was in a delirium of happiness and anguish. Diego did not ask me again about my past, which seemed strange to me but also was a great relief; I didn't have to tell him more lies. But I was afraid that at any moment he would want to know more.

Another thing. Every night, after all of us had gone to bed, he would come to my room and take me back to his own, to make delicious love to me. These were beautiful experiences, passionate ones. It was as if the seven years of repressing what I felt had become an explosion of all that hidden sentiment.

In those nights we talked, but only of ordinary things. Whenever he did touch, even lightly, on my past I avoided answering; whenever he mentioned getting married, I changed the subject. But the effort was exhausting. As a child, they used to call me the 'Little Charlie Chaplin' because of my acting ability; now it was necessary to employ all my abilities and more, to mold the conversation.

So, on the one hand I was enormously happy but on the other, I was in anguish over the falsehoods that I had created. Diego had fallen in love with a woman named Luz Maria Mendoza, from Bloemfontein, who had a Spanish father and a South African mother. He didn't fall in love with me. To tell him now, who I was, after everything he had done to regain my trust, would be sufficient cause to ruin the love he had for me. How could he marry me, if he didn't really know me? I was living in a terrible, confusing cloud.

Some months passed. I couldn't sleep. I didn't write in my journals, as I did before. I couldn't analyze things like I did before, because they were too immediate, too present. Diego occupied all my mental space, with his deep voice, his vigorous walk, his absorbing ideas.

Finally, he left on a trip and Barbara came back. Things calmed down in the house. I prepared the lessons for Adriana and Cecilio; I came to know Crespi the piano teacher; Dr. Leocadio continued his work with Miranda; everything was normal.

One day Nikita came from Morelia.

"Lea, you have to get out of here. For your own mental health." I didn't say anything. This was a refrain that I was growing tired of hearing.

Nikita inhaled forcefully, gathering her forces.

"Where is my Lea, my old Lea? The one who used to make us laugh so much? Go back to being her", she begged me. "We have had enough of Luz."

As I continued in my silence, her tone took on a bitterness.

"Rosa wouldn't recognize you now."

There aren't words to describe the effect of her words on me.

"And as much as you believe that Diego loves you, he doesn't." Nikita then repeated something she had told me many times before:

"Diego is one of those men who guesses what you most need to hear, and says it."

"No, that's not true. You don't know him like I do."

Nikita grew pensive, and hugged me. With her face a few millimeters from mine, she looked gravely into my eyes. She tried again to convince me.

"You have become fearful, Lea. Where is that girl who came to Mexico with nothing but her imagination? What has happened to her?"

"Nikita, there are things you don't know. Diego…."

"I know about that. You spend every night with him."

"How did you know?!" I was floored.

"I have my ways. What you don't know is that Diego hasn't changed. Not at all. He is the same bounder as ever", she said sadly.

"What do you know, specifically?"

"He has his women. His little love affairs."

"You're crazy."

"I'm not crazy. What I am is happy to have escaped his net. By the way, where do you think he is now?"

"In New York, setting up a new gallery for his work."

"He's in New York because he's after a woman named Lara Boon. She's the owner of the gallery. While we were in Morelia, he was involved with her, but later there was a scandal and she ended up in the hospital."

Swallowing hard I asked her:

"How do you know this?"

Ignoring my question, she continued:

"And he still sleeps with Esmé Moreau. They are together in the little house by the pond. You can see above the bed, the marks they put there with the dates of their meetings. They even give each one a grade: from one to ten, according to...."

"I don't want to hear any more."

"Diego is sick. He has a very sick way of living."

"Enough! Be quiet!"

Nikita was nearly shouting now, as was I.

"You need to open your eyes and recognize the character of your lover."

The word 'lover' bothered me. I didn't consider myself to be his lover. He had asked me to marry him. He wanted to make me his legitimate wife.

I was feeling beaten down by Nikita's words; weakened. Timidly I asked her:

"What happened with this woman in New York?"

"Diego supposedly hit her."

"Why?"

"She got angry because she found out that Diego wasn't free to contract with her for his paintings."

"And he wasn't free to do that?"

"Of course not! Diego is under exclusive contract with Esmé, here in Mexico. You must know that."

"Well, yes." But I actually wasn't aware of that particular detail.

"There was an argument. A fight. And he hit her. She was in the hospital for several days."

I felt a confusion swirling around me like a gigantic merry-go-round. From the living room came a strange music. I recognized it as a new piece that Miranda was learning. She had become obsessed with her piano lessons, practicing for hours on end. In that moment, the music unhinged me. I went hurriedly, without thinking, to the living room and shouted:

"Stop it! I can't stand it!"

Crespi and Miranda looked in my direction, surprised.

"What's wrong, Miss Mendoza?", asked the piano teacher. Miranda said nothing, but she rose from the piano bench and came up to me. She felt in the air for my shoulders and drew me near when she found them.

"Miss Mendoza is sad because my father isn't here", she explained. She patted my hair, smoothing it in the manner that I always did for her.

"Don't worry, he won't be gone long", she told me warmly.

Her words filled me with terror and happiness in equal measures. Coming face to face with Diego after what Nikita had told me, put me into a terrible nervous state. But perhaps Nikita was in error? Maybe she had misinterpreted in some way? Or been told wrongly by someone? I tried to convince myself of this. Surely there was an explanation, another version of events.

I hardly had time to compose myself when the painter returned. He immediately realized that something had changed in me. I asked him about this woman Lara Boon and what had happened in New York.

"The police found the man who attacked her. He's in custody."

"But, why did they think you were involved?"

"Misunderstandings. You have to realize, Luz, that the art world in New York is a madhouse. There are rich people, very rich people, who collect art as a status symbol, or as an investment. Art is a business with a lot of money behind it, and very few scruples."

"So, you didn't have anything to do with her?"

"Absolutely not."

Some moments of silence passed. Then Diego kissed me. He covered me with his body. He wrapped me in a silk blanket of love, his skin next to mine. He folded me like a letter into an envelope; he drew his designs on me, on my flesh and on my heart; he breathed on me; he made me feel like the most valuable woman in the world. That night was one of the most wonderful of my life.

55

Leonora
To Believe in Adriana

The day after Diego's return from New York, he told me had a very important painting to do, and that he would be busy with it for a while. With that, he went to his studio and shut the door, asking for his meals to be brought to him, and we didn't see him for many days.

It was then, that Cecilio interfered with Adriana in some way. Poor Adriana; her body had grown but her mind had not. She was the same naïve girl as always. She followed Cecilio around, begging for his attention, trying to get him involved in some activity, all without noticing that he made fun of her, mocked her, treated her most cruelly. I did what I could to protect her, but I couldn't always be by her side. The house was so large and the grounds so extensive that she could disappear for hours; she could be occupied with something in some part of the house with no sign of it in another part. Poor girl. She spent hours and hours drawing in her notebook, 'writing' things that were indecipherable. Her notebooks were full of her strange hieroglyphics; meaningful only to her, or perhaps not even to her. It occurred to me more than once that she herself might not even know what all that meant, and she 'wrote' there in imitation of me, or for some other, personal reason.

But now there was something in her notebook that she desperately wanted to show me. And this time I could see there, written in plain language, that Cecilio had raped her.

"And it wasn't just once. It was several times, on several occasions. And not just normally, but from behind as well….", I said to Nikita, my voice shaking.

"That accursed Cecilio, he's going to pay for this!", she responded in a lethal tone. "Let's get him, Lea. We can tie him up, tie up his hands…"

"But…"

"And then we can cut off his balls", she said, her enthusiasm growing.

"Wait…."

"That he takes advantage of a person with mental problems is a crime; an inhuman crime. And he's going to pay for this", she repeated.

"Yes, but…."

"I'm going to get the rope", and with this she hurried away. To her retreating back I blurted out:

"Don't you think it would be better to go to the police?", but she didn't answer.

In a few minutes she returned with a sharp knife from the kitchen and a long rope. I repeated about going to the police.

"Bah! Do you think the police would be on our side? Cecilio is the son of the famous painter, and Adriana is nobody. Besides, the police won't understand her journal."

I tried to explain that she had written in plain letters, but Nikita didn't want to hear it.

"They'll take a look at all the rest of her scribblings and conclude that she's just a poor crazy girl. Besides, this is Mexico, remember? The police don't act the same way they do in Brussels, Lea."

Cecilio was by now a young man of eighteen, tall and thin. He had continued all along with his manias and her perversities, but this was the absolute worst. Nevertheless, I couldn't let Nikita go through with her plan; it was an atrocity equal to the one Cecilio had perpetrated on Adriana.

"What are you waiting for?", she asked when she saw that I made no movement towards participating.

"Well, if you're not going to help me, I'm going to speak to Diego", she said.

I could endure it no longer. I went to Adriana and we locked ourselves in the bedroom.

After a few minutes we started hearing shouts coming from the studio. The angry voice of Diego alternated with the high-pitched shrieking of Cecilio. From the living room came a discordant music, crazy, loud sounds. It was a deafening cacophony; an expression of anguish of the most strident form.

When the explosion finally stopped, everyone came out cautiously.

"He cried sufficiently", Nikita said with satisfaction.

"And Adriana? What consolation is that for her? You can't think that it is an adequate compensation for what he did to her?!", I said incredulously.

Nikita looked at Adriana. "Well?", she asked her. "How do you feel now, Adriana? Do you feel better?"

Adriana didn't answer. Her face registered no emotion. I passed her a notebook to see if she wanted to write something, but she didn't take it. She didn't look at us; she didn't move from her position on the bed.

It was then that something new occurred to me. Was it possible that she was wrong about what happened between her and Cecilio? Or that she misinterpreted? Or worse still, that she was deliberately inventing something? Her desire for his attention was obvious, and had been since childhood. What better way to gain it than by accusing him of a terrible crime? Or maybe she was just so frustrated that she was pushed to the very edge. I could almost sympathize with her; I knew about what frustration can do to a person.

From that day, Adriana entered into a kind of trance, a sad trance, that excluded me completely.

56

Leonora
Rosa's Letters

In the days after the incident with Cecilio and Adriana, I tried many times to read her journals, but I understood hardly anything. I asked her repeatedly to explain them to me, but she wouldn't. I begged her. It was urgent that I know if something more had happened to her. Poor Adriana. I know that I've failed her; that I haven't protected her as I should.

I also wanted to read her journals to see if she was truthful in her expressions. Did Cecilio really do something to her? I wanted to understand, but without her cooperation it was impossible.

One day Nikita arrived from Morelia. She was coming often in those days; she loved the car that Diego had given us, and the freedom it afforded her.

We sat down in the patio under the mellow sunshine of the afternoon. Even on the warmest days, the patio was cool because of its position in the middle of the house, protected by the thick walls and the leaves and flowers of the foliage that surrounded it. From the beginning, I had loved the patio; loved being in it for the peace and beauty, and for the memories of all the nice things that had happened there.

"How does it go with you and Diego?, she asked. "You two seem very happy together. You haven't heeded any of my advice, but it seems it doesn't matter to you."

I was offended by the brusqueness of her words.

"I try to manage things so that we don't have problems."

"Lea! How blind you are! You only see the good in people; never the bad. You refuse to see the bad."

Nikita looked at me with a barely controlled anguish.

"You're wrong", I told her, but with no desire to continue the conversation.

"I can't believe that you don't see what's happening here. It can't be that you're oblivious."

"Nikita, don't make this moment sad. Look around you…. it's so pretty." I waved my hand to take in the whole patio. Nikita became even more serious.

"Look around? Yes, I can look around. I remember that it was here, in this place, that we discovered the letter from Fernando Blau, that letter that started everything. That catastrophe. And what's more…."

I waited for her to continue. She paused, as if to put more weight on her words.

"This house is rotten. From the inside. And you know it."

She paused again, making her statements drive themselves home.

"It's full of tunnels, of dark, secret tunnels."

"But Nikita! You used those tunnels all the time."

"Not just me", she said.

There passed a moment of difficult silence. My sister wanted to insinuate that Diego took advantage of those tunnels to observe us, to spy on us, but I knew he wouldn't do such a thing. I preferred to think that Nikita was referring to Poncia or to Cecilio. That, I certainly believed.

"All right", she said finally. "Let's not ruin the visit." With this, my sister calmed down, and began to speak normally.

"There are so many things that have no explanation. After all this time, we still don't know exactly how or why Rosa died. Diego affirms that she drank something toxic that she thought was melon water. But he didn't see her drink it. It's entirely possible that she died of something else altogether."

Nikita sighed, and continued in a rather pessimistic tone.

"And despite your relationship with him, you haven't discovered anything new. We don't know anything more than what appears in the official reports."

"I know."

"Nor have you succeeded in clearing up the mess of lies that you created. He still thinks you are someone else."

"Yes, I know."

"You spend your time writing in your journal instead of living a real life. Lea! You're buried here, and you never even go out anymore. You're completely isolated, completely enmeshed in your own thoughts."

She looked at me with a mixture of severity and tenderness.

"You've been sleeping with him for months and you've never wondered why you haven't gotten pregnant?"

"I'm taking care of that."

"You are not. I know it. Diego had a vasectomy many years ago. He can't have children with you, or anyone."

I felt very much like crying then.

"But Nikita! How do you know this?"

"Barbara told me."

"How does she know?"

"I'm not sure. Barbara and Diego have a history that predates us. Maybe she and Diego…"

Nikita didn't finish her sentence, leaving me to wonder if Barbara and Diego had ever been together. I wanted to change the subject.

"Tell me about your boyfriend", I asked her. She had come to tell me the news.

"He's good looking. Very studious. He doesn't resemble Diego or our father at all. Lea, I've analyzed myself, and that's why I mention this. Dr. Leocadio has helped me uncover a lot of hidden stuff in my psyche. Now I understand why I've been attracted to men of a certain type. Now I know how to avoid it, and I feel much more in control. What happened in Brussels doesn't affect me anymore. What happened in Paris has been erased. What happened with Diego is gone. I am the one in charge of my future, not anyone else."

My sister's voice was triumphant; it spoke of a goal met; a giant task completed.

"Look, I want you to meet him. Will you come back with me to Morelia?"

Hardly waiting for my reply she ran to get the car. The trip to Morelia was nearly four hours, and in that time we never stopped talking. We spoke of everything, in the freest of ways. Even Adriana spoke pretty well, contributing bits and pieces to our conversation. Nikita scolded me, as usual, for the errors she saw me committing, but she did it with love, with care. And for my part, I had nothing to scold her for except keeping from me the news of her love affair. She had hidden it for some time.

The young man was named Ricardo Soca. He was studying psychology, as was Nikita. He was respectable, studious, just as Nikita described him.

"But promise me not to do anything without telling me first", I told her.

"I promise. I'm sick of unexpected things."

It was getting near Christmas when Nikita visited again. We went to sit in the patio, as usual. The sun made a pretty pattern of light and shadow from the rafters above us; there were flowers blooming despite it being December. But I couldn't avoid thinking about my sister's words from before: that the house was beautiful but full of rottenness, that its beauty was the antithesis of the ugliness of its inhabitants: two sides of the same face; impossible to discern the existence of a whole truth.

Nikita opened a bottle of wine and we started to talk. All afternoon we talked about Rosa; how she was so logical and well organized; how loving and attentive she was; how observant she was. While in the background of our conversation, the household sounds hummed in their normal way- Miranda playing the piano, the chirping of the baby chicks from the rear patio, the water flowing from the fountain; all the domestic singsong making its comforting noises- the two of us were alone with our words.

"You knew that they argued a lot, didn't you?"

"Rosa and Papa?", I asked, surprised.

"Yes."

"What about?"

"Politics. What else? The socialists, the communists, President Johnson, Salvador Allende, all that."

"And Papa defended Johnson, of course."

"Of course. I think that's why she went to Chile. She wanted to see if socialism could work, like a test. She wanted to put Papa's ideology up against socialism and see which would win."

"I didn't know much about that."

"I know. We were really young. And you always preferred not to know things if they interfered with your happy character."

Into our conversation crept a nostalgia, a sense of longing for the past. The life we led in Brussels, at number 30, Rue de la Science, had disappeared so abruptly, so completely. The child Leonora who made everyone laugh had utterly changed. Our mother was dead. Our oldest sister, the ablest, most accomplished of us four, dead. Our father, disgraced, nearly forgotten. We had left to us just the little bit of family that remained in Mexico, so far from that tidy house in that tidy European city.

"I heard the name of Diego Alba mentioned several times in those arguments between Papa and Mother", said Nikita.

"What did they know about Diego in those days?", I asked, very surprised.

"That he was a successful artist; rich, but on top of that, he was linked to dangerous socialists in other parts of Latin America. That he was famous for his power to influence people in the communist party with his art and his writings."

"Do you think he's still involved in that?"

"Well, communism is in its last days. Not long ago the Berlin Wall was taken down, if you didn't know."

Nikita closed her eyes in order to think clearly.

"Everything Rosa believed in was just a dream. Socialism never functioned; it could never work."

"Are you saying that Rosa was deluded when she went to Chile?"

Nikita didn't answer except to shrug her shoulders.

Some days later, Nikita was back, this time an unexpected visit. She was very excited.

"I have something to show you!"

She handed me a manila envelope, stuffed full, and a notebook with a yellow and green plaid cover. I recognized it as one of Rosa's notebooks. The envelope was heavy.

"What is this?", I asked warily, weighing the envelope in my hand.

"Letters. Some that Mother wrote to Rosa while she was in Chile and some that Rosa wrote to her."

"How did you get this?"

Nikita looked uncomfortable. "Barbara gave it to me. She said she found it in Diego's office some years ago."

"And, how is it that now, of all times, it occurs to her to give it to you?"

Nikita struggled to find the words. "I told her, Lea. I told her about us. But I made her promise never to say anything to Diego or Miranda. Never."

I didn't know whether to feel relief or fear. The secrets that we had kept for so long were now out of our control.

"Lea, Rosa's diary explains so many things! Finally, I understand what happened to her."

Nikita's discovery sent me into a tailspin.

"Did you say there were letters that Rosa sent to Mother? How in the world did they come to be in Rosa's possession?"

"Probably Rosa asked Mother to return them to her, to have a record. You know how methodical she was."

I looked at the bulging manila envelope with fear; a presentiment that those letters could change my life.

"Go on. Take them. But keep them hidden. Diego should never know that you have them."

Nikita became pensive.

"Read the diary first, then the letters. Once you have, you will not be the same person."

That night, after my sister had left for Morelia, I took out the diary. With a deep breath, I started to read.

> *But then when Leonora, Nikita and Adriana were born in rapid succession, my father was unable to show to them the same affection he showed for me. Maybe it was because they didn't resemble him; neither in appearance nor in character. My father and I are resolute people; we are concerned with how the world is best managed, how human systems are best governed, how best to live with one another in a global sense. I love my sisters dearly, but they are frivolous; they aren't interested in those topics.*

Frivolous. Rosa's words made me feel bad. But she was right. Neither I nor Nikita was ever interested in politics, and up until recently when Nikita went to live in Morelia, we weren't much interested in the bigger world of events either.

That our father favored Rosa was no surprise as well. It was always clear that she was his favorite, so when she left and went to Chile, he was especially traumatized. His three other daughters were not much consolation.

I couldn't keep reading the diary. It was too hard to be reminded of that past. I decided to put that off for another day, and start with the letters. I took one out.

> *Mexico, D.F.*
>
> *Nov. 3, 1976*
>
> *Mother,*
>
> *I am afraid. Very afraid. I need you to go to Santiago as soon as you possibly can and get Miranda and bring her here. She is in terrible danger. The DINA is capable of anything. I'm desperate, more desperate than I have ever been in my life. Ask Papa to help you with the trip, but don't rely on him for much. I know what's happening between you and him, and I want you to know that he has put me in to this awful position. He's responsible for everything.*
>
> *Go as quickly as you can. Make sure that there is no one guarding the apartment, and that you don't attract the attention of anyone. I will be at the Hotel Geneve; we will be safe there. Call me at the hotel as soon as you land.*
>
> *Rosa*

I read her letter without stopping to breathe. I supposed that the DINA was some government group and that they had something to do with Rene's death. Did the DINA come all the way to Mexico, to Diego's house, to kill Rosa as well? How did Diego permit that to happen?

I was paralyzed, not knowing what to think. I wanted to read more despite the chaos in my head. I opened the manila envelope and saw inside a tumbled mess of letters and envelopes, some with dates, others without; so much information in a jumble. I didn't feel capable of organizing that. There was also Rosa's diary. I smoothed the cloth cover, that plaid that I knew well, but had no energy to read more. Tomorrow morning, in the clear light of day, I could start again.

57

Leonora
More Letters

But in the morning, the diary was gone. I think that Adriana took it because when I asked her, she got so agitated that she gave herself away.

As for the letters, I couldn't put them in order. There were so many, separated from their envelopes. I chose one at random. In it my mother asked about Rosa's life, and it seemed that it must be from the time when Rosa had just arrived in Chile. In another, she asked about the maid Rosa who was taking care of Miranda. In another she told Rosa not to be afraid of what Isaac was proposing to René; she doubted that he would be able to convince René to join the MIR. Who was Isaac? What was the MIR? I had no idea.

One letter made me very afraid. It was from Rosa, talking about Poncia and how the food she made, made her sick. Stomach aches, dizziness; the same symptoms that I and Adriana had. I never thought of it that way, but it was true. Our symptoms always occurred when Diego was away, just as Rosa described.

There were many letters in which I could hear clearly the voices of my sister and my mother. It made me happy to be in contact with them again, even in this removed way. But it made me angry as well. Rosa was dead. I never had the chance to know her as an adult. I was only nine when she left for Chile. I lost the person who was my best friend, who could have been my best advisor, and to whom I could have been a big help, a way for her to laugh at life, at her problems. I lost an entire universe.

One important letter left me astonished. It was dated June, 1977. This was before the trip my mother made to Chile to bring Miranda to Mexico. It was from Rosa. The letter explained in detail about the agreement between Rosa and Papa regarding the exchange of favors. It told how René would be set free in exchange for discrediting Diego. This complicated history was all new to me. I never suspected that my father was so involved in the politics of Chile. We never spoke of that in Brussels.

Finally, I arrived at the most mysterious letter. It was from my father; the only one from him that I found. It was addressed to Rosa. It asked about the Barbie doll, if Rosa had managed to get it fixed; if the paper fit; if Miranda had memorized the message to Lea. It also mentioned that my mother was on board with the plan. Clearly, there was something afoot here; some plan to bring me to Mexico. What did all this mean?

I needed to get ahold of Minx.

I waited until Miranda was busy with her piano lesson, and I went to her room. Caring not for the mess I made, I searched for the doll until I found her. I took off her clothes. On the torso, just as I had seen the day that Miranda showed the doll to Fernando, was a tiny hole. I looked for a pen to insert in the hole. When I did this, the body opened and there inside, was a miniscule roll of paper. I took it out and put it in my pocket. I felt like my head was going to explode. I didn't move.

A long while passed. When Miranda came back I offered her the doll that now no longer guarded its tiny secret.

Miranda looked at me with furious eyes. She didn't seem blind in the slightest.

"Luz, what are you doing here?"

I didn't say anything. I just waited for her to take the doll.

"What have you done? You had no right to touch my things!"

"What is the message Miranda? What is the message you memorized?"

"Give me the paper!", she cried, desperately.

"Explain this!", I said, just as desperately.

"Who are you to ask? Give it to me!"

Miranda went to the edge of her courage and threw herself on me. She was astonishingly strong. We fought for a bit and when it seemed she was not going to stop, I struggled to get the paper out of my pocket.

"All right. Here it is, for God's sake."

She took it and put it back in the doll.

"Never touch my things again", she said, panting. "Never."

We sat for a moment catching our breath.

"I know that your mother gave you that Barbie doll. I know that it's very special to you. I'm sorry."

Miranda calmed down and asked forgiveness for her actions as well.

"It's that, well, that paper belongs to one person and one person only. My mother told me that I should never, never give it to anyone else but that person, no matter what. It was a sacred obligation, a very important promise. Now you see, Luz, why I got so upset."

"And, who is that person?"

Miranda returned to her state of blindness once again. Her gaze floated in the air, her voice seemed to come from far away.

"To my aunt Leonora", she said finally. "But I don't have an aunt Leonora. My mother told me she was coming soon, that she would come soon to take care of me, but she never came."

Miranda sighed deeply.

"If it were true, she would have come just like my mother said. She would have helped me not to feel so alone here. Because I feel very alone here, Luz."

I dark cloud passed through my mind.

"You have Cecilio, and your father, and you have me...", I told her timidly.

"Cecilio is not my real brother. My father takes good care of him, the same as he takes good care of me, but poor Cecilio doesn't even know who his mother is."

"I don't understand."

"Oh, Luz. There are so many things you don't understand. Cecilio is the son of Mrs. Poncia. My father goes often to the village to see them. It's one thing here in this house; there it is another thing altogether."

My heart nearly stopped. I knew that Poncia and Diego had a long history together. I remembered that Nikita had long suspected that they were involved in some manner.

"And how is it that Cecilio doesn't know that she is his mother? That makes no sense."

"My father explained it to me. He told me that something very horrible happened to Cecilio when he was little and he had to leave his house. And he had to leave behind everything else, in order to get better."

"Including his own mother?"

"Yes. But he was little, and he didn't know too much. Besides, it wasn't the end of the world for him. She was here; they were together whenever Poncia was here. At least Cecilio has his real father."

Finally, I understood the real truth about Cecilio. I felt a great heaviness enter into me.

Miranda sighed. "My father takes good care of me, but I know he's not my real father. My real father died when I was six years old. And my mother...."

She couldn't continue.

"What was your father's name?"

"His name was René. He was very handsome. I still remember how he looked."

When I heard this, I came to see my own selfishness. In order to carry out my plans, I had taken away from Miranda what could have filled that empty hole; that emptiness that comes from having no family. I had played around with the emotional life of my niece to satisfy my own needs, my own desires. The solitude she had felt all this time was my fault.

Now had come the moment to declare all to Diego. I went to find him.

58

Leonora
Rings and Keys

"I have something very important to tell you."

Diego raised his head and looked distractedly at me. He frowned, then focused his attention.

"And I have something important to tell you as well", he responded. "You're not wearing the ring I made for you. What's wrong? Have you changed your mind?"

"How long have you noticed?", I asked him.

"Since I came back from New York, but I didn't want to say anything to see if you would resume wearing it. But a long time has passed, now. I need to know."

I felt once again between a rock and a hard place, between Scylla and Charybdis, between the sword and the wall. Whatever was written on that small roll of paper, whatever the message that Miranda had for me; I urgently needed to know, and Diego could help. But equally urgent was the need to avoid destroying the love he felt for me. I was in an impossible situation.

"I haven't changed my mind. But....Diego, I need you to do something for me. Don't ask why right now."

My worry must have been so obvious that he agreed immediately. We went to Miranda's room. She had the doll Minx in her hands still and she started when we came in.

"Is this the doll?", Diego asked me.

"Yes."

He took the doll from her and tried to manipulate the mechanism. I handed him a pen and he opened it.

"It's a roll of paper." Diego directed his gaze to Miranda. "What does it mean?"

Miranda started to shake her head slowly, a sign of anxiety.

"I can't tell you."

"Yes, you can."

"No I can't."

"YES YOU CAN", he said in a terrible voice.

Miranda seemed to shrink into herself, like a deflating balloon.

"It's a telephone number", she responded in a small voice.

"Whose?"

"I don't know", she said.

"And the message?", I asked her. "What is the message?"

"Call."

59

Leonora
Mrs. Burleigh

The prefix was a number from the U.S. Thousands of ideas passed through my mind, but I guessed that it was probably my father's telephone number. A strong feeling of uneasiness, of disgust came over me. I dialed the number with very little desire to do so.

A voice answered that I knew well.

"Lea, there have been so many times when I wanted to speak to you, but I knew that you and Nikki were disappointed in me. I thought that you would never forgive me. I thought you might never give me a chance to explain what happened in Brussels."

"That hurt us so much, Papa. And when Mother died, you weren't even sad! Didn't you realize the enormous damage all that did to us?"

A long silence passed.

"I swore not to interfere in your lives after that. I didn't want to cause you any more problems. And since I never received any answers to the letters I wrote you and Nikita, I knew I shouldn't insist."

Another silence. I had absolutely no words in my head to speak to him.

"But now that you're older, can you listen? Now that so much time has passed?"

"The amount of time that has passed is immaterial. That doesn't change anything."

My father's voice became more desperate.

"But I want to explain! Let me explain!"

"No, Papa. Nothing has changed."

I told him that we were well; I informed him that Nikita was working in Morelia, that Adriana and I were fine here. And I hung up.

I went out of the living room and didn't see anyone. That's what I asked for in order to make the call: privacy. I went back to my room and laid down on the bed, feeling a tremendous let down. That stupid doll, that useless phone call.

Two days passed. Rosa's diary did not resurface. Miranda didn't speak to me. Diego was working and on the second day he left for the city and didn't come home at night. In this way, there was a truce in the battle. I prepared the food for myself and for Adriana.

But when Diego returned, the first thing I did was to seek him out to talk. I saw no other alternative than to tell him the pure and total truth. And if he stopped loving me because I was a fraud, a liar, because I had wormed my way into his life under false pretenses, well then, I would receive my fair punishment. I was prepared for the worst.

I didn't quite know how to start. It occurred to me to show him Rosa's letters. I asked him to wait while I went to my room to collect them. There, on top of the pile was an envelope I hadn't seen. It was sealed. Addressed to Rosa; Rosa Burleigh, P.O. Box 2339, Mexico, D.F., written in the handwriting of my mother. Just as Rosa's letter to my mother had never reached her, nor had this letter been read by its intended recipient. With trembling hands, I opened the envelope.

Brussels

Feb. 2, 1977

Dear Rosa,

I have something to confess. Now that you are older, and married, you will understand me better. Do what you think best with this information. If you think that your sisters will benefit from knowing it, then share it with them. If not, then keep it from them. You will know best what to do when the time comes. In any case, my dear daughter, you deserve to know the truth.

I married for all the usual reasons, as any woman in love will have. Your father was everything I wanted in a man: intelligent, hard-working, educated. He showed me many things I hadn't seen before, things about his politics and his government that I didn't understand. These were good things, laudable things, things that made the world a better place.

I heard Diego shouting from the living room for me to return.

But I also learned that if a person is absolutely convinced of something, it is impossible for him or her to see it from any other perspective. For your father, it was impossible for him to see any merit in socialism; impossible to see that it was a better system; one that would benefit everyone, not just the rich. Because capitalism is for the rich; I know you know that too.

I heard knocking on the closed door of my room.

Your father and I fell in love, believing that each of us could change the mind of the other. Love is something that can keep people afloat for a long time. For years we put aside our differences in order to avoid hurting the marriage. But there came a moment when I couldn't keep it up. Our philosophies were too different, and I began to I feel that your father didn't love me anymore. And I had fallen in love with someone else.

"Luz! Open the door!"

Barbara had been a friend of mine for more than a year. She had a warm heart for the poor, for the disadvantaged, for the blind. She was in the process of putting together a school for the blind in Mexico. Barbara was married. But she loved me. And I loved her. We had a tie that is stronger than any ideology, any political system. She asked me to come to Mexico with her, saying she would get a divorce in order that we be together.

"Open the door, or I'll knock it down!"

For that reason, I decided to separate from your father. But I ran into problems. Your father wouldn't let me go. He said a divorce would hurt his diplomatic career. And he said he loved me, still. I didn't believe him. You know how love can unhinge a person. Barbara was in my mind, in my heart and there was no room for anyone else. I thought of a way to get free of him: involve him in a scandal.

The door moved violently.

I asked a man I knew, a painter named Diego Alba, to help me. The objective was to make his bosses in Washington believe that he was having an affair with an unsuitable woman; or better yet, several unsuitable women. Mr. Alba ran in those circles; it was easy for him to find these women. In exchange, he asked me to open the doors to wealthy people in Brussels, so that he might sell them his paintings. You see Rosa, how we all are hypocrites and defective human beings.

The door handle came free of the door and fell to the floor with a crash.

Diego Alba achieved the objective. Your father was in disgrace. But I didn't imagine it would go that far. It wasn't my intention to ruin him; I only wanted him to feel pressured into giving me a divorce. Forgive me, Rosa. Your father's life will never be the same now, nor will yours. I have been so stupid. Your father is a good man. He never was involved in any affairs; he never failed me as a husband. I failed him. And I failed the whole family.

The entire door now fell to the floor with a huge thud.

Your father is very sure of his ideology; it is his only defect. But that doesn't make him a bad man. He didn't deserve what happened to him. When I realized the gravity of what I had done, I tried to explain, tried to ask his forgiveness, but it was too late. Now I ask you to forgive me and him both. I know that the arrangement that he made with the Chileans didn't work. But Rosa, your father saw it as the only way to get René back; the only way to save his life. He was utterly convinced. When the plan failed, he was completely distraught.

Save this letter. One day you may need it. Your sisters won't understand what happened in Brussels, and later in Chile. You will have to be the light; illuminating the dark secrets. I don't want to live anymore. Barbara will not want to be with me when she finds out what I've done. I cannot look any of you in the eye. I feel totally alone. I don't want to go on.

When I finished the letter, I felt something harden in me.

"I need to talk to my father again", I said to Diego.

60

Leonora
The Air in Flames

The little paper with the telephone number was not where I left it. It wasn't on the table, nor on the floor. It was not to be found.

We heard violent sounds coming from the living room. Someone was destroying the piano. We ran in and saw Miranda striking the keys with an unmeasured fury. Her hands and forearms were covered in blood. Various piano keys were broken and lying on the floor. The noise was deafening.

Diego tried to stop her, but she didn't let him. She was like a snake, twisting and turning out of his grasp. She began running through the living room, crashing into the furniture. She fell, cried out. Diego finally was able to subdue her. At full volume she shouted:

"Minx **told** me that Fernando was bad luck. She **told** me to stay away from him, but I didn't listen."

"Miranda, what are you saying?", asked Diego.

"Fernando was from the other tribe, Papa. From the other side of the hills."

Diego and I looked at one another in astonishment.

"He came to kill you. He came to take vengeance for someone they lost. Someone in their group. That's why I had to kill him first."

"You killed Fernando Blau? That's crazy", said Diego.

"Yes, I killed him. You didn't see it, but I bent down to loosen the wheels of the ladder."

"Miranda, this can't be. Look...."

She interrupted him.

"You didn't see, but Amelia did. She saw me. Ask her."

Miranda squirmed her way out of Diego's embrace and went to the piano. She started pounding the keys again. Drops of blood flew through the air. The piano shook with the violence of her pounding.

"Call Leocadio", Diego said to me urgently.

Later, after the doctor had given her a sedative, he examined her arms and hands.

"They're not broken are they?", asked Diego.

"I'm afraid they are."

"But you can bandage them, put casts on, can't you?", continued the painter.

"I am a psychiatrist Mr. Alba, not a surgeon. She might need surgery to repair her hands. They are seriously damaged. I doubt she will ever play the piano again. No, we need to take her to the hospital as soon as possible. I'll accompany you."

We went to the city at great speed. When we got there, Diego called Barbara. It gave me a weird feeling to know I would see her now, now that I knew about her involvement with my family, with the disastrous end for my mother. And more so Diego, now that I knew about his involvement as well.

But when she arrived, she was the same as ever: caring, warm. She took charge.

The doctors told us that the mental state of the young patient was terribly fragile; they said that Miranda asked that we leave, and that only Barbara stay with her. This seemed like a bad idea to me; I didn't want to leave Miranda that way. But Diego was in agreement, for once, with Barbara, so we returned to the house.

Poncia had left our dinner on the table, but I wasn't hungry.

Exhausted by the events of the day, we sat down. Diego opened a bottle of wine and we rapidly finished it.

"Now you're going to tell me what's going on with you, and with Miranda", he said quietly.

"It's a very long story. But I only have two questions to ask you. Just two. And depending on your answers, I can tell you the rest."

"Go ahead."

"You go often to Mrs. Poncia's house in the village. Why?"

Diego's shoulders dropped and he seemed to crumble.

"If I tell you, you'll see me for the monster I am."

"You have to tell me. Are you involved with her?"

"No! Not in that way."

"But Miranda tells me that Cecilio is your son, and she is his mother. That means....?"

"No! It doesn't mean that."

"Then what?"

"Oh, I hoped this moment would never come." Diego looked very cast down.

"Mrs. Poncia is forcing me to take care of Cecilio. But he is not my son."

"Everyone believes that he is!"

"Look, Luz. Something happened years ago that still affects us."

"What?"

Diego appeared very unwilling to continue talking.

"Rosa liked to go to the village. Whenever she was anxious, she had the habit of strolling about there. You know that Mrs. Poncia lives in Comala. One day when Rosa was there, she was attacked by a man. This man was Mrs. Poncia's husband. I knew him. I knew that he mistreated her; he berated her; he hit her. She would sometimes arrive for work here with bruises on her face, on her legs. He mistreated his son too."

"And this man is Cecilio's father?"

"Yes. When I found out what he did to Rosa, it was like firing a loaded pistol. I knew where to find him and I made him pay by breaking all his fingers. He would never touch anyone again the way he touched Rosa."

"Why didn't you go to the police?"

"The police in Comala are useless. Besides, this man's uncle worked in the police station. There would never be any justice for Rosa there."

"Is that why everyone avoids you in the village?"

"Well, there's more. Somehow, perhaps from something I did to him or from something else, this man died. A few days after my encounter with him."

Diego swallowed hard.

"Mrs. Poncia told me that she would say nothing about the encounter in exchange for having Cecilio come to live here, with me."

"As your son."

"As my son."

Diego sighed deeply, as if gathering his forces to continue talking.

"To make sure that nothing linked me to Cecilio's father, I told her that we would have to change everything; all the dates and official information that could connect me to him."

"Even making it so that Cecilio stopped thinking of her as his mother?", I asked incredulously.

"Mrs. Poncia is very clever. That was her idea, and it effectively squashed any questions that people from the outside might have. Besides, it was convenient for her that Cecilio was here. But she had deeper reasons as well. She asked me for a huge salary increase. And she insisted that I adopt him, legally adopt him."

Diego became even more depressed.

"Her blackmail continues. Now she is insisting that I take Miranda's name off my will and replace it with Cecilio's. She wants to make him the sole heir to everything here. She wants to make him the owner of all that I have, when I die. Cecilio."

Diego let fall this last word like an enormous boulder that was coming down on us. A crushing silence descended upon us.

"I have to ask you the other question", I told him, forcing myself to concentrate. It was urgent that I corroborate what my mother's letter had said about him. I didn't want to believe it, and I hoped he had an explanation.

"Is it true that you are a communist?", I asked, as a way to enter into the topic.

Diego laughed, but not without a touch of bitterness.

"It's true. Years ago. But there was one thing I realized right away: I am a painter, not a politician."

"But there are people who believed that you were heavily involved in all that! People who risked their lives over you!"

"What do you know about that?", he asked me, the surprise and fear clearly evident on his face.

"Tell me, how many paintings did you sell in Brussels?"

Diego's eyes widened in shock.

"It's said that we are all hypocrites and liars in this world", I said.

Diego now shut his eyes and leaned back, as if he were suffering a great frustration.

"Let's not talk about lies and hypocrisy, Luz. Luz Maria Mendoza. Singer of country songs."

"How...?"

"I just learned this for certain. How I learned it doesn't matter."

He opened his eyes and looked directly into mine. After a long moment of scrutinizing me, he said with a strange smile:

"I don't know your real name, but I know it isn't Luz. We have much to discuss, Miss Mysterious."

Diego stood up and went to the table where our dinner still awaited us. There was a chocolate cake for dessert; one of my favorite things. He cut a slice, put it on a plate, took two forks and returned to sit next to me. Carefully, he offered me a morsel of cake.

"Try it."

"Who made it, you or Mrs. Poncia?"

"Guess."

I opened my mouth without wanting to. The chocolate filled it with sweetness.

"Do you like it?"

I felt my intestines twist.

Suddenly I felt a current of hot air at my feet. As hot as fire. I looked at the floor and I noticed something for the first time. I noticed how the wall was constructed. It didn't actually meet the floor; instead, there was a gap between the bottom of the wall and the floor that ran the length of the room. It was through there that the hot air was coming.

In that moment the electricity went out. Diego went in search of an oil lantern. After a moment I saw a point of light coming towards me.

Diego sat down next to me on the sofa.

"The cake is delicious, isn't it?", he asked. Diego Alba: expert painter, cook, and carpenter.

"Yes, it's delicious".

End (Part I)

L.A. Sosa has written three short novels: *The Solemn Vespers of the Confessor, Real Estate Kisses, The Eyes of a Thinker,* as well as a collection of poetry entitled *Ojos para adelante, niñas.* Her perspective is always personal; her passion is to tell stories that illustrate the fragility and the strength of people in a world of fanaticisms.

www.ingramcontent.com/pod-product-compliance
Lightning Source LLC
Chambersburg PA
CBHW072058020726
47501CB00003B/633